Starry Night

Isabel Gillies

Starry Night

SQUARE
FISH

Farrar Straus Giroux
New York

Author's Note

This is a work of fiction. None of the characters exist in the real world. Wren is not me, the schools are not schools I went to, and nothing in the book actually happened. Of course all of it comes from my heart, experience, and imagination, so if you know me, it might seem recognizable, but everything in the book is a mishmash, a brew, or plain old make-believe.

SQUARE FISH

An Imprint of Macmillan
175 Fifth Avenue
New York, NY 10010
macteenbooks.com

Square Fish and the Square Fish logo are trademarks of Macmillan and are used by Farrar Straus Giroux Books for Young Readers under license from Macmillan.

Our books may be purchased in bulk for promotional, educational, or business use. Please contact your local bookseller or the Macmillan Corporate and Premium Sales Department at (800) 221-7945 ext. 5442 or by e-mail at MacmillanSpecialMarkets@macmillan.com.

Library of Congress Cataloging-in-Publication Data

Gillies, Isabel, 1970–
    Starry night / Isabel Gillies.
        pages cm
    Summary: As fifteen-year-old Wren and her three lifelong best friends celebrate the opening of a major exhibit curated by her father at the Metropolitan Museum of Art, Wren finds first love with her brother's new friend, Nolan, and the relationship transforms her and her life—not always in good ways.
    ISBN 978-1-250-06822-4 (paperback)   ISBN 978-0-374-30676-2 (ebook)
    [1. Love—Fiction.   2. Best friends—Fiction.   3. Friendship—Fiction.   4. Artists—Fiction.   5. Family life—New York (State)—New York—Fiction.   6. Metropolitan Museum of Art (New York, N.Y.)—Fiction.   7. New York (N.Y.)—Fiction.]   I. Title.

PZ7.G4127St 2014
[Fic]—dc23
                                                                              2014008408

Originally published in the United States by Farrar Straus Giroux Books for Young Readers
First Square Fish Edition: 2015
Book designed by Elizabeth H. Clark
Square Fish logo designed by Filomena Tuosto

10 9 8 7 6 5 4 3 2 1

LEXILE: 790L

For Bill Clegg

"Love I get so lost, sometimes."
—Peter Gabriel

Starry Night

1

I don't think you fall in love for the first time until something—or someone—feels dangerous. I don't mean dangerous like going to jail, I guess I mean just different, really different. Different can feel dangerous, right? Like, I think it feels dangerous when your heart pounds so hard you are sure it's visible beating under your shirt. Or when you can't sleep, or catch your breath, or concentrate or listen, or when you turn a different color just thinking about his face, or when your relationships with your friends get all screwed up, or when you fight with your parents. When you change direction or your mind, or when tears fall and fall from your eyes for hours, when your whole life gets put in a Cuisinart—all because of a single person.

For me, it started at the Metropolitan Museum of Art—and it ended there too. I am not sure why the person that I was in love with ended up not wanting to be in love with me anymore. A part of me thinks it was my fault. That does *not* sound strong, but sometimes I don't feel strong. What I hear is that we are very strong, we girls. Girls can do anything. We are leaders, we are intuitive, we are brave, we are smart, and we kick ass. "If women ran the world there would be no war." Don't you hear that? Maybe it's true; I'm certainly not going to say it's not. But if it is true, then how come it can all feel so impossibly fragile? How come you can feel like you are getting it entirely wrong?

Maybe boys don't feel strong all the time either. I don't think van Gogh felt strong, and look at everything he did—look at *The Starry Night*. Maybe you can feel fragile and still paint *The Starry Night*. Or maybe you can paint it because you are fragile. Maybe you can be strong and still be vulnerable, like a tree. Have you ever seen a tree filled with birds? There seems to be one on every branch, and then all of a sudden something happens, possibly from the atmosphere or the surroundings—or maybe not, maybe it's something having to do with the tree itself, the branches, the leaves, or even the roots—that causes the birds to fly away in unison. And the tree is just left there—maybe strong, but left.

The air felt loaded in New York City. It was one of those days that you feel not only that the temperature will drop but that something tremendous is going to happen. It was a Monday in November and the sky was so blue it was violet, uninterrupted by clouds. The sidewalks reflected the shining sun, making us squint. Mostly, I remember this crazy wind. It was so forceful you knew the meteorologists were talking about it on the news. It was pushing us around. Our hair whooshed over our heads, twisting and tangling. Sometimes a gust would come and push us a few steps faster than we would have usually walked. This made us squeal. We were suited up in fall sweaters and jean jackets over our dark blue, pleated school uniforms and black leggings, scarves wrapped multiple times around our necks. Fall clothes are the best ones—I feel so much safer in a cardigan and boots than in some flimsy dress and sandals. But even in our chunky sweaters, we weren't dressed for the sudden change in weather; we weren't at all ready for it. The three inches of leg between where the stretchy legging fabric ended and my ankle booties began were red with cold, and that was just the beginning. We were not protected. We should have been wearing parkas, heavy ones.

Farah, Padmavati, and Reagan were coming over to my house after school because that night my father, who is the director of the Metropolitan Museum of Art, was hosting the opening of a new exhibit he was curating, *and*—for the first time—my friends and I were invited to the party. Charlie, our only friend-who-is-a-boy, was meeting us at my house. He was probably already there because his school, St. Tim's, is on the west side of Manhattan, where we all live. My brother, Oliver, goes there too, but he's a senior, and we are sophomores. St. Tim's is just for boys, and Hatcher, where Farah, Padmavati, Reagan, and I go to school, is just for girls. It's on the east side of Central Park. But it's not really where we met. We've known each other since we were born. Since before we were born really. We're Turtles. Fifteen years ago on the Upper West Side, five babies were born all in the same month (basically) to parents in the same reading group, all because of *Lady Chatterley's Lover*. It sounds like a reading group orgy—but really, it was because of the discussion of one hot scene and what happened when everyone got home.

Our parents called us the Turtles because turtles lay so many eggs at one time.

2

Several weeks before the very windy day, it was an early autumn evening, the first one where you knew summer was truly gone. I was procrastinating in the living room with my parents.

"Can they all come?" I said to my mother and father.

"When are they not all invited to everything?" Mom said, pointedly sliding her new orange-and-purple reading glasses farther up her nose as she dog-eared a page in the *Architectural Digest* she was reading. Dad stood up and poked the fire.

"They can come to everything here, but they have never been to a Met thing. Can we sit at the same table? Me, Vati, Farah, Reagan, *and* Charlie?"

"Darling, we have no idea how we'll do the tables now," Dad said, in his slight Dutch accent that just sounds European unless you know what you are listening to. A log rolled awkwardly off the pile and he bent down to prop it back up. Although he is one hundred percent city, he does things like kick around burning logs on the fire like someone who lives in the country. And Dad wears Barbour oilskin jackets on the weekends like Prince Charles.

"But we can all stay till the end, right?"

"Yes, Wren! Goodness, the exhibition isn't for months. Relax, this is worse than you are about Halloween." Mom put her glasses up on her head and looked at me with wide, this-is-getting-annoying eyes.

"I don't dress up anymore," I said, and pulled a random thread on the upholstered armchair I was sitting in.

"Don't pull *that*, Wrenny!" My mother kicked her leg over in my direction to get me to stop.

"Sorry." I really do pull on things too much.

"The whole chair will unravel!" She winked at me, put her glasses back down on her nose, and resumed her reading.

"It will be fun, my love. You all can dress up and hobnob with the nobs." Dad was finished futzing with the logs in the small arched marble fireplace, but before he sat back down on the love seat to read his book, he came over and kissed my head. "Are you all done with your homework?"

"No." I scrunched my nose up, knowing that he knew I wasn't and that's why he asked.

"Well, get to it and leave us to think about parties. Your B average that is *required* to apply to Saint-Rémy isn't going to materialize by itself, and I believe you have some work to do in that area." He raised his eyebrows.

I had just started my sophomore year at Hatcher, but I was already working on my application for this unbelievable, impossible-to-get-into junior-year-abroad program in France that I had been wanting to go to since the end of eighth grade, when my art teacher, Mrs. Rousseau, looked at a collage of a jungle I'd made and told me about the program. She said anyone who could draw a leopard like that (it was quite fierce and a little crazy-looking) should go to Saint-Rémy. It's an art school in an old nunnery next to the asylum where Vincent van Gogh convalesced for a year and painted one hundred and fifty works of art, most of them masterpieces. He painted *The Starry Night* there.

"Oh my god, I'm never going to get in!" I slid down the chair onto the wool sisal rug next to our old corgi, May, and curled up with her in front of the fire.

"Wren, please—you won't get in if you lie around on the floor with May. Get upstairs and Go. To. Work. That self-portrait isn't going to draw itself either, you know," my mother said.

Lying on the floor in the glow and heat, I wished I could just be May. How was I going to do that self-portrait? You had to produce a great one to be considered for this program—it had to be genius. Self-portraits are so intense. Have you ever seen Frida Kahlo's? The one with the monkey and the hummingbird around her neck? Oh my lord, she is giving such a look you can't believe it. She actually said, "I was born a bitch." And you can see that very clearly in the painting. There is no hiding in a self-portrait; everything comes out.

I put my head on May's side and her insides made a low guttural gurgle. I closed my eyes and pictured *The Starry Night*. It's my favorite painting of all time. Sometimes when I feel that I won't be able to do something, or I want something really badly, I put this painting right in front of my mind's eye and wish on one of its eleven stars. There might be more than eleven if you are counting the flashes of yellow that swirl around in the midnight sky, but I don't count those. There is one bigger ball I guess you could call a star, but I think of it as the moon. No, I count eleven true stars. That night I picked the bright one next to the cypress tree to wish on. *Please, star, give me what I need to draw a real self-portrait and get into the France program next year. Please . . . please . . . please . . .* I drifted blissfully around in the thick blue swirls of van Gogh's paintbrush marks. The fire was soaking into my face and hands and May's thumping heart beat steadily beneath my ear.

"Wren? What's going on down there?" Mom called from her chair.

"Mama?" I was shocked to hear her voice. I had been in the cosmos.

"Yes, love." She looked down at May and me. Her glasses were back on the top of her head.

"Mom," I said. She sighed like she only half wanted to hear what I would say next.

I didn't move. I just looked up into her impatient but listening face.

"Mom, what if I look inside to draw myself, and I don't like what I see?"

She took a deep breath in and let it out slowly.

"I think you will find that your insides are very beautiful, Wren. But you have to look. You have to try." She leaned back so I couldn't see her anymore. "You have to get off the floor."

May shifted like my head had gotten too heavy for her to be comfortable. I thought I should probably text everyone to see if they were doing their homework.

"And why don't you leave your phone with us, yes?" My father looked up at me over his reading glasses and stuck out his hand. I swear Dad is some kind of mind-reading wizard. They both are.

3

I am going to introduce my friends by going back in time. Then we'll get back to the present. The future will be in some other book.

Farah, Vati, Reagan, and I all started at Hatcher together in kindergarten. In seventh-grade, there is a school fair that everyone in the class organizes, hosts, and cleans up after. You vote on a charity to donate the money to: the Michael J. Fox Foundation, breast cancer, the Natural Resources Defense Council—something like that. You decide what games to have: face painting, apple dunking, guess the teacher's weight. You sell tickets, you make posters, and then one Friday afternoon it all happens in the Hatcher gym on the tenth floor.

Farah, Vati, Reagan, and I got Charlie and about six of his friends to come to our seventh-grade fair. We were the only girls in the grade who brought boys that weren't their little brothers. It was pretty awesome because having boys there made the fair feel cool and happening. Instead of helping with the cleanup, we bailed and went to Nino's Pizza on Lexington and Eighty-Sixth Street and played video games with Charlie and his friends. We didn't think a thing of it again all weekend; maybe we thought there was a cleanup committee that somehow none of us were on? Anyway, Monday morning when we got to school we got in a mother lode of trouble.

"You don't give a *SHIT* about people with diabetes!" Tyler Morgenstern yelled from the top of her desk where she was standing at the grade-wide emergency homeroom meeting that was called to discuss what we had done. Mrs. Garrison, our homeroom teacher, blanched when Tyler said "shit," but as the meeting was supposed to be an opportunity for everyone to talk about how they were feeling, she didn't say anything. "All you guys care about is St. Tim's boys!" continued Tyler.

"Are you *KIDDING ME*?" Farah stood up. "I will have you know, my *aunt* has diabetes. She has to walk around all day long with a machine attached to her with an *alarm* in case her insulin drops! It was my damn idea to give the money to the American Diabetes Association."

"Damn" made both Mrs. Garrison and Mr. Tropple half stand up.

"Girls, calm down, we are trying to work this through now," Mr. Tropple, our bald Marxist history teacher / other homeroom teacher urged.

"Oh *YEAH*—then why did you guys leave it all up to us to clean up? You just left with your little *boyfriends* without looking back," said Katie Boyer, who stood up on her chair to make that point. She wasn't the most agile of girls, so she just put one leg up on her desk. "If you *gave a shit* . . ."

"Oh, hey there!" pleaded Mr. T. "Let's watch our language, girls."

"Sorry, but honestly, Mr. T, they think they are so cool just because they know guys from St. Tim's," Katie said, in a much calmer voice.

"I don't think we think we're cool—I think we, well, I *know* we are sorry." I offered this but it was thirty-something against four, and the thirty looked like they wanted to destroy us. It felt medieval, like they were villagers and we were the outcast dragon that had eaten and spat out all of their sheep.

"Wren, give me a break, they are all just *jealous* that we brought boys to the fair and had *fun* and all they could offer up were their little brothers!" Farah said, not under her breath at all.

Tyler started to cry, which made me feel really bad. Vati started to cry too. With seventh graders, crying is contagious; in minutes you could have at least thirty hysterical tween girls on your hands.

"Okay, okay. Let's calm down," Mrs. Garrison said in her buttery monotone. "How are we going to make this right?"

Reagan's hand shot up.

"Reagan," said Mrs. Garrison.

"Okay." She got up on her desk. I guess the desks were like our podiums, but every time one of us got up there the teachers sort of put their hands in the air like they were there to save us if we fell. "It sounds like they feel taken advantage of. That is what I am hearing." All the townspeople nodded.

"If we say we're sorry, and maybe write a paper during recess about how we would feel if we got taken advantage of, maybe we can move on and let this water move under the bridge."

Reagan is so sophisticated. Her mom has spoken to her like she was a thirty-year-old since she was three. My parents practically still sing me lullabies.

I raised my hand.

"Wren?" Mrs. Garrison said.

"Um, if we are going to do that—and I totally think we should because we feel bad and everything—can I use my computer? I fully intend to write more than two pages, and I really can't write that much longhand." I get special computer privileges because I'm dyslexic and have dysgraphia. Although I can draw an owl so it feels like it's sitting right next to you, I have the handwriting of a four-year-old.

"That's fine, Wren," Mr. T said.

"I have one more thing to say." Farah didn't need to stand on her desk; when she spoke everyone in the class listened.

"I will write this paper, but I'm telling you something . . . if someone took advantage of me, I wouldn't whine about it in a shitty meeting like this. I would use my six years of tae kwon do and kick their ass."

4

Hanging out with Charlie, age twelve:

"This, you noodles, is called DUMBO!" Winston Fudge, Charlie's dad, called out from the front of the Nosh van. Reagan, Farah, Vati, Charlie, and I all went to the same preschool. But once we got into elementary school, we didn't see Charlie except on the weekends for playdates or soccer, or sometimes when Charlie invited me to ride in the Nosh van with him and his dad delivering catered meals to people. Nosh is now a huge catering company, but when Charlie's parents started it, they cooked out of their kitchen on the Upper West Side and had an online menu; then people would order dishes to have in their fridges to *nosh* on, get it? Nosh?

"Down Under the Manhattan Bridge Overpass. When I was twelve, like you guys, growing up on Long Island, this place used to be a *dump*. Nowheresville. But it got cleaned up. Big real estate honchos built swanky condos, and now"—he slowed down, looking at street signs—"some of my best customers are here." We stopped in front of a big redbrick building with lots and lots of gigantic arched windows. I would guess it used to be a factory. Now there was a doorman in a cap and a long coat standing guard out front.

"Okay, Wrenny and Charlie, do your thing!" He shoved the

gearshift into park. Charlie has a baby face, with freckles around his nose and cheeks and a thick shock of hair that sticks straight up (even though he combs it carefully down anytime he glances in a mirror) and looks like a mowed wheat field, which I think is cool but drives him bananas. His teeth, before he got braces, sort of stuck out and they were rounded on the bottom. I *never* would tell him this, but his teeth used to make him look a little bit like that *Mad* magazine guy. But he has always had sophisticated clothes and even at age twelve—even at four—he looked like an adult.

Before getting out of the van, Charlie buttoned his navy-blue peacoat, making sure all the buttons were right, and checked the cuffs at the bottom of his not-scruffy blue jeans. When we were little my mother called him "our little clotheshorse," sort of teasing him, but she stopped when we passed fourth grade and she realized his tidy, stylish appearance wasn't some cute affectation of a child. It was his nature.

"Can I carry the bags this time, Charlie, and you get the list?" I asked, making my way around to the back of the van.

"Sure, but it's more gentlemanly if I carry the bags," he said, joining me.

"Okay, why don't you give me the list? I'll read the names and what each person is getting. You check that I didn't mess up, and then we'll both carry the bags. I just don't want to make a mistake with the checking," I said, in my most serious "work" voice.

"*Don't drop these, guys! This is a soup order!*" Winston yelled back to us.

"Oh gosh, yeah," Charlie said, looking at the order form and then up at the building. "This is an important building for Nosh, there are *five* families that do business with us from here. All of them order a lot of soup. They are soup eaters, I guess."

"Soup is good food," I said, losing my work mojo for a second and laughing at my own joke. Charlie didn't really get it because it's from an old commercial that was on TV when my mother was young. She always says it when she serves soup, but Charlie laughed anyway.

"Especially if it's Moroccan turkey lentil." He smiled but then got back to business. "I better double-check this one, Wrenny," he said.

"Okay, I'll be really careful about reading the names correctly," I said. Charlie looked at me from where he had climbed into the back of the van, hovering over the many brown shopping bags full of meals for the week.

"Wren, you hardly ever make mistakes reading anymore." Charlie purposefully took a moment to look at me while he said that.

"Thanks, Charlie. I'm trying."

"Well, you're doing a good job." He went back to looking at the names on the labels stapled to the handles of the bags. "I wouldn't want to do this job with anyone else but you."

I smiled. He smiled. Charlie is a really good student. He wins spelling bees at St. Tim's and reads like a champ, but he had some kind of speech thing when he was little, he couldn't say his R's, so he is empathetic to all my learning difficulties.

"Meister is the first name. The order is for three quarts of white bean and escarole soup and a lasagna." I read slowly and proudly.

"Check!" Charlie carefully lifted two brown bags out of the back of the van. Then he paused, put one bag down, and looked in the other.

"Wait, Wrenny, Meister is the first name?"

I looked at the list again and realized I was wrong; Hermann was the first name, not Meister.

"Sorry, you are right. Hermann is the first name." I took a deep, wobbly breath. It's the same breath I take in math class when I am about to get an answer wrong.

"Could I please see the list, Wrenny—just to check, I'm sure you are right, I'm probably confused." I handed him the list and he started reading it over and looking at the bags.

"Whoops. Yeah, I think actually the last name is Hermann— it's a different family altogether. The Hermanns get the white bean soup and lasagna. The Meisters also get white bean soup, but they get crostini with theirs." He smiled sweetly at me, turned around back into the van, and exchanged a bag. "It's small type, don't worry, Wrenny." I felt tears well up—if I couldn't get the stupid names correct on a catering list, what future did I have at all? And I almost messed up the whole important-building order.

"Wren, we are a team, that's how we get it right in the end. Okay?"

I nodded. Charlie was the first person, other than my parents, to stick with me.

$\int$

Now we go back even further in time, from seventh grade to fourth.

Just being Turtles—and having this long history together—did not leave us unsusceptible to the evils of fourth grade, where all of a sudden it could be true that a girl you spent most of third grade with playing Little House on the Prairie during roof time, the next year that same girl wouldn't stand next to you in line. Reagan was in my class, which I thought was a good thing, but because of a few lucky reading-partner groupings, she ended up at the epicenter of the clique of intimidating good-at-making-friendship-bracelet cool girls headed by Melissa Ryan. Melissa ruled our class like Henry VIII from kindergarten through fifth grade, until she moved to Scarsdale. I was not in the good-readers clique. I was in the needs-to-go-to-special-English clique, which wasn't really a clique, more like a one-man band. To blame my marginalization on my learning disabilities might sound delusional and paranoid because it has been drilled into our heads since we were in first grade that everyone "learns differently," but if you ask me, kids who "learn easily" feel good about themselves, and confident in a way that I know for a fact I never have.

Lunchroom at Hatcher: supervised insanity—lower-school girls looking like Eloise in navy-blue uniforms and puffy-sleeved white button-down blouses, sitting at long white linoleum fold-out tables. Pitchers of ice water and heavy plastic plates of "rabbit food" (cut-up carrots and celery, but the ladies in the lunchroom called it "rabbit food" even though I don't think a real rabbit has ever seen a piece of celery in the wild) grace every table to accompany the main course of pale roasted chicken and boiled rice. I was at the end of the table, wishing I were closer to where Melissa and Reagan were sitting.

"So, guys, what do you want to talk about?" I said, throwing my voice like a stage actor so I could be heard in the center of the hub.

I got a blank stare and a possible are-you-kidding-me squint out of mean-Melissa's eye.

I continued, not being as good as I might have been with social cues yet. "How about . . . if we were horses, what color would we be? I would be a dappled gray one." I laughed nervously and thought I might pee in my pants.

"Wren, what are you even *talking about*?" Reagan said, to the tune of all the alpha (maybe-as-insecure-as-I-was-but-sure-didn't-look-it) girls laughing in unison. Reagan and I had *just* had that very same, totally fun what-horse-would-you-be conversation over the summer in my garden and I knew she would be a chestnut brown one, so I looked at her like, *Huh?*

"I can't quite tell, Wren, but are you"—wait for it—"retarded?" Melissa said, like a Marine-trained sniper.

Retarded?

I laughed at my own expense to fit in with everyone else, but it felt like someone had just made me swallow a clementine. Before I actually wet my pants or cried or vomited, I heard a clear, strong voice behind me.

"I would be a black-as-night thoroughbred with four white socks and a star," said Farah, from a kinder, gentler table, throwing her voice way more effectively than I had. There was a big blister of a pause. The girls were silenced.

"I can see that," I said, as the clementine made its way out of my esophagus and down into my tummy, where I could still feel it but where it didn't hurt so badly.

"We can be in the same barn," Farah said, smiling at me as a few tears fell by mistake out of my eyes.

6

Summer after kindergarten.

Padmavati's house was my favorite. There was always a moss Diptyque candle burning in the front hallway that made me think I was in a sophisticated place. My mother wasn't a fan of scented candles. She said they were "too expensive by half," a fire hazard, and made rooms smell like a brothel. The one at Vati's house smelled like a place where relaxed people lived—people who ordered in sushi and had guitars in the living room.

"'And for all I know he is sitting there still, under his favorite cork tree, smelling the flowers just quietly. He is very happy.'" Padmavati's mom, Dipa, closed the worn cover of *The Story of Ferdinand* by Munro Leaf, put it down on her skirt embroidered with a Mexican village, tilted her head to the side, and sighed.

"Oh, how I love Ferdinand," she said. "He just wanted to be himself, right, girls?"

"When I am six, I am going to wear flowers in my hair just like the ladies at the bullfights," Vati said.

"I don't think I would want to sit alone under the tree," I said.

"How come, Wrenny? I think of you as a very thoughtful person who would be happy under a cork tree, drawing or reading."

Padmavati's mom is an editor at a fancy publishing house. Even when I was five I felt pressure from her to like books and reading. I looked at the very small gold and red bindi dot she always wore on her forehead. Everybody thinks it means you are married, but it doesn't; it's just there to make you look pretty. Even babies can wear bindis.

"I think I would get lonely under the tree," I said.

"Did Ferdinand seem lonely?" Dipa asked.

"No."

"Yes."

Vati and I had different responses. I think because I have a brother and a baby sister, I think doing things by yourself seems lonely, and since Vati is an only child she doesn't. I don't know why I think that, as I am alone all the time when I draw, but somehow that never feels lonely.

"Can you read that one about the mermaid and the whale?" I asked, and re-tucked one of the tassely ikat pillows under my head.

"Oh *yes*! Please, Mommy!" Vati knelt and put her hands together in begging prayer with a *huge* smile on her face.

"Pleeeeeeaaase," we both said, giggling because we knew it would work like a charm.

"Oh my goodness! I don't like that book!" Dipa said, but she went to get it anyway.

"Her hair is like Rapunzel's," I said. "When I am an older girl, I am going to grow my hair like that."

"But are you going to chase a crotchety, mean old whale and try to make him love you when clearly he doesn't?" Dipa snuggled in between the two of us on the big red velvet sofa.

"I don't get *why* that whale doesn't love her," Vati said. "She can talk to fish!"

"I know, sweetheart. She's smart, she knows all the tides . . . she's beautiful, she looks like a supermodel of the Atlantic Ocean whose best friend is a dolphin, and yet she spends her whole life chasing that good-for-nothing whale."

"But maybe if she tried harder, the whale *would* love her," I said, hoping there was a sequel to the mermaid-and-the-whale book.

"Wren, dear heart, if a man doesn't love you, there is nothing you can do to change that. You should just let him swim away." I remember thinking that *clearly* Dipa wanted us to glean something from this piece of wisdom. Vati's parents were divorced but were still great friends—they both stayed in the book club even after their split. I think Dipa might still love Vati's dad, Jordan, but ever since they were divorced he has always been with Summer, his girlfriend. He never has married Summer, but he never goes back to Dipa either. Confusing.

"Oh never mind, that is silly." Dipa shook her head, took a deep breath in, and then said with a twinkle in her eye, "Maybe, Vati, you should write a storybook about a mermaid who is so talented, funny, and beautiful that every single creature in the sea falls in love with her and wants to marry her."

She wrapped her hands around our shoulders and squeezed as she said the next part. "But instead, she goes to Ocean College and graduates Summa. Cum. Laude." She released her grip. "Wrenny, you can illustrate it. Until then, we'll just read this antiquated book." She flipped open the cover, looked over the title page, turned it, and as she did said slowly, "Here we go. 'Once upon a time . . .'" Dipa licked her long, elegant finger and got ready to turn the page.

Whoosh, I really just went down memory lane. But I kind of had to for you to get where we came from, for you to see who we all were, who we have always been. Sometimes I think people change in only the smallest ways over time. My mother says that kids are basically the same from the moment they come out, and I think that's true. I hope it's not altogether true though. There are so many things about myself that I hope one day will change.

7

Back to the day of the museum party. Or, much more important, the day I met Nolan.

"We have to get a move on, my mother is just going to drop off the dresses on her way to the airport," Farah said, quickening the pace as we walked up the last hill in Central Park before we got to the West Side.

"There are four hundred people at my house at the moment so someone can take them. Where is your mom going?" I said, checking my phone. It was almost four o'clock.

"Napa. There is a gentleman there apparently," Farah said in a no-big-deal way. I didn't say anything. Farah's mom's "adventures" are beyond what I can understand in my parents-have-been-married-my-whole-life brain.

"Oooohhhh! I am very excited for the party!" Vati skipped a few feet ahead, clapping her hands.

On the day of the party, the day with the life-changing crazy wind, something else was happening in our house that was making the afternoon feel chaotic. My ten-year-old sister, Dinah, was shooting an episode of her cooking show, *Dining with Dinah*. Dinah is a celebrity—for real. She is definitely the most famous person I know. Her show is shot in our house on average every eight days for fourteen weeks during the school year. Our mother likes to think she is the kind of person who believes your name should only be in print three times in your life—when you are born, when you get married, and when you die—so the fact that her younger daughter has a hip little "Ask Dinah" cooking column at least three times a year in *New York* magazine and her own blog is really ironic.

The whole TV thing started, to Mom's horror, because one day *Eyewitness News*, a local newscast, went to Hatcher to do a report about how kids were participating in cooking school lunch. It was some kind of feel-good news story about healthy food awareness. Anyway, Dinah caught their eye. She is one of those adorable kids with almost unimaginable looks-like-it-was-dyed blood orange hair (which she inherited from my maternal grandmother), heavy-cream skin tone, and, of course, freckles—a pretty Pippi Long-stocking. She sparkled and charmed the camera chopping away at an onion like Morimoto when she could barely see over the counter. It was just weird how adept she was—AND she has an incongruous New York accent that no one else in the family has. It's like Fran Drescher raised her. So a day later, when the broadcast ran, a star was born. All you could see was Dinah. She was saying "but-tah" and her twinkly sapphire-blue eyes grew in size two or three times when the turkey meat loaf (which is what they were cook-ing) tumbled perfectly out of the pan. I mean, we knew she could cook—she was eight when she started and could whisk egg whites into stiff peaks like Julia Child. She's a prodigy—a Mozart of mozzarella. But when all-the-world (pretty much) saw it on the news and then on YouTube (where it went viral), suddenly she wasn't ours anymore; she was a sensation.

I think kids watch Food TV more than cartoons, which is probably why, very soon after Dinah was on the news, Bravo called to say they were interested in having Dinah host a thirty-minute cooking show. Mom was repelled, but Dad, who is more relaxed about publicity and media and sort of everything, convinced Mom that it would only be *good* for Dinah. I remember him saying at dinner, "Nan, love, it's a wonderful life *experience* for her. I don't see how we can stand in her way." My mother protested, "I can stand *directly* in her way, David. She is only NINE!" Dad laughed and put his bent pointer finger under her chin, looking her in the eyes. "Oh, I love you, Nan, my little worrier . . . Maybe she will be a *hit* and we can all retire!" Mom laughed too. He had won. *Dining with Dinah* airs on Saturday mornings. Some of her recipes, like her caramel sauce, you can buy on Gilt.com. She is so famous she wears sunglasses to the Museum of Natural History so the under-eight set doesn't mob her.

"I feel like I'm about to see Beyoncé and Jay-Z or fall off a cliff or something! This party is freaking me out, I feel all *crazy* inside. I have never been to a party this big!" Vati said, and skipped again.

"I think it feels more like going to the prom, or staying up to watch Jimmy Fallon," I said, huffing. The park is hilly.

"Staying up to watch *Jimmy Fallon*? You are such a nerd," Reagan said, laughing.

"What, we weren't allowed to till, like, last year," I said.

"None of us have ever *been* to a prom, nor will we ever *go* because we go to an all-girls school, Wrenner," said Farah, quickening her pace. "No, no, no, no, I have a more ominous feeling about tonight, in a good way, but I feel like something disastrous will happen, like a flood." There was a huge field to our right, where people were walking their dogs and kids were doing after-school sports.

"Floods aren't good, Farah," Vati said.

"I know, but they are exciting." Farah raised her eyebrows and winked at Vati.

"You're weird," Vati said.

"What are you going to wear, Wren?" Reagan said, checking her phone.

"I don't know. My mom said she had a plan."

"Sc-AIR-ree," she sang.

"Well, I know you all borrowed Farah's mom's dresses, but my mother didn't want me to. She thinks Alix's clothes are *too sophisticated for a fifteen-year-old*. I can't help it. You know my mom. She's uptight."

"Your mom is *so not* uptight, Wren," Padmavati said, putting her hand out so we wouldn't jaywalk across Central Park West.

"I know she doesn't look like that on the outside, but she completely is. I'm not even allowed to be on Facebook."

"Um, hello? She lets Bravo come into your house every week," noted Farah.

"And Oliver has dreads!" Vati said, releasing her arm when the light turned green. "I loooove the dress Alix lent me. It's pink!" she said, crossing the street.

"Dinah's TV thing and Oliver's dreads are totally different. Remember when she made me give back that little bracelet to Andrew Goodman in sixth grade?"

"Oh yeah—what was up with that? It was weensy, and he was *asking you out*," Farah said.

"I know, but it was gold, and Mom thought it was inappropriate. She let me keep the Hershey bar he gave me with it."

"Oh god, she's going to be home when we get to your house, right?"

"Yes, Farah, Dinah has her show thing," I said, and looked at my phone.

"Wren! *Just help me.* How am I going to stay downstairs with your mother hysterically lurking around the set?" We were now two blocks away from my house. Farah's sudden and obsessive application of the palest pink sparkly lip gloss every block was giving away the fact that she was about to see Tom-the-camera-guy. She took a deep cleansing breath in preparation.

"Farah, we don't even know if Tom-the-camera-guy will be shooting. And we have to get dressed anyway." Farah had a massive crush on the DP (director of photography), Tom, who was so old. I'm pretty sure he was in his twenties.

"Um, will Oliver be home?" Padmavati asked, with the subtlety of a ram. Padmavati has loved Oliver, my brother, since we were in kindergarten. Now that we are sophomores, she is absolutely sure she will marry him. We plan their wedding every time everyone sleeps over. Because she is Indian-American, in all likelihood some part of her wedding will be Hindi and traditional. Her husband might even ride in on an elephant, or maybe a horse. For the American half of the wedding she wants barbecue and coconut cake. Farah is the get-married-at-the-Carlyle-in-Carolina-Herrera-eat-filet-and-drink-champagne-wedding kind of girl. Reagan says she doesn't want to get married because she doesn't believe in true love or God or any institution really. Charlie blushes at any talk of weddings at all. Sometimes, when we talk weddings, we forget he's there until he turns such a violent crimson color from embarrassment that he starts glowing.

"I don't know what you will do about Mom, Farah. She's a fixture. And yeah, Oli will be home, Vati. He promised he would come home right after school so we won't be late for the cars taking us to the mus-e-UM!" I said in a singsong crescendo.

"Oh my god!!" Farah joined me in a shrill call to the wild. And then she said, "I want Tom to come with us. Would that *ever* happen?" She looked at me as seriously as she could, knowing full well how off-the-wall she was.

"Oh, well, maybe . . . yeah, no," I said, looking at her like she was insane because she was. "Farah—*yuck*! He's so much older than you!"

"Spencer Tracy was seven years older than Katharine Hepburn," she shot back.

"Who?" Reagan said. She was walking just ahead of us because four people can't walk in a row down a side street in New York City. The sidewalks are too narrow.

"What? How do you *not* know who Katharine Hepburn was?" I said. Reagan's parents never make her watch black-and-white movies.

"She was in only one of the greatest movies of all time, Reagan," said Farah. *"Gone with the Wind."*

"*What?*" Full stop from me. "Farah, Scarlett O'Hara was *not* played by Katharine Hepburn, it was . . . oh gosh, well, whatever, it wasn't her."

"You guys are missing the point. First of all, Katharine Hepburn was in, like, ten of the greatest films of all time. My mother has all of them on her iPad and we watch them in bed. And," Farah said, clearly trying to have the last word, "Spencer Tracy was older than Katharine Hepburn and he was married to *someone else* and he and Katharine *still* had one of the greatest love stories of all time."

"But I bet Katharine Hepburn wasn't in tenth grade, Farah," Padmavati noted.

"Seal is eleven years older than Heidi Klum," Farah hissed.

"THEY BROKE UP!" Padmavati and Reagan roared in unison.

"Vivien Leigh!" I yelled. "Vivien Leigh played Scarlett O'Hara . . . Jeez." I can never get names until at least ten minutes after I need them. It's one strain of my other learning disorder: dysnomia. I have that along with the dyslexia, dysgraphia, and a dollop of ADD. I do eventually get it right, it just takes me longer than most people.

"Oliver is only seventeen . . . perfect," Padmavati mooned dreamily. Reagan turned away from Vats and rolled her eyes secretly at me. Padmavati's love for Oliver was sadly one-sided.

As we arrived at my house, I saw Charlie standing on the fourth step of our brownstone's staircase holding up the dresses that Farah's mother, Alix, must have just dropped off. His arm looked like it was shaking, either because of the weight of the garment bags or because he was afraid of having them touch the ground. Charlie was already dressed for the party in a brown velvet suit, a French-blue button-down shirt, and his favorite purple tie that he can't wear to school.

(At St. Tim's you have to wear jacket and tie. Beat-up blue ties, not slick purple silk ties.)

"I'm going to drop these!" he teased in a quivering voice, teetering on the step and making us run up the stairs to relieve him of the finery.

"Thaaaank you, Charllleeeee," Vati and Farah chanted, taking the bags from him.

"Good boy," said Reagan, patting his head like a dog as he handed the last dress over. Charlie rolled his eyes at me and reflattened his hair.

"Hey, Wrenny," he said.

"Hey, Charlie. I like your tie," I said, because I knew it would make him feel good after Reagan treated him like a dog.

"Purple is the color of royalty," he said proudly.

"Right. What were you doing with all those dresses?"

"Farah's mom spotted me down the block on my way to your house, and without even asking me, she hurled these out the car window and zoomed away. I think I heard her saying 'Thank you, dahhhhling' as she went back to her phone call."

"Oh. She's a trip," I said.

"No kidding." He pointed at me with his index finger held out like a gun.

Charlie and I walked up the remaining six stairs, following the girls. When we reached the landing they moved aside for me to open the outermost door with my key.

"Why didn't you just ring the bell?" I asked Charlie.

"I was scared I'd mess up a take like I did the last time they were shooting here."

About a week before, we were watching *Dining with Dinah* being shot and the theme from *Twilight* came blaring out of Charlie's phone. It totally blew the take of Dinah showing off her golden-brown sear of a tilapia filet she was frying, mortifying Charlie and aggravating the crew that we worshipped because they were straight out of NYU film school and lived in Brooklyn. We think Brooklyn is so cool even though we haven't been there very much. But if you are a teenager growing up in Manhattan, you are supposed to like Brooklyn and want to live there when you get out of college. You can hardly read an issue of *New York* magazine that doesn't have a story about some bearded guy making artisanal pickles in Gowanus.

"That was horrible." When Charlie says "horrible" it sounds like "whore-i-bul." It's a lingering effect from his speech impediment and although it bothers him, I think it's so cute.

"Hurry, Wren, it's freezing out here!" Farah whined as I fiddled with the key, which always sticks in the lock.

It *was* cold. Colder than it had been all fall. It was that wind. That sharp, serious wind that makes the reservoir freeze and tells you with a discomforting certainty that there are forces greater than yourself in this world. Big ones. Ones that you better pay attention to.

Forces that can change the course of your life.

8

"Girls!"

My mother twirled around at the sound of the door closing. She rushed at us, kissing and saying hello, taking our backpacks off—a vestige of when we were ten. May skidded around on the wooden floor and leaped up on our legs, imitating my mother. The house smelled like curry.

"Hi, guys!" Dinah called from the kitchen, where she was sitting on the counter next to the stove surrounded by Bravo people. "We're done!" She thinks the whole world revolves around her show, and actually, in our house she's not wrong.

"Oh, my darlings—feel you!" My mother had both hands on Padmavati's cheeks. "You are frozen, come in, come in, we just finished. Whoosh—that wind came in with you! Charlie darling, close the door! Let me help you all with these dresses. Look at these garment bags!" She lifted her eyebrows like some big fun was inside them. "Go put them upstairs, everyone!" She made a shooing motion upward. "We have to get going! The cars will be here right at six-fifteen. Dad is meeting us there. He's been there all day. I had to bring his evening clothes over because he ran out of time. Are you hungry? What time is it? Already quarter to five!" She frantically turned her attention back to the set.

Through the huge double doorway between the entrance hall and the open kitchen, you could see the BlackBerry-checking producers sitting on the vanilla-pudding-yellow sofa that sits at the far end of the room, nestled in the bay window. Beyond them the crew, dressed in dingy worn-in T-shirts and carpenter pants, were packing up lights and hauling cords around. Leading the charge was Tom-the-camera-guy. Farah spotted him as soon as she walked in the door. She threw her garment bag over the banister. "I'm going to say hi to Dinah!" she said, as if she had been longing to see Dinah all day. *Please.*

Padmavati and Reagan also draped the garment bags they were holding over the banister and, with Charlie, went to poke around the kitchen for the leftovers of whatever Dinah had made. She has to prepare at least three or four servings of whatever they are shooting, so if one gets ruined they have backup. It looked like my mother was about to oversee the producer, who was giving final notes to Dinah, but she twirled around again, took my hand, and led me away from everyone to the stairs.

"Wrenny." She looked like she had something biggish to tell me. I got nervous for a second. I don't always know when I have done something wrong. Once when I was little I thought it would be cool to make stained-glass windows, so I used colored Sharpies and drew what looked like stained glass all over my real glass windows. My mother hit "a ten." A ten is when she really loses it. She looks insane, screams things like "*What in god's name is the matter with you!*" Fire comes out of her nose. And then she calms down and cries and feels so terrible for what she said when she was in a ten. She went to a shrink about it and he said she couldn't do that, he said it was against the law, so now if one of us inadvertently enrages her, she tries to go to her bedroom until she is at a three or four. That time when I drew stained glass all over the windows, she hit a ten, but later, when she was at a three, she said it was actually beautiful and wept that I was a genius.

"You know what I thought?" my mother said.

"No—am I in trouble?"

"No, oh heavens no! Why do you say that, sweetheart? Do I look mad?" Sometimes my mother *does* look mad when she isn't. Like, sometimes she will taste soup or an éclair and her face contorts so you think she is about to say, "Oh disgusting—it's inedible!" And out of her mouth will come "Oh good lord, this is possibly the best thing I have ever eaten." She has big bursts of either love or anger, and sometimes it's hard to tell which one will be coming at you.

"No, forget it, I just—what were you going to say?"

"You know my red Oscar de la Renta dress?"

Of course I knew this dress. The greatest piece of fabric hanging in my mother's closet is a muted poppy-red strapless Oscar de la Renta silk taffeta floor-length gown that she wore to the first gala she and my father went to when he had just become director of the museum. The dress is as old as I am and since I was a little girl I would sneak into my mother's cedar closet to find it. I would sit at the bottom of the dimly lit closet that smelled like earthy warm juniper and like my mother, because of the faintest hint of orange blossom left over on the clothes. I'd carefully leaf, one by one, through pants, kilts, and kaftans until I got to that beautiful red dress that lives in the back. I would run my fingers along the bottom of its finely sewn hem and picture my mother dancing in it with my father, who looked so handsome in his evening clothes and slicked-back jet-black hair. The dress has a huge skirt made with yards and yards of light, swishing, crinkly silk that almost forces you to dance and spin around. I've tried it on before for fun, years before it would actually fit, and every time the dress takes me away to someplace I have never been—balls in London, Bette Davis movies, the Oscars.

"I think it will fit you now." Her eyes welled up with tears.

"Oh, Mom, I would *love* to wear it!" As if this was what she knew and hoped I would say, she opened her mouth and smiled, nodding her head. "I know, right? Isn't it a *marvelous* idea?" She was now sort of laughing and crying at the same time, as if I had achieved something. My mother has a huge mouth and cries very easily. My father says she looks like Carly Simon. She has a lot of hair and big teeth. I was looking at that big mouth and all those teeth when suddenly my stomach contracted to the size of a walnut. I had always wanted to wear that dress, but now that the moment was here, a bajillion questions raced through my mind. Was I nervous to wear the dress? Was I old enough to wear the dress? Would it really fit? Was I pretty enough to wear a dress like that? Would wearing a dress like that change me? I felt like Laura in *Little House on the Prairie* when she was getting dressed on her first day as a teacher. With one single costume change she went from a buck-toothed little girl with braids in an apron to a real-life woman with her hair in a bun, a proper calico dress like Ma's, and a look on her face that said she meant business. I was going to wear *the red dress*. Once I wore that dress, I would never again be the girl who hadn't worn it yet.

One flight above, as if he had been cued, Oliver turned on his music. (He actually probably had been cued. The show's assistant director texts us when it is okay to make noise and when it's not.) The tightly wound, rhythmic thumpings of Eminem made their way down the stairs from the second floor and it felt exactly how I was feeling inside. It was as if I had my very own sound track. Rap has a kind of battle cry about it. Eminem tends to scare me—he's so angry. I'm more of a Kelly Clarkson/Beyoncé gal, and I even like country because of Sugarland. But that evening the muffled pounding was appealing.

"Guys!" I called to my friends, who were spooning mouthfuls of rice and soupy yellow chicken curry into their mouths from one big flame-red Le Creuset pot on the stove. "Let's go get ready."

9

Like a herd of goats, we galloped up the familiar stairs to my room on the fourth floor.

My parents, Oliver, Dinah, and I live in a five-story brownstone my parents bought when my father became the museum's director. One of my mother's favorite things to say about it is "It's too much house, but we thought we would need to entertain more for David's job and the children could be upstairs." She stops talking and does this fluttering thing with her hands indicating that we would all be up "there" somewhere and they would be downstairs amusing the art world. Then she pushes her hands away from her in a whooshing motion, like all of that was garbage, and says, almost showing off about the closeness of our family, "But we are always piled in this kitchen whether there is a party going on or not, so we didn't end up needing all the floors."

Oliver's room is on the second floor, where the living room is. To Padmavati's dismay, the door was shut. The muted music was the only way you would know he was in there.

Vati looked at me with a sad-dog face.

"Oh, all right," I whispered to her. Reagan, Farah, and Charlie passed us and continued up to the third floor, where Dinah's and my parents' bedrooms are, then the fourth, where my bedroom is. And the fifth floor is just a tiny landing that has a door to the roof, which we are forbidden to go on.

I knocked loudly. Nothing. I knocked again. He usually opened it just a crack so I wouldn't know whatever he was doing in his room. He was in a "private stage," my mother would say, as she reminded Dinah and me to respect it and not bother him. Maybe he was masturbating. Gross.

I knocked for the third time and the door opened, and a guy that totally wasn't Oliver was standing there.

"Oh—hi, um—"

Oh my god, what-the-fluke is going on? This was no random friend of my brother's, this was—he was in a whole other category. He was extraordinary.

"Hi, I uhh—" I am stammering. I'm disoriented. I actually heard Padmavati take a sharp breath in as if she had seen Justin Timberlake.

"Um, I—" I continued pathetically.

Who are you who are you who are you who are you?

He was so beautiful.

His beauty, and a cool-guy vibe that I had not yet encountered in real life, only in movies, assaulted me. He was tall, taller than me. He had once-my-hair-was-normal-boy-length-but-I-let-it-grow-out-like-two-years-ago long choppy brown hair that fell below his shoulders. His bangs were studied. He swept them to the side with his hand, tucking them up and around his ear, which had a perfectly round, small golden hoop imbedded in it. When he tilted his head ever so slightly forward, his bangs fell off his ear and covered his enormous root-beer-brown eyes. His eyes looked Italian, like Michelangelo eyes, big lids, soft. Can you picture those? Have you ever seen Michelangelo's David? This boy had eyes from the Renaissance, and they were looking right at me. He was wearing a worn athletic-gray BRONX SCIENCE T-shirt. Bronx Science is a really good public high school in New York. I think it is one of the best schools in the country. I think geniuses go there. Did this guy go to Bronx Science? An unfamiliar feeling shot through my gut, as if an octopus had darted from one end of it to the other.

"Hi there." His voice was friendly, and a little gritty. It was the voice of someone older than he looked like he was.

Oliver popped his head into the hall, breaking the spell.

"What's up, Wren?"

I looked at him like, *Um, who is this?* Because the thing is, this guy wasn't Samson or Benjer, Oliver's goofy friends that had been coming over after basketball practice and playing Dungeons & Dragons in Oliver's room for the better part of the last fifty Saturdays. This guy was *new*. It was like Oliver had brought home the *Twilight* guy.

"This is Nolan."

"Oh. Nolan. Hi." *Nolan.* Who would have thought that I would ever meet someone named Nolan?

"Hi, Oliver!" Padmavati almost shouted.

"Hey, Padmavati," Oliver said, with nothing in his voice but a hello.

"Mom said we should be ready to go to the . . . um . . ." I was almost positive *Nolan* was kind of *smiling* at me. He had put his arm up so it rested on the frame of the door. I had to take a very subtle deep breath—unlike Padmavati's earlier sharp and loud one. ". . . party."

"I know. It will only take us five minutes to get ready. We have, like, almost two hours. It's not even five." Oliver shot a glance at Vati, which she would be using as proof of interest for the next few hours.

We? Was this guy coming to the party with Oliver?

"Okay, well, I'll, we all will be, you know," and I pointed my finger upward.

"Yup," Oliver said. Nolan, who didn't say a word, gave me an honest-to-god real smile, revealing adorable kind of big teeth, one of them chipped in the front. Oliver closed the door. Padmavati and I stood looking at the door in our face. The music got louder from behind.

"Oh my god, Wren. Who was that?" Vati said. "He has a chipped tooth, and still his hotness is devastating."

I looked at her, speechless. My heart started beating a strong, distracting beat, like there was someone furiously pounding on a door in my chest. It felt exactly like I was about to recite a poem that wasn't one hundred percent memorized in front of a class, or even like I was riding a bike down a steep hill and was just out of control enough to be unsure of my outcome. Or it was as if I had lost my footing climbing and almost fell out of a tree. Have you ever felt any of that? Like something thrilling was about to happen?

10

The instant Nolan's mouth formed a smile in my direction, I wanted to tell Charlie and the girls. My first impulse is to tell. I am very impulsive. I blurt. I am a teller. I am an impulsive teller. But this time, I used my hard-won-in-therapy tools and pulled myself back. If this were any other day, I would have put Farah's hand on my heart so she could feel the new beat, discuss, and figure out what was to be done about it. I would have shouted up two flights of stairs, "Guys! Something is happening to me and it's because of some guy in Oliver's room!" *But I didn't do it.* Padmavati and I did rush up the stairs, but with each step I took, this fast-acting, unfamiliar feeling of wanting to be private and keep him to myself was building in my bloodstream.

When you get to the last flight of stairs before my floor, along the walls of the stairway are my drawings. Some are framed, some I just stuck up there randomly with blue wall tape. It's my "gallery." My mother gave it to me as a free space in the house that I could use any way I wanted. I mean, my room has my drawings all over it too, but there are too many of them. I had overflow. There were some drawings up there from as far back as third and fourth grade, and some from as recently as last week—black chunky cityscapes with yellow dripping windows, antelopes jumping, and many pictures of the stars in the night sky.

I had run past those drawings countless times, and seeing them was like looking in a mirror. But that day, they all looked unfamiliar. As if I was someone new. As if meeting Nolan had changed who I was even from that morning. Why the big change? I don't know. Why do dogs that look like they are just checking each other out suddenly erupt in a growling explosion? Why do you sometimes have such a violently bad dream you bolt into your parents' bed even though you are fourteen? Why can a song—a really cheesy one that you hear by mistake while your parents are watching the Country Music Awards on TV—make you cry, and move you so much you then download it so you can listen to it for the rest of the night up in your room? *I don't get it*, but I am here to say that life—or a person—can unexpectedly change who you are very, very quickly.

I had only minutes to process this feeling before we got to my room. It wasn't enough time. Padmavati rounded the corner into my bedroom at the end of the hall and jumped on the bed where Charlie and Farah were lying platonically all over each other.

"Reagan, get in here!" Vati called to Reagan, who was in the bathroom showering. Vati was going to blow it about Nolan and there was nothing I could do. I closed the door and flopped on the window seat on the far side of my room. It's my go-to place of safety. Good for daydreaming, texting, and sketching the rooftops of the Upper West Side. Not good for homework, as my mother tells me almost every day.

"So something is up downstairs," Vati said, sitting crisscross applesauce on the bed.

"We were assuming you were spying on Oliver," Charlie said, unearthing himself from under Farah's leg and putting one of my European squares behind his back. Farah, still reclining, shoved a sausage-link-shaped pillow embroidered with loopy pink ribbons under her head.

"Well, first of all, I really think Oliver looked at me—like, *looked at me.* It was ever so slightly different than any time before. He looked at me like this." She relaxed her body, slouching like Oliver does, and said, "Hey, Vati."

"Whoa hay hoe," Charlie teased. "I see a marriage proposal any day now."

"No, no, I'm quite serious. He has never given me this look before." She relaxed again and then smiled with one corner of her mouth tilted up, exactly like Oliver does.

"I saw it, it was a nice smile," I said from the window seat, hoping that maybe Vati was going to run with the telling-everyone-about-Oliver thing and forget to mention Nolan.

"Yeah, thanks, Wren, it was the real deal, I think. But—*but*, there is this *other* guy down there . . . *Nolan*, and he is so freaking gorgeous. He was wearing this Bronx Science shirt, like all cool and faded and worn in. And he had purple high-tops on, and he had this long, cool sort of black-brown hair and he's tall, right?" Vati looked at me for confirmation.

"That is Nolan Shop. I'm sure of it," Reagan said in a towel, standing in front of my *Starry Night* poster with my Tweezerman in her hand.

"How do you know?" I asked, with a little more edge to my voice than I meant to have. (That's another ADD thing, or maybe it's a big-feeler thing, but not having a lot of control over the emotion in your voice.) That is what Reagan is like. It can't just be my thing that I had an encounter with a hot guy in my house, of course Reagan knows him. It felt like she was ever so slightly taking something from me. She does it even with random things, like magazines. I'll have just cracked open a brand-new issue of *Vogue* and she'll ask to see a picture for "just a second" and then she'll end up reading the whole thing.

"It's *got* to be him," she said, gesturing with the tweezers she was holding like some teachers do with their reading glasses. The octopus in my tummy was going bananas.

"There's a sort of famous Nolan that goes to Bronx Science. How many Nolans could there be? He's all over Facebook. And Facebook is all over him," she said. I felt like I was going to murder my parents that I had to wait until I was sixteen to have a Facebook page. I rushed into the bathroom to look at myself in the medicine cabinet mirror that was completely steamed up because of Reagan's shower. *Who am I if I don't even know what is all over Facebook?* The mirror had no answers. All I saw through the steam was that my hair looked wild and unruly from the wind.

"*Who.* Is. Nolan. Shop?" I heard Farah say from the bed. I saw my eyes in the mirror open wider and then I kept going with that and opened my eyes as wide as I could. I mouthed *Nolan Shop* so I could see my lips form his name.

"Oh! I think I know who that is!" Charlie chimed in. I turned away from my reflection and looked back into the room to see Reagan whip her hair up over her head and then back down again so I got sprayed with tiny darts of water.

"He's in a band," she said.

"*Yes!*" Charlie jumped off the bed.

Reagan opened her towel to readjust, showing everyone on the bed the Crenshaw melons that are her boobs.

"They're called the Shoppe Boys—like P-P-E shoppe—because his last name is Shop: S-H-O-P," Reagan said.

"*Yes!* Yes, yes, yes—my guitar teacher totally told me about them. They're still in high school but they are incredible. Yes, that is definitely him," said Charlie, who got back on the bed happy that he knew what he was talking about. He was oblivious to Reagan's boobs, which I couldn't believe because I could hardly stop myself from staring at them.

"You seem to know a lot about that band, Reagan," Farah said, like she was getting to the bottom of something. I leaned against the sink to listen. But before Reagan could answer, I heard someone pounding on the door of my room.

"Wren!" Dinah yelled, at the top of her lungs. "Mom wants you to come downstairs and try on *the dress!*"

"Dinah! Come in here." Farah and my other friends had spent so much time with Dinah she was like everyone's little sister. Dinah skipped in, followed by May.

"Did you see anyone come home from school with Oliver today?" Farah asked her.

"Um, no? I was *shooting*, if you didn't notice."

"I know, you little fish fryer, I just thought you could be helpful to us, but . . . never mind." Farah plays Dinah like a tiny fiddle. The last thing I wanted was Dinah getting all up in my business, so I intervened.

47

"Shhh, you guys, come on. Let's go see the dress." I left the bathroom, passing Reagan, who was headed back in.

"I hear he's adorable," Reagan said.

I felt a flash of annoyance rip through me again, as if she had just taken my magazine.

"Who's adorable?" Dinah has ears for boy-talk like a bloodhound has a nose for a missing person.

"Wren's got a crush on a rock star in Oliver's room," Reagan said, popping her head out of the bathroom.

"Reagan!" I looked at Padmavati like, *Thanks,* and she looked at me like, *What?*

"That is just so wrong," Dinah said, cracking up.

"Let's go to your mom's room and look at the dress," Farah commanded.

"I'm doing my makeup," Reagan called from the bathroom.

"I think I won't go into your mother's boudoir while she's dressing, thank you," Charlie said, and pulled a math textbook out of his knapsack.

"*What is going on?* Who does Wren have a crush on?" Dinah whined, scrambling to follow Farah.

"Dinah, please—go downstairs and do something else! We have to *get ready.*"

"'We have to get ready,'" Dinah mimicked, rolling her eyes and following May out the door, her blunt bob swinging. Dinah wasn't invited to the party.

11

Anytime someone compliments our house, my mother mentions what a wreck it was when she and Dad bought it. My first memory is being held by my father and looking around the kitchen that had eggplant-colored wallpaper peeling off the walls and very heavy drapes the previous owners had left on the French doors to the garden outside. I must have been two years old. I remember the feeling of his scratchy tweed blazer on the bottom of my thighs and putting my hand out to touch the dust drifting around in the light coming through the French doors. The scattering of particles in air is called the Tyndall effect—I learned eleven years later in Mr. Chin's eighth-grade Earth Science class, but as a child I had no idea it was dust or particles, I thought it was just what light looked like up close. The glass in one of the panes was broken and Dad must have thought I was going for the sharp edge. He pulled my hand back and said, "Don't touch it, my darling, it will surely cut you." Sometimes both my parents think I am going to do something dangerous when I am really just trying to touch the light.

Now the glass in the windows is clear and storm-proof, and the walls are a deep butter-yellow—"like Rome in an August sunset," my mother often sighs. There are Persian rugs running down the halls, and under those rugs the beaten-up floors are made from smooth, wide wooden planks. Photographs and paintings hang on the walls from the floor to the ceiling, all mixed up. There is a picture of Oliver in his purple West Side Little League uniform, right next to a Sylvia Mangold drawing of a tree—a present my father gave my mother when I was born. In every room (including my parents' bathroom), deep, soft upholstered chairs and sofas are arranged so you can gather and talk, read, or take a nap—and you are encouraged to do all of those things. And on every side table are lamps with kraft-paper lampshades. All the lamps are different: eighteenth-century Dutch white and blue porcelain tabac jars, Italian owls from Siena, metal milk jugs found in barn sales, blown thick smooth Simon Pearce glass. It's a real mishmash, but the shades are exactly the same. "Having uniform shades saves this room from looking hodgepodge," I can hear my mother saying. We don't have any overhead lighting because that is for hospitals and department stores—not for homes.

The real reason why we live in such a big house and have all those beautiful things is not only because my father has an important job, it's also because long ago, back in Holland, my great-grandfather made a boatload of money as a banker. That money is why we can live where we live in New York City, and why most of my family can work in the arts.

Mom was seated at her dressing table in a pale pink silk robe, getting her hair blown out by Dinah's hair-and-makeup person, Rachel. Hanging on the door of the closet was the red dress. Compared to the mayhem of my room, my parents' spacious creamy wall-to-wall-wool-sisal-carpeted room, with the whirring white noise of the hair dryer, was peaceful and calming. Even Farah and Vati quieted down when they came in. It was a sanctuary of grownup-ness.

"Do you girls want your hair done? I'm almost through here," said Rachel, with a soft lisp from her tongue piercing.

"*Yes*, girls—you should take advantage of *marvelous* Rachel and have her do something fantastic with those locks," Mom called over the hair dryer, signaling to Rachel in the mirror that her hair was done and to wrap it up. I lay down across the bottom of my parents' bed to stare at the dress. I would never flop on their pillows that were plumped to perfection by Hailey, our housekeeper. I had been taught that lesson a thousand times. I'm not sure my mother has a harsher bark for someone who messes up the pillows, but like May, I am always allowed to sit or lie on the goose-feather duvet folded at the foot of the bed. The hair dryer came to a stop.

"It gets more beautiful every time I look at it!" my mother said, getting up from her little upholstered dressing-table chair and gliding over to the dress.

"I know. I can't believe it." Flashes of Nolan in the doorway assaulted me. I felt like I had to squeeze my stomach.

"It's a rocking dress," said Rachel.

"It's huge!" said Padmavati, as she sat in my mother's chair and considered her hair. Rachel swept Vati's long black hair up in both her hands and twisted it into a chignon. Vati smiled.

"I wish I was Indian. Look at this hair!" Rachel tumbled Vati's heavy, thick hair in her hands like every strand was solid gold. She practically put her face in it and rubbed it all around, looking like she might weep. "Hair like this is the reason I get up in the morning to do my job."

"Put the dress on!" Farah flopped next to me, dangerously close to the plumped pillows, and pinched my butt. My mother clapped her hands like a preschooler and reached over to take the dress off the hanger. Farah leaned over and whispered in my ear, "I bet Mr. Music Man is gonna *love it*," so I smacked her on the bottom as I sat up on my knees.

"Shouldn't I take a shower or something first? I feel so dirty and yucky."

"No, no, you can quickly try it on to see if it fits and then take a shower. Don't you want Rachel to do something with this?" Mom came over and took a handful of my unbrushed hair and held it up to Rachel, who looked over with bobby pins clenched in her teeth and raised her eyebrows.

"No, no, I'm going to wash it and then let it dry with that stuff in it so it curls a little. It will be fine, Mama."

"Up to you," she sang in an I-don't-think-you-are-making-the-right-choice voice.

"It's my hair," I sang back to her. We looked at each other in a standstill.

She tweaked my nose. "Okay, Wrenner. Take off those clothes."

I undid my uniform skirt in the back and wiggled out of it so I was standing in my leggings. I pulled off my sweater and tank top at the same time and threw them on the bed. Then Farah pulled them apart and folded each one properly. She could work at the Gap. I was wearing a camisole top with a bra thing in it. I really don't have enough boobs to wear a real bra. Truthfully, it felt awkward standing there, like a little girl in a dressing room with her mother trying on school clothes.

And that is probably why I blurted out, "Mom, how does Oliver know that guy in his room?"

My mother, who had taken down the dress and was looking at it as if she was remembering herself wearing it, turned to me and said, "He is quite something, right? Did you meet him? He just came home with Oliver today, just walked right in as if he had been here all his life. I've never seen him before. I guess they met at a party or something? He goes to Bronx Science—which is *impressive*, sort of the Harvard of high schools. His name is . . . wait, it's like a girl's name."

"Nolan!" Farah and Padmavati hooted in unison.

"Shhh! Oh my lord, what if he hears you!" I said, blushing like crazy. My mother looked at the girls and me like she was in on something. She sort of giggled and put her hand over her mouth, which she then uncovered to whisper, "He's coming to the party tonight!"

"Oh my god." Now I felt out-of-control-dumb, standing there talking with my mother about boys in my leggings, which you should never really be in without a long shirt on unless you are in a yoga class.

"Mom, just—"

"Did you meet him, Wrenny?"

"Yes, Vati and I did. It's no big deal, we just saw him for a second." (God, why did I even say anything?)

"Who is he?" Mom said, like she was asking the universe.

"He's in a band!" Padmavati said, as Rachel wove a braid in the front of her head that looked very fashion forward.

"Oh my god—why are we all freaking out about a freaky band

boy upstairs in greasy Oliver's room? Yuck," Farah said, and hoisted herself up from the bed. "I'm going downstairs to get some almonds, I have low blood sugar."

"I'm sure the crew has left already," I said, totally catching her drift that she was going to see if Tom-the-camera-guy was still around.

Farah winked at me—"We'll see"—and flounced out of the room.

Mom looked at me like, *Huh?* She had no clue about Farah's burning desire for Tom-the-camera-guy. She turned her attention to the dress, which was getting too heavy for her to hold up off the floor. "Well, let's get this going—oh my goodness, look how great this thing is."

Mom laid it down like it was my wedding dress and took it off the quilted hanger. Then she unzipped it on the bed. "Come and help me, Vati." Rachel quickly tucked a bobby pin into Padmavati's braid, fastening it to her head, and released her to help my mother. Vati and Mom maneuvered the dress around to the foot of the bed where I was standing and I took the camisole off. I am trying to get relaxed about being naked in front of my mother—post-puberty—but I haven't quite gotten there yet. It's like, in growing, I did something without her and she's dying to know about it. Sometimes I can feel her checking out my development. I guess she grew me in the first place, so she's interested, but *yuck!* I left my leggings on. Like ladies in waiting, my Mom and Vati crouched down before me, protectively holding the bodice so I could step into the dress that was pooled on the floor like an enormous fallen parachute. I put my feet carefully through the top and steadied myself on Padmavati's and Mom's shoulders so I wouldn't fall. Slowly they stood up, lifting and fitting around my waist, up and over my breasts. Then Mom zipped up the back. I could feel she was being careful not to catch my skin in the zipper's teeth. The dress fit perfectly. I picked up the skirt and went over to the full-length mirror. My hair, even though the wind had made it look like I'd slept in a barn, was almost to my waist and was doing something good that made me reconsider the shower. My mother stepped into the mirror's reflection.

"Oh, Wren. I feel like I'm going to cry. Look at you." She came up behind me and put her hands on my shoulders. "You look like a *dream*, Wren. It fits you so beautifully." She slowly spun me around and inhaled as if she had just seen Christmas tree lights being turned on. "Let me get my phone. Dad will want to see you. He gave me that dress, you know, picked it out himself." She left the frame of the mirror and Vati came in. "Wow, Wren. You look amazing. You look like a princess or a Southern belle or something—like Scarlett O'Hara."

"It's so pretty, right?" My hand drifted down and felt the fine weave of the silk that I had touched so many times before, sitting on the floor of my mother's closet.

"I think tonight's going to be particularly amazing, Wren." Vati's eyes shone as much as her smile. "And think about it"—she lowered her voice to a whisper—"*he's* going to see you in this."

12

Farah was still downstairs or somewhere else in the house when Vati and I took the dress and her new hairstyle back up to my room.

"Vati." I was holding the dress in my arms like I was carrying a wounded soldier, but I managed to reach out and grab her sweater with a few fingers before she went up the last three stairs to my door. "I'm having a weird fantasy."

"Oh yeah? That's okay."

"You know when you said," I whispered, even though I could hear Reagan and Charlie doing some kind of rap from my bedroom, "*he* will see me in it?"

"Yeah, totally. He will, like, soon," Vati said, standing up on her tiptoes and lifting her eyebrows at the same time.

"I know, but here's what I'm imagining. I am imagining myself walking up the Met steps like Lady Diana Spencer walked up the steps of St. Paul's Cathedral before she got married to Prince Charles."

"You mean Kate Middleton and William?"

"No, noooo. His *mother*."

"I didn't see that wedding."

"I know—nobody did, it was like thirty years ago, but Mom

made us watch it the night before Kate and William got married. She said you couldn't watch one without the other."

"I didn't know that," she said, like she had missed that day in class.

"Yeah, well, personally, I liked Lady Diana's dress better than Kate's," I said. Vati's eyes widened.

"Because it had such a big skirt and she wore a *big time* tiara," I said.

"I don't remember Kate Middleton's tiara."

"Right—it was like a sparkly headband. She was trying to be understated, but if you are going to marry the future king of England, let it rip, right? Diana's was like six inches high."

"Kate is so cool." Vati sighed.

"I know, but the point is, I'm thinking, what if Oliver and Nolan leave for the party before we do?"

"Have they?"

"I don't know, but what if they do and when we get there, they are there waiting at the top of the steps because they are too cool to go into the party right away," I said.

Vati sucked in air through her nose, squeezed her shoulders up to her ears, and squinched her face in sheer excitement.

"Nolan would see me in my red dress getting out of the car and then watch me walk up the steps, holding my dress, so I wouldn't trip on it, I guess. That is what you have to do in this kind of dress."

"Yes, you totally do," Vati confirmed. I nodded.

"And maybe that big wind would be making my hair fly wildly around so I would have to gather it coyly to the side of my head, laughing because it was out of control."

"And I will be right next to you but my hair won't be flying around 'cause of this." She pointed to her braid.

"Right. Oliver will see you too." We were not on the stairs of my house anymore but in a full-blown fantasyland of love.

"What if—" I felt like I was going to jinx something, but I couldn't help it. "Because we are all dressed up, they fall in love with us?"

Vati's shoulders relaxed, her eyes looked up to the heavens, and she shook her head gently back and forth.

"That would be so great," she said.

"I know . . . Is it stupid that I am thinking that?"

"Uh-uh. I think about stuff like that all the time."

It took less time than you would think for us to get into our dresses and do our makeup. Regan was still in her underwear. By six o'clock we were sitting in my room not wanting to move too much so we didn't smudge or wrinkle. We had so much time to kill that Charlie started doing his homework again.

"So, anyway, Tom said that he would definitely be shooting the next episode here, *and* he told me it would be on November 18!" Farah said.

"So?" I said.

"So? *So*, he obviously wants me to be here or he wouldn't have been so specific about the date. That was a not-so-subtle flirtation and invitation!"

"Invitation to what? Farah, yuck, he's so old, he's out of college."

"Vati, like that matters—attraction is attraction," Farah scolded, like an older sister.

"Another term for attraction is statutory rape, Farah. He's a sicko to flirt with you," Charlie said, as he erased the shit out of a wrong answer to a math question.

"Where is Bronx Science?" I asked.

"In the Bronx," Charlie said. He looked up at me and laughed and I stuck my tongue out at him.

The only thing my parents didn't change when they renovated the house was the intercom system. Dad thought it was stupid and that we'd never use it. But of course we use it all day long, even though it's so old that it's almost impossible to hear what anyone is saying. The boxes look like the equipment from old *Star Trek* TV shows from the 1960s. The loud, scratchy noise it makes before someone speaks into it interrupted our discussion about Tom-the-camera-guy's age.

"Girls"—static hissing, beeping, and scratching—"the car is here! Oliver, Nolan, turn the music *off*! We are leaving!" More lost signal sounds and static.

"Oh my god—are we going to run into them on the stairs?" I asked everyone.

"Oh my god, are we?" Vati repeated.

"Jesus, you guys," said Reagan, finally wriggling into her ace bandage of a dress that she left off until the last second. "Let's just go. I want to see if this guy is who I think he is. Where's my clutch?"

As cool as she sounded, she made sure to look in the mirror and check her makeup with the meticulousness of a Renaissance art restorer.

"How am I going to get down the stairs?" I felt like I had only been dressed in shorts and a T-shirt my whole life and suddenly I was rocking a red-carpet ball gown. Everyone else had a short dress and teetered ahead in their high heels.

"Here, Wrenny, I'll take your purse and walk in front of you so you don't fall. Can you even see your feet?" Charlie said. He had his backpack on.

I looked down at the hem of the dress that reached the floor. "No!"

"I'm having a hard time seeing you as a *lady*," Charlie said, holding my hand to guide me.

"What? Shut up, Charlie!" It embarrassed me that he called me a lady. At least he didn't call me a *woman*.

"No, you look different. You look like a, well, like a woman."

"Oh, yuck, Charlie! That sounds frumpy and weird and wrong and I don't even want to go now!"

"No way. You don't look frumpy, you look . . ." Charlie patted his hair down and to the side, to no avail—it still stuck straight up. "I don't know, you look ripe—like an apple."

I winced. "Oh man, just go," I said, and pushed him in the direction of the stairs.

"Don't fall, that dress would pancake me," he said.

"Shut up," I said as Charlie slowly walked down the stairs.

"You shut up," he said, looking behind him to see that I was okay.

"You shut up." I laughed and put my hand on his shoulder so I wouldn't fall.

13

There were not one, but two sleek black sedans humming outside our door on Eighty-Fourth Street. Rachel-the-hair-lady was going to babysit for Dinah and the two of them bade all of us goodbye, with Rachel making last-minute fixes to our hair and Dinah taking pictures with her phone.

Yes, it's weird for a ten-year-old to have a full-on iPhone 12 or whatever model it is, *but she is a TV star*, and somehow it got justified as part of her "work." As annoying as it is that she gets to throw the "work" word around and get a souped-up phone, she has already paid for a hunk of her college, so.

"Oh, doesn't everyone look nice!" My mother was *decked* in a tight-fitting, floor-length brown dress with very long sleeves—they went to her mid-hand. She wore chunky sage-green tourmaline earrings that hung to her shoulders and a bracelet made of the same green stones, coiled around and around her wrist like an Amazonian snake. Her nails were short and painted a dark cocoa brown. "Wren, you and . . ." She looked around at who was ready to go. Reagan was almost out the door. "Reagan, go ahead and get in the car with Oliver and his friend, and Charlie and Vati, you come with me. Oh, Vati, look at you! You girls have gotten so grown up, I'm telling you." The disappointment that she didn't get to ride in the car with Oliver was all over Vati's face. She did look really pretty in Farah's mother's pink halter dress and her braided raven hair. I hate to say it, but she sort of looked like one of the younger Kardashian sisters—the taller one. I hoped that sometime during the party Oliver would notice too.

"We'll get there at the same time," I assured her, heading for the door. "We'll all go in together." The enormous red dress thing was feeling very wrong as I watched Reagan slink and sway her way down the stoop stairs and click over to the first car.

"Can you manage the stairs, Wren?" I heard my mother call from inside.

"Yes!" I hissed. "Yes, sorry, Mom. Yes, I can do it." I wasn't convinced. I was worried that, even though it was a strapless dress and it was freezing out, I was going to make sweat stains on the silk under my armpits. My unruly hair, which I previously imagined I would elegantly twist to the side and hold in place, was at the mercy of all that wind and was sweeping violently across my eyes, plus I was holding my clutch and a shawl my mother lent me, making the risk of a total wipeout closer to a terrifying reality. To make matters very, very much worse, I looked ahead and saw Nolan by the car. He took Reagan's hand and guided her into it. She gave him a big smile and did the suave ass-first-get-in-the-car move that you see people like Angelina Jolie do on *Access Hollywood*.

By the time he looked up at me, I had gotten onto the sidewalk in one piece and had quickly been able to get ahold of some of my hair.

"Ho—ly!" Nolan, who was way out of his floppy T-shirt and

Chuck Taylors and way into a dark blue full-on suit, called to me over the wind and city street sounds. "That is one serious dress!" And then he didn't walk, he ran—a cool run, not a teenager mad dash, it was an English-gentleman-coming-to-get-his-girl-out-of-the-rain run—over to the stoop where I was standing holding my breath.

"Here, let me help you." He took my hand.

"Oh thanks, no, I'm fine. It's okay, I just had to get down the stairs, but I'm totally fine now." But he didn't let go of my hand until we got to the car.

"Here, I'll get in first and sit on the bump in the middle." He opened the car door and did a head-first-guy-get-in-the-car move. I turned to see my mother watching me get in the car, as she was getting into hers. "See you there!" she called, and waved her brown satin evening purse in the air. I copied Reagan and turned around, trying to elegantly seat myself in the car, gathering my dress and making sure it didn't touch the leafy gutter between the curb and the street. I felt like one of those practical-joke snakes getting shoved back into the peanut tin.

Oliver was in the front seat with the driver.

"To the museum?" the driver guy said.

"Yes, sir!" said Oliver. I was staring at his hair, which between sophomore and senior year had morphed from an out-of-control ringlety blond mop to dreadlocks. He turned around and smiled in an I'm-about-to-make-fun-of-you way.

"Is that *Mom's* dress?"

I flushed. Jeez, Oliver.

"Yes." I smoothed it down, trying not to touch Nolan's leg that was one centimeter away from mine, but he didn't know it because he couldn't see my leg. He could sure see Reagan's legs, which were toned and comfortably crossed on his other side.

"It's really pretty," Nolan said.

"Oh thanks." I looked up briefly but with enough time to see the same smile he'd given me in the doorway. I shot my head back down as casually as I could. "Um, yeah, she wanted me to wear it, so." The car turned into Central Park and accelerated through the winding transverse to the East Side.

"I love these parties," Reagan said, looking out the window at the trees rushing by.

Huh? I thought. *What is she talking about? I* had never been to one of these parties and I was fairly certain she hadn't been to any either, let alone many.

"Yeah, they must jump off. I've seen pictures of them in the *Times*," Nolan said, seeming to believe that Reagan knew what she was talking about.

"Yeah, this isn't the Fashion Institute thing, but it will still be cool. Cy Dowd will be there," Oliver said. He had been to a few of these parties with Mom and Dad, but what was he doing dropping Cy Dowd's name?

"I've never been to a party like this, but the museum is like my second home, sort of," I said. Then, sotto voce to Nolan, "And I really don't think Cy Dowd, the most famous living contemporary artist in the world, will be hanging at the kiddie table with us, but whatever."

"Who is Cy Dowd?" Nolan said, kind of to me.

"The Met is one of my favorite places on *earth*," Reagan pronounced before I could answer.

What? What was Reagan doing? And so loud? I bet the last time she went to the Met was in third grade when her class took a trip to see the Chinese Garden Court with Ms. Rios.

"What do you love about it?" Nolan asked in a real, curious way. Oh, okay, he's going to love Reagan.

"Oh my god, what *isn't* there to love?" She took her cat eyes away from the park and flashed them up at Nolan. I think she even batted them. Now I was getting hot and felt super crunched. I involuntarily pushed out a little like I needed space and sort of elbowed Nolan. "Oh, here—let me move over, you look jammed in there." He shifted toward Reagan. *Why did I wear the dress?* "I'm fine, I think my leg is just falling asleep."

"I have some room over here," Reagan purred, sliding her narrow figure over toward the door. I felt Nolan's leg that had been so close to mine move away. "Thanks," he and I said at the same time.

"We're almost there, kids," Oliver announced, looking out his window at the huge alabaster museum. It took up almost three blocks opposite the fancy apartment buildings on Fifth Avenue.

As our car approached the Met, I could see photographers' cameras flashing and a steady stream of yellow taxis lining up to let out their partygoers. *Forget Nolan,* I thought. Reagan obviously had her sights on him. She'd get him, with her dark, silky hair, intense green eyes, and big boobs. Reagan is *Teen Vogue*'s wet dream, and probably a boy like Nolan's too. I love her, I really do—she's one of my oldest friends—but she's, well, she gets what she wants.

The car eased along the curb and came to a barely noticeable stop. My mother's car must have arrived first because Vati, Farah, and Charlie rushed up to our car and Charlie opened the door on my side, before the driver could do it. I realized that those fifteen minutes might very well be the only ones I would ever spend so close to that gorgeous Bronx Science boy. As Charlie swung open the door, all of the mixed-sexes-new-boy-hot-car-close-proximity energy flew out like heat from an oven and the sharp November chill slapped some sense into me.

"Wrenny! Come out, this is *so cool*. Look at the photographers!"

"Oh god, Charlie, don't say that out loud—how *uncool*, of course there are photographers," Farah said, and bonked him on the arm with her clutch.

"Oh sorry, Miss New York City, I think I know that. I might remind you *Nosh* is catering this event." He patted his hair down again.

"I think photographers are cool, Charlie," I said. "Maybe we can get one to take a picture of all of us. *Right, Farah?*"

Farah headed for the stairs. "I'm sorry, Charlie, I know your dad does these things all the time and of course you know about them."

"I do." Charlie bucked up and straightened his tie.

Last-minute adjustments happened in front of the mighty, illuminated museum as we tugged our dresses, wraps, and hair. Oliver and Nolan started heading up to the party. Senior boys, even if one is your dreadlock-haired brother, are old—they are like adults. Nolan put his hands in his pockets and swaggered.

An event organizer dressed in a tux with a microphone in his ear pulled my mother away from a quick hello she was having with another elegantly clad woman and escorted her up the stairs to my father, who was trotting down, hair slicked back, and smiling. Dad looks as natural in a tux as a country singer looks in jeans and a T-shirt. He thanked the party planner, took my mother's hand, lifted it up to admire her, and then brought her in to kiss her on the cheek. She smiled and said something to him just as they got to the top of the stairs, then Dad turned around.

"Darlings! Come inside!" He beckoned to us. "Wrenny! You look beautiful down there!" That made Oliver and Nolan look back at me to see what Dad was yelling about. I must have been purple with embarrassment, because Nolan gave me the thumbs-up and I couldn't tell if he was agreeing with Dad or making fun of me.

"I saw that," Farah said, as she screwed the lip-gloss top back on and put it in her clutch. "He's into you. Let's go." My heart leaped with hope. Farah may like inappropriately older guys, but she's smart about looks and the vibes people give.

"Wait," Charlie said, not hearing what Farah had said to me. "To keep body and soul together"—he pulled a small brown paper bag out of his blazer pocket—"Swedish Fish."

14

"Well, well, well," said Bennet, by far my favorite guard at the museum. He was standing right at the entrance when we walked through the gigantic doors.

Bennet sounds like Usain Bolt, the Olympic runner. He's Jamaican. "Look at cha, Wren, all grown up!" He leaned back, clapped his hands, and laughed out loud. "Whooo, you look like a ripe peach, dear. Someone might pick you toNIGHT." Bennet has been a guard at the museum for forty years. My *father* asks *him* where certain works are because Bennet knows the place better than anyone.

"Bennet!" I gave him the high five he was waiting for even though his peach comment made me flush.

"Go have a good time tonight, little one. It's a big pa-ty," he said, leaning in and lifting his pointer finger up into the air. "Ha haaaaa!"

When I was eight or nine, Bennet used to give me Life Savers when I came to visit Dad. He knew I liked cherry so he would sort through all the other colors with his thumb until he got to a bright red one. "Here's one with your name on it," he'd say, and press the hard candy into the palm of my hand. Even though I had the sweet red taste of a Swedish Fish left over in my mouth and I was too old for a special treat, the gigantic party ahead of me gave me a funny feeling in my gut, like maybe I wished for just a second I could be eight years old again and loose in the museum, running in my Tretorns and pigtails through the hallways, holding on to a sticky, melting Life Saver.

"I'm going to find my parents and say hi," Charlie said.

"Okay, we'll be in here, I guess, until we go in to dinner?" I said, looking at the girls.

"Right, I'll find you. Make sure to try the Peking duck rolls. My dad said they are insane."

"Good," I said, looking into the sea of silks, furs, and clinking glasses. I scanned the waiters' trays to see if I could identify the duck thing, and at the same time I looked for Nolan.

"Where is Oliver?" Padmavati said, not thinking, like I did, to mask her obsession by looking for a tray of roaming hors d'oeuvres.

"Vati." Farah took her by the hands. "Listen to me, okay?" She was speaking to her like a life coach. "You look exceptional to-night. That pink color is doing something amazing to your skin and you are like eleven feet tall, but I am telling you, Oliver is *never* going to notice you if you are acting so puppy dog-ish. Never, ever, not ever."

"Oh yeah, okay. So what should I do, look busy? But how? I don't have my phone."

"No, Vati," I said, and fixed her dangly, sparkly Indian beaded earring that was twisted in a weird way. "Just be yourself. Hang with me. Let's go see if there is anyone famous here or something."

"Just stick with me, guys, okay?" Vati said, and touched her earring.

"*Totally,*" I vowed. And then everyone nodded their head, confirming that nobody would leave her side.

"Come on, let's do a circle and see if we can't take a glass of champagne from one of the waiters. The bartenders probably won't give us any," Reagan said, leading us into the party.

"I'm sure my parents will let us have a little champagne at dinner, you guys," I said. Sometimes they do let me have a glass of wine at dinner, I guess because my father is European.

"Oh, Wren, come on! Look at this party!" Reagan said and hooked her arm in mine. "We need a glass of champagne *immediately!*"

Photographers were asking to take people's pictures (and then writing down their names, which meant they were important enough to be in the paper the next day), swank, literary-looking couples, artists, the mayor of New York, Troland Johnson, who was standing with the Met's blog guy and Cy Dowd—the most prominent artist at the opening. The show had at least seven of his paintings in it, all of them new (all of them written about in *New York* magazine and *Art World* and *The New York Times*). The idea behind the show was to present the old masters and the new masters. It was unusual for the Met to exhibit so many current artists, which was one of the reasons the show was such a big deal.

Reagan released my arm to snake her way through the crowd and I let Vati and Farah move ahead of me. They didn't recognize Cy Dowd. He looked younger than I would have thought, even though he had gray hair on the sides of his head. He wore heavily framed black nerd glasses, which didn't surprise me, and a navy tux. You might not notice it was navy, but because Cy was standing next to the mayor, who was in a normal black tux, I could tell. I think it's some sort of statement to wear navy instead of traditional black. George Clooney does it all the time at the Golden Globes. *And* Cy Dowd was wearing blue Vans sneakers. I wondered what he wore when he painted. I wondered if he liked these big parties, or if he was an introvert who wished that the evening would be over and he could go back to his massive studio in Brooklyn, drink red wine, and paint his next masterpiece with his pet teacup pig by his side (I read that he had one in that *New York* magazine article).

The cavernous, marble entry hall was loud. All the party guests were talking to each other intensely, as if they were in the most important conversation of their lives. Some people would explode in laughter. What were they laughing at? Politics? I wanted to retreat to my bedroom and draw an owl or something. I felt like that big wind of the day was in the hall with us, blowing everything and making me feel like I had to hold on.

Suddenly I heard my father's voice in a microphone.

"Hello . . . Hello, everyone!"

Nan and David Noorlander (at these things they seem more like Nan and David Noorlander than Mom and Dad) were standing at the foot of the large white marble stairway leading to the upstairs galleries that held Vermeers, Manets, Monets, Jackson Pollock's *Autumn Rhythm* (I wrote a paper on that painting in an art history elective once), and of course, a large number of van Goghs.

"Ladies and gentlemen, esteemed guests, Mr. Mayor, dear friends, it is my greatest pleasure and honor to welcome you all tonight. It is rare, even at this great institution, that we can erect a show with the work of so many vital contemporary artists. How lucky we are to be living in a time when we are globally connected and have the technology and resources to be in an active, alive, real-time conversation with artists from around the world who, it seems to me, are working together as if in a master class. Some, like Rosanna Zelman, live in Kyrgyzstan. Tony Une resides in Tokyo. Alexandra Sheere, in Paris. For the first time at the Met, we have tried to continue that conversation in the galleries you are about to see. We are truly fortunate to have with us tonight Cy Dowd, who has seven works in this show."

The room exploded in applause. Vati, Farah, and I were, totally by accident, standing so close to Cy Dowd that it felt like everyone in the room was looking at us, which of course they weren't. Cy lifted his glass to my father and then took a small bow to the crowd. But then, when he lifted his head, he unmistakably looked in our direction, not at me, but at *Farah. They caught eyes.* You could see it as plainly as if it were a scene in a TV show. Was it because Farah was in a silver dress? I looked around to see if anyone else had noticed, and there was Charlie who was now back with us. I took his sleeve and pulled him closer to me.

"Did you see that?" I didn't really have to lower my voice because the whole room was still applauding.

"What?" He had found the duck things and had a pyramid of them in a napkin. "Why do you guys have champagne?"

"I don't," I said.

"They do." Pointing his pile of duck in Farah and Padmavati's direction.

Farah was now coyly poised with her knee bent like a fawn and *smiling* at Cy Dowd. Thank god Dad was talking again or she might have taken her spindly legs and stepped her platforms right over to him.

"As a boy growing up in Amsterdam, I spent hour upon hour in the Rijks, studying and falling in love with the masterpieces of the Golden Age. How I wished I could have met these artists. How I wished I could have spoken to them, asked about their technique, their visions, what they ate for dinner!"

Titters rippled through the great hall. I looked over at Cy, who was laughing and *side looking* at Farah, who caught his glance and was throwing a bigger one in his direction.

"It is like a dream come true for me, but I am quite sure for all of us."

More applause.

"The board of directors and I welcome you. We hope you enjoy what you see in the gallery, and later, we invite you to join us in the Temple of Dendur for what is sure to be a delicious celebratory dinner. Proost!" Everyone in the great hall echoed the Dutch toast back to my father.

"Proost!"

As the guests raised their glasses, I finally caught sight of Oliver and Nolan standing at the entrance of the Egyptian gallery. I watched them say something to each other and then Nolan disappeared through the small arch that leads to the tombs and pharaohs.

"I'll be right back. Stay here," I said to Charlie.

"Have one of these, I'm not kidding you, they will blow your mind." He looked at me and nodded like his family had invented Peking duck.

"Oh thanks, I'm starving." I took the tiny, still-warm egg roll and, without thinking for a second about what I was wearing, crunched into its middle. Of course the very amazing-tasting, but hot, goopy brown duck juice squirted out both sides of the roll, flew up into the air, and landed like a Rorschach test splatter on both sides of the skirt of my dress. Had I been wearing a little fitted dress, the juice would have hit the floor. *Or* since I was dressed in a one-of-a-kind vintage Oscar de la Renta, I *could* have paused to consider cause and effect, like a careful person.

"Charlie! My god." I sucked air in. "Ohhh, look!"

"Oh crap—I should have told you they were sort of juicy."

"Shoot shoot shoot. Do you have another napkin?"

Mortifyingly enough, a mom-looking woman next to us grabbed cocktail napkins from a passing Nosh waiter and started blotting my skirt.

"Gracious, it's really in there. Let me just . . ." blot, blot, blot, ". . . never scrub or it will stain *forever*. You might have to take this to a very good dry cleaner, dear, but it will come out, I am sure of it. Oh what a shame, this is a beautiful dress."

"Thanks," I said anxiously. At the opposite end of the hall, Oliver was making his way toward the bar.

"I'm *really sorry*, Wren." Charlie had his mouth full with another duck bomb.

"It's not your fault." I looked at the concerned woman. "Thanks, I just have to catch someone."

"Don't do *anything* until a professional can get their hands on it."

"Okay!" I bolted through the maze of people to Oliver, who was now at the bar getting himself a beer. I had to wedge myself between grownups to get to him.

"Having a beer? How do they even serve you?"

"Yuuuup." He smiled and I thought he might burp because that is something he would do at a moment like that. I was extremely aware of the plum-brown stains that were drying and deepening into the fabric of my mother's dress. "They don't know how old I am, it's not like we're at a bar. It's a private party."

"Oh. Can I have a sip?"

"Sure." I took the glass filled to the top with the just-poured foaming beer and took a big swig. Bitter and bubbly.

"Easy there, sister."

"Yuck." I handed back the glass and got down to business.

"So who is Nolan?"

"Why do you want to know?" He smiled.

"What? I just rode in a car with him and, nothing. I'm just interested—he's at this party like out of nowhere."

"He's in this band I went to see last weekend. We hung out afterward."

"Why did you invite him?" I said, reaching for his beer for another sip and then changing my mind.

"Benjer couldn't come because of some swim meet he has tomorrow—his mom wouldn't let him, so I invited Nolan."

"But why? You don't even know him."

"So what? And I do know him, sort of. He friended me on

Facebook at the same time Ben said he was out, so." He took a sip of beer.

"What's the band called?" I asked.

"The Shoppe Boys."

My heart started beating in that weird way again. "Are they good?"

"Hell yeah they are. They are so good. And he's so good."

"He is?"

"Yeah, man, he's like Eddie Vedder. He's got a sick voice—I don't know if he'll even go to college. They might get signed and go on tour or something. I'm getting him a beer too."

"Why didn't he come get it himself—what are you, his groupie or something?"

"No." Oliver had no reaction to my dis because he was a senior and not much flustered him. He was a math guy who would probably get into MIT early-decision. He took a calculus class at Columbia just for fun. I don't get genetics. "He went to look at the hieroglyphics with Reagan."

"What?" I said in a way-too-elevated way. I felt my hand tighten into a ball.

"You have something in your hair." He pulled out a shred of a leaf.

"Nolan was with Reagan, like, *with* her? I mean, no, I don't care, but . . ."

Oliver cocked his head. "I guess. No, I don't know."

"That's cool. She looked like she liked him in the car," I said tentatively.

"I didn't think she did," he said.

"No?"

"No."

"Okay, well, I'm going to find Vats. I said I wouldn't leave her side, and I did."

"Okay, you do that." Oliver, with his dreads and his beer, could be so dismissive.

15

Padmavati was standing by herself in the middle of the room holding a full glass of champagne.

"Have you been holding that the entire time?" I said, watching Oliver go into the tombs.

"No, this is my second glass." Her already enormous Betty Boop eyes opened even more.

"That is nuts, Vati, you are going to throw up."

"I didn't know what else to do. You disappeared and then so did Farah."

"I was talking to Oliver," I said.

"What?" Too loud. "Where is he?" She turned around and was in danger of sloshing her drink on my skirt. This skirt—I am telling you.

"He's with Nolan and Reagan looking at Hatshepsut."

"Bummer." She swigged her champagne. "You did see him give me that meaningful look, didn't you, Wren . . . earlier today . . . at your house?" She sounded sort of sloshed.

"Yes, I totally did, but wait, Reagan is going to go for Nolan. I can feel it."

"You think? Nooo. She seems so bored by the thought of him," said Vati, suddenly sober.

"You weren't in the car with us."

"No, I wasn't. I listened to Charlie talk your mother's ear off about the summer bird-watching internship he wants. Does he think your mom can help him or something? What connections does she have to Central Park? Your parents' deal is all art, right?" And she swung the champagne flute up and around, indicating that "the art deal" was the museum.

"*No*, she can't help him—gosh, Vati, watch it with that glass—he tells my mom everything, sort of." She swigged from her glass. I lifted my eyebrows at her. "Where *is* Farah?" I said, searching for her in the sea of fabulousness funneling through the large archway. I couldn't see my parents or Farah or Charlie or Charlie's parents (who were invited guests because their company was catering) or Reagan or Oliver or Nolan.

"No idea."

"Maybe she's with Charlie." And then I remembered the stains. "Look at this!" I held up my skirt for her to see.

"Spaz."

"I am a spaz, but it was really Charlie's fault with his duck rolls."

"It doesn't show if the folds go this way." She fiddled with my skirt for a second. "Is your mother going to freak?" And then, out of the corner of my eye, I saw Reagan walking in the crowd going into the show, not with Nolan but with Oliver.

16

The Temple of Dendur is in a gigantic room with long, rectangular pools of shimmering water meant to look like the Nile in Egypt. The temple itself looms in a background strikingly lit from underneath, making the warm sandstone look even more ancient and mysterious. That night glittering dinner tables, crowded with silver and glass, glowed in the candlelight of many small votives. The tables closest to the temple were the golden ticket tables, the ones where the museum's biggest benefactors, famous people, the artists, the mayor, and my parents would sit. Down a few steps there was another level, with more tables alongside the pools. On that level a string quartet was playing. White roses and hydrangeas were at the center of each table, and place cards made of heavy white card stock with the guests' names written in jet-black calligraphy were centered at the tops of all the place settings, just above the dessert spoons. One entire wall on the far side of the temple is a window. Through it you can see Central Park. I think it's one of the most famous windows in the world. It must be fifty feet long and thirty feet high. There are a lot of movies shot right in front of it. Thousands of kids have gaped through its thick glass on school trips, people have proposed in front of it, tourists from all over the world have taken pictures of it.

"Wren, I have been looking for you, darling!" It was my father, who was talking to three other art-worldy people when I entered the room with Vati.

"Hi, Dad." I gave him a hug. I hadn't talked to him since breakfast.

"My goodness, you look radiant! Look at Mom's dress! It fits you as if it were made for you. Vati, don't you look pretty too. You girls are growing up way too fast for my comfort. Here, come meet these fine people." Dad talks like that normally because he is a gentleman, but it gets amped up a bit at these kinds of parties.

"This is Mr. and Mrs. Siegal. I think, Wren, you might remember their house upstate? We went there when you were very young. You destroyed the hay bales in their barn," he said, and winked at Mr. Siegal.

"Oh yeah, sorry! Well, hello! I'm Wren." I am really good at shaking hands and looking into people's eyes. I've been trained like a dog. It took me years, but I got it.

"Hi, I'm Padmavati." Vati waved, but gave them a *huge* charming smile, which counts. They enthusiastically shook our hands and smiled at us and one another, the way adults do when teenagers are obviously making an effort.

"And *this*, Wren, is *Dev Brocklebank*." He said that with emphasis because Mr. Brocklebank runs the van Gogh program in Saint-Rémy, France, that I was applying to for my junior year abroad. He's not an artist or anything, but I think he is the head of their board. He's like the Oz of the place, a banker pushing the buttons behind a big art curtain.

"Oh my gosh, *hi*!" Not cool, not cool, too much. But I still shook his hand heartily and looked smack-dab into his eyes.

"Wren, hello. What a pleasure it is to meet you." He had a heavy French accent.

"I'm applying to your program!" Again, way too much, I reined it in by introducing Vati. "This is Vati."

"Hi!" Another wave from Vati.

"Well, that is marvelous. Your father has told me you are very talented."

"Oh yes! I mean, I hope so. I, well, I don't know if I am or not, maybe not, but I've already started my application." Truth: I had been studying the website for this school since I was thirteen. And I have been plotting the work for my application with Mrs. Rousseau, my art teacher, for a solid year. Only one girl from our school has ever gotten in, Elizabeth Wilson. She is a legend of the art room. She graduated three years ago and went on to the Rhode Island School of Design. A drawing of hers is still up on the wall, like it's a part of the permanent Hatcher collection. The Saint-Rémy school only takes ten of the best high school students from all over the country each year. It's almost unimaginable to get in, but you have to try. Or I had to try. I don't have much to be proud of except for my art, not really, and *van Gogh* painted the irises there; all the field paintings—the ones with the peasants bent over working all that gorgeous wheat; those curvy cypress tress with about twenty shades of green in each one of them—the *very* famous one of his bedroom in the asylum, the one with the bed with the red blanket? Do you know it? It looks so cozy in there even though it is an insane asylum. And he painted *The Starry Night* in Saint-Rémy.

"When Wren puts her mind to something, not much can get in her way, right, Vati?" Dad winked at me.

"That is true, Mr. Noorlander. Totally."

"You girls should find your table, and we should find ours, yah?" Like an army taking orders from its general, all of us dispersed.

"Have fun, Turtles!" Dad said, as he skipped up the three shallow stairs to the higher level of the room where the guests, and my mother, were waiting.

"Oh my god. That makes me want to go home and start my self-portrait this instant," I said, like the wind had been knocked out of me.

"Huh?" Padmavati was pressing her fingers to her head, checking that her cool braid was still in place.

"The hardest part of the application for that school is you have to do a self-portrait. I bet lots of people are good at them." An image of art students all over the country looking deep into the mirror at themselves flashed in my head. "But I'm scared."

"Why? *You are such a good artist.*"

"No, it's not really about that." I noticed that in fact a strand of hair had fallen out of the braid, but Vati was missing it with her weird pressing. I tried to tuck it into a hidden bobby pin behind her ear, which is easier said than done. "It's more about, well, revealing *who* you are." I gave the bobby pin a shove.

"Ouch!"

"Sorry, but it won't stay in." I struggled until she became still, closed her eyes, and let me properly anchor the pin into her hair.

"You have to look way into yourself to do a good one. It's not just being able to draw what you look like, it's way deeper. It's like van Gogh's self-portraits are revelations of who he was as a *man*, it's not just anatomy. There, that looks good."

"Oh man." She fingered her braid again to feel the adjustment.

"Yeah . . . What if I look deep inside and I don't like what I see? I might not." Even though this was kind of an important conversation, I could feel myself wanting to look around the room for Nolan.

"*No way*. No way, Wren. You are going to do a great job and you will like what you see in there." She pointed to my heart. "And so will that French guy. I see who you are all around you—your aura. You just can't see it, but everyone else does."

"Thanks, Vatter."

"Do you think Oliver liked my dress?" she said in a sad-girl way.

"I'm sure he did."

"Is it stupid that it's Farah's mom's? Maybe I just should have worn one of my own. I should have worn a sari—my mother said she would have one made. Maybe that would have been nicer."

"Maybe. Gosh, I want a sari too, but whatever, Vati. I'm wearing my mom's dress, you're wearing Farah's mom's dress. It's that kind of night. Now come on." I took her hand. "Let's go eat. Everyone will be at the table."

17

Charlie and Vati were at my table and Reagan, Oliver, and Farah were seated at another scrub table next to ours. Both the tables were so far out of the spotlight they were practically in the American Wing. We were not only on the lower level of the room, but hidden behind the temple, so if you were seated where my parents were you wouldn't even be able to see us. We were at the kiddie/random people tables, which was what I was expecting. But what I was not expecting to see as Padmavati and I circled the table to find our own names was a white folded card right next to mine with the name *Nolan Shop*.

"Hi," I said helplessly, standing three feet away from the table, too terrified to move closer to the golden bamboo chair next to his.

"Hey," he said happily, and pulled the chair out so I had no choice but to move forward and take my seat. Luckily, I was getting a handle on the full skirt and managed to sweep it around my legs gracefully, fitting myself between the table and the chair. When he leaned forward to usher me in, between my naked shoulder and his face was a force field. If force fields had colors, that one would be pearly and sparkly.

"I switched the place cards," he said, pushing me in. I took in a breath and held it.

"I was sitting next to some dude named Earl." I looked up and across the table to see Earl-the-intern from my father's office next to Padmavati, who had begun to use her dinner party manners and was clearly in the "What do you do?" conversation with Earl.

"I wanted to sit next to you, so I switched them, " Nolan said.

The volume of the string quartet and the roar of three hundred people talking got turned way down by God or someone so the words "I switched them" could penetrate into my soul. The only place to look was down, into a bowl of butternut squash soup with a swirl of cream on the top and a fried sage leaf floating in the middle.

"I think you're not supposed to move place cards," I said.

Nolan looked at me without a shred of regret. "Yeah, I know," he said. "But to hell with that, right?"

"Right." I looked around the table to see if anyone else was tuning in to this. *Nope.* It felt like three years in slow motion for my ass to hit the seat, but when it did, Charlie was on the other side of me talking to an Asian woman I didn't recognize but I figured also had a low-level job at the museum or why would she be sitting with us?

"This smells good." Nolan gave me a huge I'm-blowing-your-mind smile and gently blew on a spoonful of soup before he ate it up.

18

"I'm a flexitarian."

"You are? What's that?" I asked, just before putting a fork jammed with beef fillet, mashed potatoes, and green sauce in my mouth.

"I would rather eat things that didn't have a mother or father, so I do that at home and at school and stuff. *But* if I go to someone's house and they are serving ribs, or like this steak tonight, I'll just eat it, because I don't want to be difficult." He crunched into his fennel-raisin semolina roll.

"Are you against it in like a moral way? Or for health reasons?" I said with my mouth still a little full.

"No, no judgment. I just saw this movie at school that would turn any thinking person into a vegan, so I'm mindful of what I put in my body, but I don't want to be rude so . . ."

"Oh." I swallowed and thought for a second about two cows standing in the field watching me chew on their kid.

"So, Reagan said you are in a band?"

"Yeah, you guys should come see us sometime. We're playing the Harvest Festival up at Columbia soon, like next week I think. Can I ask you something?"

"Uh-huh." I held my breath, in anticipation of I had no idea what. I could feel myself breaking out in a tiny sweat.

"Who are you?"

Now, this might sound weird, but Nolan's "who are you" did not come out badly. That question sounds a little asshole-ish or pretentious and Dr. Phil-ish, like, "Who *are* you?" but it was more like he was asking because he was *enchanted* with me, so that was wild—*and* nobody had ever asked me who I was before, so I was way into it.

"Um, well, I—"

"Like, what kind of name is Wren?" he interrupted.

"Oh, my aunt named me."

"How come?" He took a drink of water but still looked at me, waiting for the story.

"So, after I was born . . ."

"What hospital?"

"Columbia Presbyterian. We were all born there."

"Okay."

"Where were you born?"

"Columbia Presbyterian."

"What!" Kismet . . . "Wow. When's your birthday?" I asked.

"May 10. When's yours?"

"September 25," I said. We sat there looking at each other for longer than it's normal to without talking.

"So, your name?" I am not exaggerating when I tell you that he was looking at me like I was a luna moth emerging from a cocoon or like I was the only living girl in New York City. Has anyone ever done that to you? Nobody had ever done that to me, ever.

"So my mother was holding me in the hospital bed, and she said to my aunt that compared to holding Oliver, who apparently was the size of a baby hippo, she said I felt like a . . ." His elbow was on the table and he was resting his chin and cheek on his hand. He had a silver ring on his pinky that I had not noticed before. ". . . tiny bird. And my aunt said, 'Like a wren.'" He smiled. "So that was what they called me. I think I was supposed to be named Lillian, after my grandmother, but . . ."

"At first, I thought your brother said he had a sister named Gwen."

"Nope, Wren."

"I am so going to write a song about a girl named Wren."

"You are?" I started fiddling with the salt and pepper shakers on the table.

"Yeah, man." He sat up, picked up his fork, nailed the last piece of beef, and put it in his mouth. "Who do you know named Wren?" Chew chew chew. "It's out of a fairy tale." Chew chew. "In fact, *you*"—he pointed his fork at me—"look like a fairy tale." He put the fork back in his teeth upside down. "Like Rapunzel."

Charlie elbowed me, jolting me out of the spell that was being cast on me.

"Hello? How good is this?" Charlie was holding up a roasted parsnip. I didn't think he had heard Nolan call me a fairy tale.

"Yeah, it's good, Charlie," I said without even looking at him or my own parsnips. I'm not even sure I had tasted them yet.

"Wren! It's a parsnip *fry*, have you even tried it? Are you even listening to me?" I looked at the parsnip Charlie was holding in my personal space. I had the instinct to whack that fry out of his hand and into the wishing pool at the other end of the room.

"It *is* good, man," Nolan leaned in and said sincerely. "Your father is a great chef. Your dad's the chef, right?"

"Yes, thank you, he is." Charlie took a bite of the root vegetable. "I get really proud of him at things like this. He started out as a school cook."

"That's impressive, man. See—you have to pay your dues." They were now talking over me, so I leaned back and watched Nolan be totally awesome to Charlie.

"Oh, yeah! Well, if you want, I mean if you are finished, I can go find them. I think they are sitting up there—or I can show you the kitchen! I can go back there anytime I want," Charlie said.

"Thanks, I totally want to do that. I have never been backstage at one of these things, and maybe there is more of that carrot soup around!" He lifted his eyes at Charlie like maybe he could hook him up. It totally worked.

"Butternut squash . . . there probably is," Charlie said sheepishly.

"Cool. But first I'm going to"—he pushed his chair out, took my hand, and pulled me up—"take Wren on a stroll."

I let Nolan pull me, looking at Charlie for approval. I felt a little guilty leaving him at the table, but despite that I lifted away like a balloon being released from a little boy's hand.

"Wanna take me somewhere, Wren?" Nolan asked.

"Oh sure, I mean, yeah."

"Oh okay, well, after then," Charlie said. "You can see the kitchen and maybe we can get a sneak peak at these insane lace cookies they are serving with coffee."

I looked to where I thought Farah was sitting at the other table, but her chair was empty. Had she gone to the bathroom? It was all a blur. I couldn't focus on where anyone was. I had been in a twilight zone of boy-ness all through dinner and now everything was distorted. Even the Temple of Dendur, a place I thought I knew by heart, was as foreign as, well, an ancient Egyptian temple.

Nolan started walking toward the American Wing, pulling me like I was one of those kid toys, like a duck on wheels that you can drag, but he paused right before we got close to the guards. "Can you take me somewhere in here?" He pointed his finger in the air and spun it around, meaning the museum. "Someplace you like? You said this was your second home."

The room suddenly burst into applause and I saw my father walk up to a podium. The chances that he would see me standing there with Nolan and not in my seat where I was supposed to be were high, thanks to my red dress, not that he could do anything from a podium. My parents were in Nan and David Noorlander mode, not Mom and Dad mode, but I still had to make quick moves.

"Okay, come on—not that way, just follow me." I let go of his hand and rushed down the far side of the room, away from all the tables. I darted in and out of waiters moving to bus the dinner plates and guests making their way to the bathrooms before dessert. It was like we were in a James Bond movie. We reached the entrance, where we had all come in to dinner and that would lead us out of there. I turned around and heard my father say, "Excuse me, ladies and gentlemen."

I froze with fear that he was about to say, "You see that girl in the red dress running off with a boy who is unrecognizable to me?

That is my naughty daughter, Wren." But he didn't. He said, "If I could take you away from your dinners for just a moment to introduce our honored guest, Cy Dowd." More exploding applause.

"Do you want to stay?" Nolan said.

I should have stayed. I shouldn't have left the party without telling anyone where I was going. But every impulse in my body said go.

"No." I looked back. Could I see my mother's silhouette sitting at one of the tables? Could she see me? Was she watching me? Nope. "No. Let's go!" I took his hand and bolted around the corner to the Egyptian gallery. We had to run through at least six rooms before we got to the main hall, and to the big stairs that lead to the master paintings. We ran farther and farther away from the party. I felt like the space shuttle blasting up into the atmosphere. As it gets farther away from Earth, pieces of metal start falling off it, like it's being freed from everything that was keeping it grounded.

When we ran by the cases of amulets—tiny good luck charms that Egyptian people of the Middle Kingdom carried around with them or stuck in their coffins—I had to screech to a halt. Some of the talismans are as small as a fingernail—carved bats, cats, and falcons, coins, little jewels, statues of people standing up very straight.

"Look at these. Have you ever seen them?" I said breathlessly. Nolan didn't seem to know what I was talking about. "These!" I pulled him in, pointing to the hundreds of teeny figurines. "When I was little, I used to hope that if I was very good, my father would open this case with a special museum key and give me one of these."

"I guess that didn't happen?" he said, a little winded too.

"Yeah, he doesn't have a key. I'm not sure there is a key, and anyway, I don't think I was ever really good enough to deserve one of these."

"What?"

"Oh, nothing." I supposed I wanted him to hear that, but I also wanted to take it back the minute I said it because it's kind of weird to tell someone you think you are a dud.

"Which one would you have now?" Leaning in close to me with his face flushed from running, he looked hot. I wondered if he played a sport. "Pretend I have a key." The thought of a game made me smile.

"Oh, okay. Well, let's see." I totally focused on choosing, like maybe he *could* give me one. "I like those amber bees." He smiled at me like I had picked well.

"Which one would you choose?" I asked. He scanned the case, giving each ornament a good hard look, and then he said confidently, "Definitely that blue eye. I want that thing around my neck."

I turned and looked at his neck. His skin was smooth and maybe had leftover tan from the summer. Even though his tie was still fastened, I imagined what the base of his neck looked like. That bone at the bottom that is shaped like a U. I involuntarily swallowed and willed myself to breathe.

"I think they do have reproductions of those in the gift shop," I said, looking back up to his eyes.

"Well, that makes me feel uncool and unoriginal. I bet they don't have the bees in the gift shop."

"No, they don't." I smiled because I had looked for them before.

"Is this where you wanted to take me?"

"No, no—come on." I started running again, past the kneeling high priestess, past the masks and the coffins, back into the great hall, and up to the wide, milky marble stairs. If you had an image of the yards and yards of red silk billowing behind me as I ran through the oyster-colored galleries, you were right.

19

Van Gogh's *Starry Night* is *not* at the Met. It lives at the Museum of Modern Art on Fifty-Third Street. My disappointment that *The Starry Night* does not hang in the museum where I spend the most time is quite real. Once when I was six or seven, around the same time I believed Dad had keys to the cases that held the world's tiniest treasures, I asked if he could trade one of the museum's great works—a Sargent? a Picasso?—for *The Starry Night*. I thought it was a reasonable trade. Dad was and still is nuts about Picasso, but I found all those exaggerated noses and blue paintings scary. I thought the museum would be better off with one less Picasso and *the* most glorious van Gogh. Anyway, you might be thinking that I would take Nolan to see *The Starry Night*, but we were in the wrong museum. I never ended up showing him that painting.

The Great Hall, compared to what it looked like two hours before, was nearly empty. There were people dodging out of the party early and quite a few museum guards and party planners milling around, but all the action was in the Temple of Dendur room. Near the entrance where Bennet had been standing there was a long table that was being set up with gift bags for people to take home with them when they left. Nolan and I were on the other side of the room from that action. If we went upstairs, there easily could be a guard who would send us right back down. It's not like you can just waltz around the museum as you please—it's the Met—but I had a crazy feeling in me that even if we saw a guard, I would be able to talk my way into going where I wanted to go. I felt empowered.

"So, we might get busted, but let's go upstairs," I said.

"I think that is a supremely good idea," Nolan said, and held out his hand for me to take. No, that isn't right. Really, he reached out and took my hand. I know that is how it went because even though I was emboldened enough to blow off my parents' dinner and sneak upstairs to forbidden galleries filled with priceless art, I definitely didn't have the courage to voluntarily put my hand in his. No, he took my hand. My hand. My hand. He. Took. My. Hand.

We dashed to the side of the stairs and climbed them together. They are so white and huge that it is impossible to believe nobody saw us, but we made it up to the third stair from the top before we saw a guard. Her back was to us.

"Wait, stay here," Nolan whispered and pulled me to the wall, where the names of benefactors are carved. I started to giggle.

"Shhh. Wait, wait, wait. Let's see if she sees us."

And like in a movie, the security guard, whom I didn't recognize, started walking in the opposite direction from where we were standing.

"Go!" he said.

I shot up the last three stairs and made a beeline, taking off past the Asian court to the rooms where the European paintings hung on the walls. I had to hike the skirt of the dress up a little to run, but that made me feel even more like a Bond girl.

There were no guards in the rooms where we stopped. Bizarre, but true.

"Let's just stay here," I whispered, winded. We were standing in front of Vermeer's *Study of a Young Woman*. "I would take you to the van Goghs, but we might be pushing our luck to go over there." I pointed into the next dimly lit gallery, which housed some of the museum's most famous paintings. "And"—I still couldn't really catch my breath, I motioned in front of me—"she's so beautiful, right?" We both looked at the painting of the sweet girl with the pearl earring staring at us. It was like she was amused that people had come to see her when there was a party downstairs.

"She is beautiful." He put his hair behind his ear. "Her eyes are so wide apart."

"I've always thought she looked nice." I paused and looked at the girl, who was probably my age. "And you know what's weird?"

"What?"

"She looks like someone you could go to school with or who's on your soccer team. I never picture people from the 1600s being so friendly." I looked at him to see if he agreed with me. "Don't you think she looks normal?"

"You know what I think is weird?" Nolan asked. I shook my head back and forth. "You know this was painted in the 1600s without looking at the sign."

"Well, sort of, yeah, I mean that's when Vermeer painted." He smiled at me. "But, I have also looked at the sign before."

"You guys are all cool," he said.

I shrugged my shoulders.

"Yeah, Oliver is a math freak, your sister is a TV star, your parents run the frigging world, and you know when this random painting was painted and all about tiny Egyptian artifacts."

"My parents don't run the world. Mom runs a pottery studio, and, yeah, the museum is cool, but Dad works really hard. I don't think it's easy running this place, but it's not like he's secretary of state or something." I hoped he wasn't going to launch into some kind of foreign policy talk because I just threw the secretary of state thing out there. I wasn't prepared to hold my own in a discussion about the Middle East.

"I'm sure it's not easy, but it's the frigging Met, so." There was almost a don't-be-stupid tone to his voice.

"I know." I didn't know what else to say. Dad had been at his same job since before I could remember. I knew it was unusual, but it was also just what my father did every day. I made a mental note not to be blasé about it. "Though Oliver *is* really good at math, which I guess is cool. We used to give him impossible math problems, like 124 times 53, and he could do them in his head."

"Hold on." Nolan closed his eyes and concentrated. He put his pointer fingers and thumbs between his eyebrows and his lips were moving a little. It was so quiet in that room.

"You are not going to . . ."

"Shhhh." He kept his eyes closed and held his hand up like, *Hold on.*

"6,572."

"*What!*"

He laughed.

"I'm sort of good at math too."

My mouth was open. "I suck at it!"

"No! You could do this, it's not that hard." He was laughing. "You just do 120 times 50, which is 6,000, then multiply 4 times 50, which is 200, and then 124 times 3, which is 372, and then you add those all together and you get 6,572."

"Yeah, see, I couldn't do that, like ever."

"I bet you could."

"No, I really couldn't. If someone said if I could get the right answer they would give me that painting, I still couldn't."

"Awww." He reached over to pat my shoulder in a jokingly patronizing way, like poor-little-spaz-girl-who-can't-do-math. I batted his hand away before he could touch me.

"Shut up." I was beaming at him. We calmed down again.

"Do you want that painting in your bedroom?" he asked me.

"Um, yeah. I really do."

"I wouldn't." He was smiling.

"Well, then you aren't such a smarty-pants because it's priceless, it's luminous . . . it's a masterpiece!" I looked at the adorable froglike girl with her creamy skin. "I would love to lie in bed and look at her."

"She's your bud from the 1600s," he said.

"Yup."

"You're funny."

I was smiling at him like a goofball. Out of the corner of my eye I saw *Bennet* looking at us from the entrance to the gallery. He raised his eyebrows, put his finger up into the air like he had when

I saw him at the start of the party, turned on his heel, and walked away.

"Why wouldn't your dad give you one of those little Egyptian things? I mean if they weren't the museum's obviously."

"Um?" I couldn't get over Bennet. It was like he had given me a red Life Saver all over again. Nolan didn't notice him. His relaxed posture and mellow disposition made you think he *always* came on up to the galleries after closing and hung out. My insides felt like there was a pack of electric eels swimming through my ribs.

"You said that even if he had a key, you didn't think you were good enough to get one."

"Oh no, I don't know. I just . . ." He was looking at me like he really wanted the answer.

"Sometimes when I was little, and even now . . ." He was still looking right at me, listening. I'm telling you, the guy listens like you hold the secrets to everlasting happiness. "I just can screw up."

"You don't look like a screwup," he said.

"No?"

"No, you look like her." He pointed at the famous painting.

"Well, how do you know she wasn't a screwup?" I said, all the while taking in the amazing and unbelievable fact that he had just compared me to a Vermeer.

"Why do you think *you* are a screwup?"

"I'm like an apple. I look perfectly good from the outside, but when you bite into it, it has mealy insides."

"Mealy apples are the worst."

"Yeah, I know."

"I don't believe you have mealy insides, but you do look like an apple."

Charlie and Bennet said I look like fruit too, I thought.

I looked down at the skirt of my dress that did look like the glossy skin of a Gala. I also took that moment to subtly shove the stained fabric back into the folds. My heart got momentarily heavy because, no matter what that lady had said about finding a good dry cleaner, those stains were never going to come out.

"Well, thank you, but you should believe me. I'm so dyslexic you can't believe it," I stated almost too loudly.

"So?"

"So I have ADD too."

"So? So do I."

"You do?"

"Yeah. I'm not really into labels though." He raised his eyebrows at me.

"Do you take anything for it?" I said, surprising myself because I don't usually talk about my medication.

"I used to when I was younger, and then my mother got sick of it because I couldn't sleep so she chucked the bottle in the garbage can. But I still can't sleep."

"I can sleep. I'm on drunillian. It helps me, I think."

"Are you on it now?"

"It's worn off. It wears off around seven."

"I remember that feeling. It felt like a dip. It was kind of too big a dip for me to handle. It bummed me out a lot. I felt like I couldn't play my guitar, so that was unacceptable."

"Yeah, I was on one like that when I was littler, like in fifth grade. But then I started seeing Dr. Trout."

"Dr. Trout!" He laughed.

"Yeah, I know, she's my pediatric neuropsychologist . . ." I felt like maybe this wasn't such a good conversation anymore.

"Go on."

"Well, are you going to make fun of me or something?"

"Hey, no, no . . ." He shook his head gently and pushed his bangs out of his eyes. "Tell me."

"It's just that she put me on this other stuff where there is no dip, and it really works. I do much better in school. I feel more like a citizen on it. And I'm not on it during the summer. And it totally doesn't mess with my drawing."

"That's good," he said. Sometimes I have a hard time looking people in the eye, but not with Nolan. It was like the only choice at that moment was to look into his eyes that were warm and kind and loving. "I have no judgment about that, Wren, I mean it." I kind of felt tears gathering, so I blinked.

"Well, I may not take it forever," I said.

"No, people can use it for a while, learn stuff from it, and then ditch it when it doesn't serve them anymore. Happens a lot."

"Yeah. So do you play guitar or sing or . . ."

"Both."

"Right, that makes sense, that's what people in bands do, like, um . . ." He reached out and rubbed the fabric of my skirt between his fingers. It was as if he had touched the inside of my thigh. I shivered.

"Jimmy Page," he said.

"Yeah. Who's Jimmy Page?"

"*What!?*" His reaction was like a fire alarm had gone off in the room. He grabbed my shoulders and fake-shook them. "*Jimmy Page* in many people's opinion, including mine, is the greatest, most brilliant genius rock guitarist that ever lived. He is the lead guitar player for Led Zeppelin. You have heard of Led Zeppelin, please tell me."

"Yesssss. God, yes."

"Thank god. This might have had to end right here if you didn't know Zeppelin."

I couldn't even respond. If it could end that meant something had started. And then his phone must have been on vibrate because he pulled it out of his pocket and read.

"Listen, my boy from Pittsburgh is spinning down on Houston Street at this club. All these Pitt kids that I know came up for it and it's going to be . . ." And then he did this move that I can't really describe, but I guess it's a cool-music-guy dance move you make if something is going to be off the hook. "They are wild, those kids from Pittsburgh. Do you want to go, like, right now? It's"—he looked at his phone again—"nine-o-five."

"Well." A spell had been broken. "Wait, how do you know people from Pittsburgh?"

"I spend a weekend a month there. My dad's a professor of biology at Pitt—the university."

"Really? But don't you live here?" All this time I hadn't even asked him about his family or anything.

"Yeah, my mom lives here. My dad and stepmom live there, with my half brother, Bruno. It's not far on the train."

"'*Stairway to Heaven!*'" I said, way louder than anything else we had said since we were in that gallery. "Led Zeppelin sings that song 'Stairway to Heaven.'"

"Bingo." He leaned forward, smiling, took my head in his hands and kissed me, right in front of the Vermeer.

Think of any girl who has gotten kissed in any movie you have ever seen by any dream of a boy. I was that girl. I was the girl in the movie.

"I think you should come downtown with me."

20

My phone was still on the table under the roses and hydrangeas, which was where I left it when I sat down.

"But I don't have my phone—or my bag," I said, keeping up with him as we scooted down the staircase that we had just run up.

He turned around and caught me by the waist.

"You totally don't have to come if you think you'll get in trouble." I was sort of suspended over him, still on the stairs, but leaning into him like I was a ballerina and he was going to lift me into the air.

"Well, I mean, I *will* get in trouble, right? How could I not?"

"You won't. You won't because—because, don't you think one of your friends will get your bag? Or, here"—he let go of me so I had to make sure I wouldn't tumble down the rest of the stairs—"text one of them from my phone. Tell them to get your bag and phone and tell them you are going with me for an hour."

"But—"

"*Then*, leave a message for your parents at home saying that you went with me to see a friend play music, just for an hour, and I'll have you back before you would have been home from this party anyway."

"Why don't I just go tell them now?"

He looked at me like, *No, don't do that, dummy.*

"They are hosting a huge party! Not only will they say no, but they are busy and probably don't want to be bothered, and it doesn't matter because I will have you home before midnight." He took my hand and looked at his phone that I was holding. "That is in more than two hours."

He had a huge this-is-a-good-plan smile on. He handed me his phone.

"Text one of those girls."

This felt like the universe of someone else. Other people do things like this. Or maybe this is like the teenage version of doing something sort of bad, but not really bad, like licking a subway pole, which I did all the time as a little kid. Or like touching the light. Maybe my teenage self reaches out of her father's arms by going downtown to dance with a bunch of kids from Pittsburgh.

"I only know Charlie's number by heart."

"So text him."

Lots of voices inside me were screaming, "Nooooo, don't dooo thaaaaattttt . . . baaaaddddd ideeeaaaaaa." But a *much* louder one screamed, "*Do it!*"

> Hi, it's Wren. Nolan is taking me to a dance thing, but I will be back home by midnight. Could you please get my bag and my phone on the table and give them to Oliver?

"Now call your home and leave a message for your parents. They will be cool if they know where you are. Parents only freak out when they *don't* know where you are."

That felt true to me. In fact, I could clearly recall at that moment my mother saying something like "I don't care where you are as long as I know where you are." Or it was something like that.

I called home. Rachel-the-hair-person answered.

"Oh, hi, Rachel. It's Wren."

"Hey, Wrenny. How's it going?"

"Good, it's good. But will you leave a message for my parents?"

"Sure." No big deal, no big deal, no big deal. Sound like this is no big deal.

"Okay, so will you tell them that I am going with Oliver's friend to a dance and I will be back before they get home. I am just calling to say where I am, so they don't worry. Okay?"

"Sure." She sounded like what I was saying was no big deal, so I must have pulled it off.

"Oh, great! So, thanks, Rachel!"

"Sure. Have fun!" And we hung up.

"What about Oliver?" I said.

"What *about* Oliver? He's cool, I think he would rather stay here with Reagan," he said, like he knew everything.

"*What?*" I kind of punched him in the arm when I said this.

"I think he and Reagan were maybe going to hook up. That's what it looked like before." He held on to his arm and laughed at me.

"Where? In the temple?" I said, still flabbergasted.

"Yeah, before dinner. Does that not seem right to you? It looked like they were into each other."

Reagan and Oliver?

"Come on. Let's get out of here. I have to get you downtown and home before you turn into a pumpkin."

21

Kissing.

Frankly, I didn't think you could kiss someone for such a long time. Nolan hailed a cab in front of the museum, and from the second we finished piling my dress into it we kissed with him on top and me leaning against the hard door of the taxi until we got to Houston Street, which is almost a hundred blocks away. Here is the thing about all that kissing. Since I had never kissed someone for so long, I didn't know what happened to the rest of your body when you kiss. It's really not a mouth thing. It's a *body* thing.

I'm not going to gross you out with details about what happened to my body, or Nolan's body, but I will say that it felt like nothing else feels in your life. It doesn't feel like running really fast or falling asleep when you're extremely tired, or dancing, or doing yoga, or eating a spoonful of Nutella. When you kiss a seventeen-year-old boy, who has clearly kissed other girls in his life because he is very confident about it, in a cab zooming down Fifth Avenue, and during all the red lights and while stuck in the traffic that comes around the New York Public Library, your body goes into a state of sensory overload. You kind of feel like a lion.

We talked a little during this extended playlist of a kiss (so if you can bear it, picture this conversation while we are kissing).

"Do you have a boyfriend?"

"Noooo."

"How is that possible?"

"I haven't had a boyfriend since eighth grade."

"What was that guy's name?"

"Thomas Friedman."

"Do you know that is the name of a *New York Times* columnist?"

"Yes."

"How do you know that?"

"My parents thought it was funny that I was going out with a mini Thomas Friedman. He was even on his school paper."

"I will never be able to read that guy's column again. The real Thomas Friedman, I mean."

"Do you read it a lot?"

"Yeah, for current events. He's a genius."

"I don't think my Thomas Friedman was a genius."

"I think you're a genius." Giggling, kissing, giggling, tugging, squeezing, breathing, giggling, kissing.

22

The club was really a loft space on the third floor of a walk-up on Houston and Varick Street. The building was run-down and scary-looking, like maybe it looked like a crack house (or what a crack house looks like in my imagination, which I am sure is not really what one looks like), but I figured it wasn't actually dangerous because there was a very trendy barbecue restaurant right next door and the 1 train was right on the corner. During the day, this neighborhood is as normal as toothpaste, but to me it felt like I was in a Chinatown in another city, like I was in Paris or in a P!nk video. I felt out of my league.

"Here we go!" Nolan said, not like a mom starting a long drive; it was like hip-hop talk.

"Wait." I suddenly felt *super* self-conscious in my big red dress. "I am fairly certain I am not wearing the right thing for this." I pointed to the dingy, banged-up door with chipped paint.

"Oh, you never know what people will be wearing at these things. Who cares, you look like Guinevere."

"I can't believe I don't have my phone. Did Charlie text back yet?"

"Ummmmm." As Nolan scrolled his messages, I thought that

he sure had a lot of messages. I get the same four people texting me all day, but it never adds up to as many as Nolan seemed to be scrolling through. I wondered how many friends he had.

"Yup." He held out his phone so I could read it:

You left?

I looked up at Nolan like, *Yikes.*
"Wait, there's more." He continued to scroll, then:

I'll get bag/phone but you are insane

"Oh golly." Everything about the small groups of hip-looking, downtown kids going into the club was making me think I had done something stupid. I should be sitting at my table with Earl and my brother and my friends at the Met. I wasn't one of these people. *But* I was standing there with them, so maybe I was cool and hip and exactly where I was supposed to be.

"I wonder if Charlie told the girls, or, oh god, my parents," I said, still looking at the nose ring of a kid talking to his friends about skateboarding.

"We do not know." He stuck the phone in his inside pocket. "All we know is we have an hour to dance before I am going to take you home. Nothing bad is going to happen in an hour."

He smiled and went to grab the door. "In fact, I think a whole lotta good is going to happen in the next hour. Come on, this is my museum."

There were two flights of narrow, steep stairs that went directly up. If you went to the left on the first floor, there was a record store. A handmade sign in the shape of an arrow pointing in its direction said LUCKY LOUIS'S VINYL.

"This," said Nolan, pointing into the shop, "is the only place in the Village you can buy vinyl anymore. The guys who own that place have thousands of records. We'll come back here. It's its own universe and you have to have, like, three hours to dig around."

"Why is it still open so late? It's like ten-something." The steep stairs were a challenge in the dress and I was starting to speak loudly because the music coming from where we were headed was becoming louder and throbbier.

"Oh, they just opened. They'll be open for the rest of the night."

"Has Oliver ever been here?" I was starting to shout.

"This is where I met Oliver!"

"Are you sure about this whole Reagan, Oliver thing?" I didn't even like saying that out loud, much less screaming it.

"I can only report on what I saw. And it was a vibe thing. I pick up on shit like that, so yeah, I'm pretty sure." I had a pit in my stomach for Vati.

I nodded, as it was getting too loud to talk. We were almost in front of a biker guy sitting on a stool on the next landing up from Lucky Louis's. This mammoth, hairy man was wearing a leather vest with no shirt on under it. His wide, beefy arms crossed over his middle on top of a long, mouse-colored beard. He had a classic worn-in blue bandanna on his head. On one of his upper arms he had a tattoo of the outline of a state. I am not quite sure, but I think it was Indiana.

"Nick!" Nolan shouted. The biker guy stood up and man-hugged Nolan. They slapped each other's backs.

"Nick, this is Wren!" I tried to make a neutral face so I didn't look frightened.

"Pleased to meet you, Wren." Nick stuck out his hand and I shook it enthusiastically, just as if he were one of my parents' friends. I made sure to look him square in the eye.

"Hi!"

"That is some kind of dress," said Nick, like maybe he knew what he was talking about, like maybe behind all that bikerness was a couturier.

"Oh, yeah, thanks!" And then I noticed that Nick had a round yellow pin with a light blue squirrel attached to his vest. This was weird because Reagan has a little obsession with squirrels. She's all badass and then she'll see a squirrel in the park and take a picture of it. She must have five hundred pictures of squirrels on her phone. Farah once said they were like rats, and it made Reagan cry.

"Did Mikey start?" asked Nolan.

"Yup, go on in." Nick heaved open a door that had to have been made of iron. A tsunami of sound and heat rushed at us. Nolan led me into it, full-on.

"Mikey is a *genius!*" Nolan shouted, pointing at the bent-over boy at a turntable in the front of the room. I could only see Mikey's ski hat and earphones. Nolan took off his coat and tie at the same time and threw his stuff near the mixing table as he pulled me into a mass of sweaty bodies. His movements were fluid, like his body had already, instantly, adapted to his surroundings. He seamlessly and quickly fit in. I don't feel like my body does that. I am like the fish in the bag. You know that rule? When you bring a fish home from the pet store to put it in an aquarium with other fish, you can't just dump the new fish in. You have to gradually replace the water in the bag with water from your aquarium so the fish can acclimate. The fish needs an adjustment time. Nolan didn't seem to require any time to adjust to any new circumstance. He just fit in.

"Mikey's a madman! Listen to this!" Nolan jumped up and down with everyone else.

I felt like Dorothy in *The Wizard of Oz* when she gets to that first Technicolor other-universe, where the flowers are as big as houses and everyone sings in unison. Except, my dress was ridiculous in that place. I should have been in mini-shorts and a tank top but instead I looked like the chick from *Enchanted.* I'm sure hipsters were looking for my wand. Thank god it was dark in there. I was oblivious that a mysterious club sludge was seeping into the bottom of my dress.

"Oh ye-ah!" Nolan saw a dancing girl who clearly was his friend, and pushed her shoulder. She looked up and was all "Yo Yo!" From the crouched dancing position she was in, she jumped like a poison dart frog into his arms, wrapping her legs around him.

"Nolan!" she screamed. Then she catapulted off him and the two of them jammed out like J-Lo and one of her dancers.

A little too much, you say? It turned out to be Emme, one of his best girlfriends from Pittsburgh.

He stopped her mid–jam out and turned her in my direction.

"This is *Wren!*" he shouted.

"*Gwen?*"

"*Wren!*" we both shouted.

She waved to me, pointed to herself. *"Emme!"* She smiled and kept dancing. She was in really short shorts, a tank top, and Doc Martens. When I tell you she was dancing, I mean she was on fire. She was doing the Dougie and this crisscross thing with her legs, her arms tucked up around her ears. And then I realized there were ten or so cool dancing girls all in a pack. Heads down, glistening, tight and really kind of crazy-looking, but not chaotic. It was more military than that. I didn't know from this kind of pack dancing.

If you are worried that Nolan left me out and danced with his Pitt friends and I stood on the side like a loser, don't be. He totally didn't. He did the opposite—he pulled me in.

"Are these your friends? How come they are such good dancers?" I had to shout. It was hard to say anything, especially because I was trying to do the Dougie in an Oscar de la Renta.

"It's a Pittsburgh thing! They grow up dancing like that!"

"Why?"

"It's just what it's like there! Look at you! *You* are a good dancer!" Oh, what? But you know, that music sort of does make you feel you are a good dancer. I would hate to have seen myself in a mirror, but it felt good. I felt cool.

The music changed from some kind of Skrillex dubstep to a Rolling Stones song, something my parents got all excited about when they heard it on classic rock radio stations in the car. It was "Let's Spend the Night Together." But all funked up with other mixes of things. Everyone freaked out. I did, too. It was the most fun I had ever had, and I forgot about absolutely everything.

23

Nolan did what he said he would do—he got me home before midnight. We rode the 1 train up Broadway and he told me about his parents' divorce as the train rocked and screeched into station after station all the way to Eighty-Sixth Street.

"I can't believe we were born in the same hospital," I said, with my leg over his leg.

"But we missed each other by two years and 138 days, I think, if my math is right." He mentally counted. "Yeah, 138."

"You really are crazy good at math."

He raised his eyebrows at me. "By the time you were born, I was living in Louisville, Kentucky."

"Why?" I had pictured him growing up in New York like me.

"When I was born, my dad was getting his PhD at Columbia, but then he had to get a teaching job and it took him a while until he landed a good one, so we moved around a lot."

"Oh." I felt bad about that the way you do when you hear about Army kids having to go to a bunch of different schools.

"Yeah, so before I was seven we lived in New York, Kentucky, and Santa Barbara."

"How come? Did he keep getting fired?"

"No, no, just the only academic jobs that came up in his field were non-tenure-track, so they only lasted a year or two and then we had to move again. It stank—I think. I don't really remember."

He looked so sweet, and I did something I had never done before. I kissed a boy because I wanted to show that I felt for his experience of having to do something hard, like move around. Up until that point, kissing was about Truth or Dare or it just came with the territory of going out with someone. Kissing was an awkward part of what you thought you were supposed to do, even if you didn't know why. This kiss was different. I kissed Nolan because it felt like the only response to what he was saying. It felt more appropriate than words. He smiled sweetly, blinking his eyes slowly. He was touched. At least I think he was.

"How did you end up living back here?" We were so close to each other, all snuggled in one of the two-seaters on the train. Nolan had given me his suit jacket when we left the dance/rave thing. I felt like I was his girl.

"Well, so when I was seven, my dad finally got an assistant professorship at the University of Pittsburgh in biology. We lived in this little brown house on Tremont Street, where my dad still lives now. It's right next to campus. He used to walk me to the elementary school where lots of the professors' kids go, which was next to his office in this gigantic gray cinder-block building. I remember I thought it was NASA, the center of the scientific world. There were so many labs and computers. Sometimes, he would do experiments with me there, little stuff, like make electricity with paper clips. And my mom could take psych classes at the university too, for free I think, or for half, I'm not quite sure, but the psychology department was in the next building, so we were all close."

"She was in school?"

"Yeah, grad school. She's a shrink now."

"Whoa. That's cool."

"Yeah. Anyway, I think we all thought we were all right. It was a big deal that Dad's job was tenure-track, because it meant that in a few years he could maybe get tenure. Then we would never have to leave, and my mom could take classes easily, and then she could be a shrink there in Pittsburgh." He was explaining this like he had it down, like he had had a few shrink appointments himself on the topic. "I had two great little girlfriends that lived next door with their mom and—oh yeah! One was Emme! That girl you met tonight? She's one of my oldest friends. We used to climb this little apple tree in her backyard and eat granola bars up there. Her dad owned Terry's, the pub where all the college kids go."

"Apple trees aren't really that big, are they?"

"I know, but we were so small, so . . ."

"Oh." Big smile out of me, I loved thinking about him small. "Does her dad still own the bar?"

"Totally."

"Do you go there when you visit your dad?"

He nodded. God he was cool. He just was. Nodding is cool, and I thought, even though this doesn't entirely make sense, if you nod at someone instead of talk, you are connected. Nodding is confident.

"When did you guys come back to New York?"

The train stopped at Times Square and about half the people got off. Even close to midnight, tons of people ride the subway in New York, especially the 1 train. A new batch of people got on the train. Some looked tired, like they were heading home. But most looked shiny and energetic, like their nights were just beginning.

"Only my mom and I came back to New York. It was unexpected because, well, things got screwed up. I am pretty positive that my mother wasn't planning on ever moving back."

"No?"

He shook his head and bit the side of his lip. "Nope. I remember my mother painting my bedroom there. She let me choose my own color and I chose a Kermit the Frog green. 'Are you sure?'"—Nolan imitated his mother—"'Because it's going to be this color for a long, long time.' I remember thinking that I would always want my room to be that color."

I smiled at him.

Nolan checked out a guy who had just sat across from us and was taking out fries from a McDonald's bag. The salty, savory smell that is so distinctly McDonald's had overtaken the subway car. Most new Yorkers of my generation have been trained to think Mickey D's is gross because of the documentary that guy made about it, the one where he ate McDonald's every day for a month and almost died. Nolan looked a tad offended by the guy eating on the train, and I couldn't figure whether it was because eating on the subway is gross, or that he thought McDonald's is gross. But secretly, I think Big Macs are freaking delicious. And sometimes, like after a long, exciting night when you didn't finish your dinner and danced in an unfamiliar part of town with someone who can only really be described as a demigod, the smell of McDonald's is comforting and makes you ravenous.

"But then, one night, I heard my parents fighting in the kitchen, which was weird because I never heard them fighting, or saw them fighting. Our house didn't have a fighting vibe at all, it was more of a pancakes-in-the-morning-reading-*Garfield*-comics-in-the-afternoon kind of house. Like your house."

"Oliver reads a ton of *Garfield*, or he used to."

"Yeah, Garfield is the man."

I smiled. "He's actually a cat."

He smiled. "So I had gone downstairs because I had to pee, or I wanted to watch the Food Network with Mom, which sometimes she let me do at night even though I was supposed to be asleep." He turned to me with his whole body, putting his arm up on the top of the seat, and leaned his cheek against his hand.

"They definitely didn't know I was there because my dad wouldn't have ever said this to my mom if he knew I was there . . . He said, 'I love her, and I'm going to be with her, Nolan.'"

"Wait, he was talking to you?"

"No, my mom's name is Nolan too. I'm named after her. Weird, right? It's actually her maiden name, her real first name is Jessica, but Dad used to call her by her last name when they were dating—it was like his special nickname for her—so." He shrugged and looked out the window as we came out of the tunnel and into the next station.

"That's sweet," I said. The doors opened to the Fifty-Ninth Street stop. We were only four stops away from when we would have to get off. I felt butterflies in my chest. I didn't ever want the train ride to end.

"Anyway, my dad told my mom he was in love with another professor in his department and by the end of that semester, my mom and I were living in New York City in a tiny rental apartment on 145th Street. It was the only neighborhood she could afford, and it was close-ish to Columbia, where she still had friends from when my dad taught there. Eventually she started taking classes again."

I was stunned. It was not every day that I heard people talking about being unable to afford to live where they want. It was not every day that I heard about single mothers who were going to have to go it alone without a big fat child-support check every month, like Reagan's mom. Talking to Nolan made me feel like I had been in a cocoon, wrapped up in the finest silken thread all my life, asleep.

"I remember having to go to a new school in the middle of the year, which wasn't so bad, but sometimes I saw my mom crying when she thought I couldn't see her."

"Oh gosh."

"No, but here's how cool my mom is. The first weekend we were in that little apartment, she painted my new room, this little tiny room off the kitchen that had a sink in it, Kermit the Frog green."

In one day, I was in love. Not that I was fully aware of that then, but looking back, I was. It wasn't like when people in books and movies say, "I grew to love him." I was hit by a subway of love.

Stupidly, I believed that because I was having this big feeling and knew with the greatest certainty that my life had changed, somehow my parents would be able to see that too and understand it, so they couldn't be mad, because how could you be mad at love?

"Here we are," I said, looking up at the ivy clinging to the outside of our brownstone. Nolan insisted that he walk me all the way to my door, and I thought that was yet another reason why my parents couldn't be mad at me. How can you get mad at your daughter for falling in love with someone with such good manners? It was freezing out but I gave him back his jacket. My skin felt like it was being burned by the cold.

"Wow, it looks really big when you just stand looking at it from the outside. Inside it feels smaller, cozier," he said, looking up at the five floors of house.

"I know, it is big, but my parents bought it a long time ago, and . . ."

"Hey, no, it's fine." He rubbed my arms and pulled me toward him to get me warm. "Your dad works hard. It doesn't surprise me you live in a nice place," he said plainly, hugging me. "You better go inside. I don't want you to get in trouble." He said it like he didn't think I was going to get in trouble, so I believed him.

"Oh, I don't think I will, I don't even think it's midnight." I looked up at him. "And I spoke to Rachel, right?"

"Yeah. I'm just going to kiss you quick."

The front door flew open at the top of the stairs as my mouth was curling into a waiting-for-a-kiss smile.

"*Are YOU KIDDING ME?*"

Nan screamed that.

"Wren—get in this house *immediately*! Right now . . . right now, *RIGHT NOW!*" She was repeatedly pointing at the stairs as if she were calling in a naughty dog.

"Mom, I . . ." She was at a ten.

"*GET IN THIS HOUSE!*"

Nolan was already walking quickly away up the street, but

backward, his eyes on me. He wasn't running away from the she-wolf at the top of the staircase, but he probably sensed that sticking around would make things worse for me. The last thing I saw was a look of horror on his face.

Phone-less, bag-less, and in a now downright filthy dress, I ran up the steps.

"Get in here," she hissed, still in her party dress.

"Mom, I . . ."

"Don't you speak. Don't you say a word."

Oliver and Dad were sitting on the yellow sofa in the bay window. All the downstairs lights were on, even the ones in the dining room. I pictured them coming home and furiously turning on every light, maybe thinking I would be in a dark corner. Oliver looked at me like, *I wish I could help you but you screwed yourself, lady.*

I saw my phone and clutch sitting on the table, and—this might have been the worst—neatly folded under them was my mother's ruby-red cashmere wrap I had also borrowed, and completely forgotten, on the back of my chair at the party.

"First of all, *look at my dress!*"

"Nan, please, let's keep our eye on the ball here."

"It's ruined, David, look at it! What is on the bottom? Is it wet? What the—?"

"Nan." Dad reached up and took my mother's hand to stop her from waking Dinah and perhaps running to strangle me. She started to cry.

"Okay, Wren. What were you thinking here?" my father said with crippling austerity. I stood, breathing hard, not knowing at all what to do. I looked at Oliver again. He wasn't going to make a peep. "We didn't know where you had gone. You put Rachel in a terrible position. You put Charlie in a terrible position . . . I am confounded by this."

"You ruined your father's big important night, Wren," my mother growled through her tears.

"How is that possible?" I said that softly, but my mother shot a crushing look at me. "I'm sorry, I thought . . ."

"I don't believe you were thinking, not at all, Wren," my father continued. The room was filled with ungodly silence and tension. "Do you know we were so worried we asked Bennet if he had seen you and he, dear Bennet, had to confess that he had seen you and Nolan in the upper galleries? In the galleries that were off-limits to guests? Bennet was mortified that he had been involved with your shenanigans, and he too didn't know where you had gone off to, so now he is at home worrying as well."

The thought of Bennet worrying made me cry. Had I thought I would upset Bennet, or *anyone* . . . well, I wasn't thinking. And continuing with the not-thinking thing, I chose an iffy line of argument. I should have stayed with the quiet weeping but instead I said, "I told Rachel I would be back before midnight and I *am*." My choice of offense over defense wasn't a strong one.

"*Rachel?*" My father was losing his cool.

"Yes!"

"*Rachel was in charge of Dinah—NOT YOU!*" Mom exploded.

"Someone has to be in charge of me? I am *fifteen*!"

"By the grace and generosity of your father, you and your friends were invited to the museum tonight and you took *advan-*

tage and left without telling anyone. That is *hardly* evidence of maturity!"

"Nolan said—"

"Nolan?" My mother howled. "Oliver, who *is* this Nolan?"

"He's just a new friend. He's a cool guy. He's, I don't know, I think he really enjoyed being at the party, but I guess—"

When you have made so many wrong turns, something happens to your brain, or to my brain at least, and they start to feel like perfectly good turns, so you keep making them.

"He is an amazing person!"

My mother laughed at me. My father put his head down and Oliver stayed quiet for two unending seconds until he too cackled with laughter.

"Go to bed, Wren," my father said, sizzling me and my stupid declarations about Nolan's amazingness into oblivion. "Your mother and I will tell you your punishment tomorrow, but for now, and for the foreseeable future, this phone is no longer yours, and the Internet will be deactivated upstairs."

I turned around and headed for the staircase.

"Take off my dress and leave it in front of our door," my mother said icily. "And you better get yourself up and ready for school tomorrow and be on time. I don't want to see you until you are walking out the door."

In the morning, I thought I heard the front door close from the top of the stairs. It's a rattling, slamming sound that has a finality to it. My mother leaves the house at 7:25 a.m. with Dinah and walks her to the Hatcher school bus on Columbus, a half block east of our house. (I used to take that same bus, but at the start of seventh grade I was allowed to take the public bus with Reagan and Vati. Farah has always been driven to school by her mother's driver.) Mom then goes downtown to a yoga class before she goes to her pottery studio. I thought they were gone, but I was wrong. The door closing was Mom coming back from walking May. Dinah was waiting at the bottom of the stairs with her hat, parka, and backpack on.

"Your ass is grass," said Dinah.

"Dinah, you stay out of this," Mom said, unhooking May and rising up to look at me like an evil queen (in yoga clothes) might look at the waif girl.

"Wren, this afternoon you come right home. Do you understand me?"

I nodded.

"You are grounded from now until we are not quite sure when. You will do nothing but be at school or at home. Absolutely no phone. If you need to use the Internet for your schoolwork you will do it at the kitchen table . . . none of your friends are welcome to come over." She paused as if she might be finished, but she wasn't. "And don't even think about seeing that boy."

24

When I got to school, Farah careened around the corner as I walked out of the stairwell and onto the fifth floor of Hatcher, where the ninth and tenth grade homerooms are located. Girls were standing in front of their lockers and sitting in groups on the floor, cracking open binders and snapping the rings back together. The stairwell door repeatedly opened and more girls filed into the hallway, screaming hello or quietly making their way to their lockers to prepare for class. In the upper grades students still have to wear a navy-blue pleated uniform skirt, but we are free to choose any top we want as long as it has a collar and is reasonably conservative. Farah and I had both chosen gray turtleneck sweaters. The fierce wind the day before had brought winter to November.

"I really have to talk to you." She grabbed my hand and took me over to her locker, which was at the end of the hall where fewer girls were milling around. She turned around and looked right at me. "I *know* you have something to tell me too."

"Yeah, I do, Far. It's all kind of awful but wonderful."

"I have to go first," she interrupted. She was doing the Farah thing of leading the discussion. "You didn't respond to any of my texts."

"My phone was taken away, but—"

"Just listen. First, have you seen Padmavati?"

"No, I just got here." I pulled my parka sleeve off with my teeth.

"She's a wreck."

"About Oliver?" I spat the parka sleeve out.

"Yes. How do you know that?"

"I live with Oliver, but that is not how I know. Nolan—"

"Shh shh shh, we will get there, but I have to get through this first."

"Okay, but mine is really good! And bad." I dumped my parka and backpack on the floor.

"Okay, first, Vati looks like Wednesday Addams. She's gutted, and Reagan is *such a bitch*." She said that in a whisper.

"What happened?"

"I will get to all of it, but I have to get to this other thing first."

"What?"

"I went home with—" Oh god, I knew what she was going to say before she said it. My stomach turned into a garlic knot.

"Cy."

"Farah!"

"Do you think that's really bad?"

"Oh *god*. He's *Cy Dowd*. Farah—he's old! Like really old, and famous and, oh my god."

"Wren. Listen to me right now. You can't tell anyone."

"Have you?"

"No. And you can't—at all. Ever." She pointed her finger at me, the nail still smooth and pearly from the manicure she got for the party.

I started laughing.

"Oh my god, stop."

I couldn't. I got the giggles.

"Wren, what is happening to you?" she said, like an annoyed mother of a seven-year-old boy.

I leaned against the locker, laughing my ass off.

"Stop it!"

I slid down my back against the metal, bumping along the vents and the locks until I hit the cold linoleum floor. I slumped on my backpack and gave into fits of halting laughter. Farah stood above me with her hands on her hips.

"I chose you to tell, Wren. And you are acting like a chimp."

"Okay, okay, I'm sorry." It took me a minute to calm down and then I felt sick; suddenly I felt my empty tummy. I definitely hadn't bothered to stop in the kitchen for a yogurt on my way out the door, which was stupid because I had taken one of my pills, and I definitely should eat something with it.

"That was a weird response."

"Well, what you told me is off the charts, Farah."

"I know." She bent to scratch at a nonexistent stain on her Uggs, anxiously looking down at me. I noticed that her mascara, which is usually impeccable, was smudgy on the corner of her left eye.

"How did it happen?" I whispered. Girls around us were making moves like classes were about to begin. The last thing I needed was to be late, and I was still in my hat.

Farah's eyes filled with tears. She had a moment of looking troubled, like she regretted what she was about to tell me.

"Well, he smiled at me before dinner, when your dad was talking." She breathed in and the tears receded.

"I saw that."

"You did?" She smiled, and her eyes got big and perky.

"Yup."

"Well, and then—" She really whispered here. Mrs. Garrison, our homeroom teacher, was in the classroom ten feet away from us with the door open, and she was writing something on the board.

"I could kind of feel him knowing where I was in the room all night—even after we went to our tables."

"He was sitting with *my parents!*"

"I know. That did not seem to matter to him."

The first bell rang loudly, startling us.

"Jesus," Farah said. We had five minutes to be in our first class. I visualized the schedule in my binder. *What did I have first?* Studio. My whole body relaxed. I had a double period of studio art with Mrs. Rousseau. All I had to do was get my stuff into my locker and go up to the seventh floor.

"I have calculus," Farah said. "I totally have to go, I think we are going to have a pop quiz. I didn't even look at my books yesterday. *Jesus.*"

Farah shot up, opened her locker door, and pulled a fifty-pound math textbook out of an impeccably organized library. Farah is in Math A, I am in Math C. Math C is full of kids the school has given up on mathematically. Reagan is in C with me. We mostly learn how to balance checkbooks and read the stock tables in *The New York Times.*

"When is your lunch?" she said.

"Fifth period. Farah, how did your mom not know?"

"She's away, remember? Marta just came in this morning, but I came home before that, at like six. I have lunch in fifth, too."

"Oh man. I'll meet you in the cafeteria," I said. "I can't believe Marta wouldn't pick up on something," I added, sort of to myself. "She knows you better than your mother." Marta has been Farah's nanny-now-housekeeper since she was born.

"Wrenny." The tears came back into Farah's eyes. "I slept with him."

25

The art department takes up half of the seventh floor. It's made up of three rooms filled with light, chalky dust, big shiny-leafed jungle plants, stacks of newsprint for drawing, paintbrushes of every shape and size, oversize jugs of blue, yellow, and red paint, and Mrs. Rousseau, our blousy art teacher, whose personality pervades the entire space. There is also the very shy and slight ceramics teacher named, funnily enough, Mr. Size. He is balding and wears wire-rimmed glasses, all tan clothing, and an apron that he never takes off. I don't think I've ever seen him in the rest of the school. It's like he lives in the art room, sorting glazes with one hand resting on his tiny hip, like an art hobbit. As a third grader, the moment I smelled the oily wax of the Cray-Pas, my body opened up and all the anxiety of Mrs. Paynter's rigid, impossible, and *infuriating* math class oozed out. But today I wasn't sure if any art supplies in the oasis had the power to make the insanity in my head stop.

"We must start, girls!" bellowed Mrs. Rousseau, waving her arm over us. "One believes that a double period is an endless reservoir, but it ends all too soon. We must get to work."

Mrs. Rousseau sounds like that old movie actress Lauren Bacall, and looks like a round version of the Wicked Witch of the West. You know how that witch was sort of beautiful? Mrs. Rousseau is too. Every day, she wears a black gypsy dress and the same well-worn neutral-colored smock that tucks under her ample bosom and wraps around her middle, tied in the exact same way, year after year after year. Her emotional outbursts are mimicked all over school. There are even *Saturday Night Live*-esque skits about her at talent shows. But she is all real. She can be brought to tears by a student's work. I've seen it. And I'll tell you something—her reaction makes *you* cry too, because it's authentic. If someone truly feels something, everyone does.

"We don't have much time." Mrs. Rousseau slowly circled the room, her plump hands together as if in prayer resting on her huge chest. She wears silver and turquoise rings on every finger except for her ring finger, where the gold wedding band Mr. Rousseau had given her years ago is embedded.

"Now before you start, please take a moment to lie on the floor. It's colder today, I know, but give yourself space to lie down and let the *ten-sion* and *tur-bulence* of your morning rush drain down, down into the floor until it seeps into Mr. Matheson's social science class." She laughed at her own idea, as if she had some beef with Mr. Matheson. "Take this time to find *the truth of who you are*," she said, delivering her most important and repeated message in a chocolaty baritone voice while slowly walking around the tables.

I didn't want to get on the floor.

I was too anxious about what Farah had vomited on me, and I was worried about poor Vati and starting to get infuriated with

Reagan, and maybe even Oliver? And I didn't have my phone, which gave me that horrible feeling like I had forgotten something, or like I was naked. I hadn't not had a phone in my backpack since I was twelve. I was feeling terribly guilty about Charlie and Bennet and even Rachel-the-hair-lady. What would happen when I got home from school? "Mrs. Rousseau, I think I should just start working, I can't get on the fl—"

"*Douwn, Wren,*" she commanded with the Irish-sounding accent she uses when she is being especially dramatic.

The floor was cold and hard but it had a mellowing effect. It felt like when someone puts a soaking washcloth over your fevered forehead. I sucked in air through my nose.

I could smell Nolan. I swear, I could smell him. I almost shrieked. I was bombarded with flashes and images of him kissing me in the cab. I let out an audible sigh/moan.

"That is right, Wren, let it all out, let out whatever you are holding on to so you are *free* to work from an *open* and *available* place. One more minute, girls."

I lay there, shut my eyes, and thought about Nolan looking at that luminous Vermeer. He really studied it, like he wa trying to figure it out. What boy does that? I breathed in deeply, hoping I would be able to smell him again. A beam of sun burst through a cloud outside and shone in through the window onto me. If I had opened my eyes it would have been too bright, so I kept them closed and felt the warmth on my face.

"Ooooookaaayy. Find your places and let's begin," said Mrs. Rousseau.

We were all drawing the same still life that was set up in the middle of the room. Wooden bowls, fruit, glass jugs, spoons, books. It was an exercise in shape and we had been working on it for ten days. Although I drew the light and dark, found the negative space, and worked with my chalk to define edges, mine had morphed into a medieval village. I added buildings jammed together and rivers, some bridges, and I even stuck a dragon in there, snaking through the cobblestone alleys. My picture also had an inordinate number of owls tucked into windows and perching on spoons.

"*This* has become a wild mastah-piece, Miss Noorlander. Wow, wow, wow," Mrs. Rousseau said, reaching into the pocket of her smock and taking out her tortoiseshell reading glasses to get a better look.

"The detail, Wren. I looove it. What is it with you and these delicious owls? Look at this one with all his plooommage."

"Yeah, I don't know if Harry Potter had some kind of influence on me or what, but I just can't get enough of drawing owls . . . Mrs. Rousseau?"

"Hmmm?" She was following the spine of my dragon with her finger up around the side of the bowl that I had turned into a road.

"Last night, I met Mr., um, Saint-Rémy Broc-someone?"

"Hmmm?"

"Yeah, well, he runs the Saint-Rémy program?"

"Oh, Mr. Brocklebank."

"Right. It was pretty cool to meet him."

"I'm sure it was. But meeting him will not get you into the program. How are your grades?" she asked, still engrossed in my drawing.

"I'm not sure I'll do so well in chemistry, but I think my English and history grades will be good, at least fine. Well, I think I'll pass. I hope."

"If you submitted this piece you would get in," she said softly, so the other girls wouldn't hear.

"I have to do a self-portrait and two other drawings of a bike and a shoe," I reminded her. I took my chalk and darkened a line that was bothering me.

"What an adventure that self-portrait will be, yes?" She looked at me over her reading glasses.

"Uh-huh . . . I'm sort of scared of it though."

"Technically, Wren, you have nothing to fear. You have a deep and solid understanding of light and dark and how to render."

"Well, but it's not really about just drawing something that will look like me, right?"

"Right you are, dear. It's about drawing"—I knew what she was going to say so we said it in unison—"the truth of who you are." And then I laughed, stupidly, because she takes that truth-of-who-you-are thing seriously.

"You laugh, Wren, but being able to find that truth, the truth that is in here." She stuck her finger in my gut. *Oh my goodness, she is so dramatic,* I thought, and her fervor was getting the attention of the other girls.

"And here." She pointed to my brain. I stood very still while her pointer finger was on my temple.

"But mostly, here." She thrust her hand onto her own heart. Obviously I knew she didn't want me to draw what was in her heart, but what was in mine. I got it, even though she was skating on the edge of cheesiness.

"*That* is the challenge. That is where your work lies."

The only thing that I felt in my heart at that moment was this boy that I would probably never be allowed to see again.

26

On my way into fifth-period lunch I ran into Vati walking out of the cafeteria. She must have had fourth-period lunch that day. She saw me, lifted her arms in the air, and flopped them down, so so sadly.

"Oohhhh, Vatter. What is going on? Farah only told me a tiny bit, and well, that guy, Nolan did too, a little."

"Wren—are you insane? Do you know how much your parents freaked out? Have you gotten any of my texts?"

"No, well, I mean I know they freaked out but I got home late and they sent me to bed like I was five and took away my phone that I actually hadn't seen in hours, so no, I really don't know what is happening."

"Well, it all *sucks*." She burst into tears.

"Oh my god, Vat."

"Freaking *Reagan*—who isn't even in school today."

"She isn't?"

"No, you know her mother doesn't care what she does."

"Oh, gosh, well."

"Did you see Oliver?" She looked at me like, *Well?*

"No, I didn't." She gave me a look like *BS, lady.*

"I did *last night*, but, Vati, I am in so much trouble."

"I bet you are. I would ground you."

"Wow, Vati, you are so mad."

"I know!" She scrunched up her face, stamped her feet, and shrieked at little.

"What happened?" I asked.

"She flirted with him at dinner, *so* intensely, I could *see it* from our table." She wiped her eyes on her sleeve. "And he ate it up. He was looking at her like she was Gisele, and I don't get it because he has seen her every day or something since we were born and she's never even, *god*, he's *my* crush." She started weeping again so I hugged her.

"He's my crush," she repeated quietly.

"I know, Vati. You have been so devoted to Oliver for years."

"I have, I really have." She nuzzled my shoulder and cried. She was doing that two-quick-breaths-in-one-bigger-breath-out crying. Girls were walking in and out of the lunchroom, but nothing is shocking about a girl crying at Hatcher or probably any other high school in the country, so nobody stopped.

Then she jerked her head off my shoulder and looked at me with wet, wide eyes. I swear she looks so much like an Indian Katy Perry sometimes. "What *did* happen to you?"

"I'll tell you, but are you okay enough for me to talk about myself?"

She nodded, took a deep breath, and stopped crying. "I'm going to be late for chemistry, but I don't care."

"So, first I took Nolan upstairs, to show him some paintings."

"You *did*?"

"Yeah, but then we left."

"No kidding," she said sarcastically, which made me think she was kind of better.

"Well, we did, and he took me all the way downtown to this party, rave thing, that his friend was spinning at."

"*What?*"

"Yeah, I know, and it was so totally amazing and cool and kind of scary. I mean, I would have been *so* scared if I was alone, or even with you guys."

"Wren—promise me you won't ever be friends with Reagan again."

"Oh, well, Vat, that's . . ." She restarted to cry. The second bell rang.

"Oh ratso-rizzo, I have to get upstairs," she said.

"Okay, but let's walk home together. I have to go straight home. I'm in major trouble."

"Yeah. Getting in trouble sucks." Vati had gotten herself together again and was pulling her chem book out of her backpack.

"It will be okay, Vati. You are so awesome." I gave her a huge hug. Vati *is* awesome, and my brother was an idiot.

27

Farah was already sitting at lunch with one of her complicated salads from the salad bar.

"Hi, let me just go grab something." I wish I liked all those different textures and could get chic salads, but I really don't. It's something to do with my ADD, I think. Mouth-feel is imperative to me. I can eat a lot of things, but anything I eat has to feel good in my mouth. This is what does:

> Pork chops
> Steak on a baguette
> Pizza with no cheese
> Very hard cheddar cheese
> Raw carrots or broccoli with no dressing
> Pears, but there can't be any soft spots
> Black beans and rice
> Meat sauce
> PowerBars but not granola bars

Other stuff too, but basically I need my food to be hard or chewy, except for chocolate pudding. Lunch was meat loaf, which I do like, but it can't have sauce and it has to be on a roll, which this was. I put my tray next to Farah's and sat.

"You should have something colorful, Wren." I sighed, got up, went to the salad bar, and got a small bowl of raw spinach.

"Happy?" I asked. She smiled at me and handed me a CD.

"What is this?"

"Your boy."

"What?"

"I told Mr. Weiner I had to use the computer lab for some calculus thing, and I went and found these songs on a Columbia website. Last night Oliver told me that Nolan is playing there for Harvest Festival, so I looked and there was a link to *Nolan's* website so I downloaded three songs. I always have blank disks in my binder."

"Farah, whoa, you're like a love spy."

"Not really. I didn't have time to listen to the music because I was being rather clandestine." Holding the CD felt like I was holding his hand.

"Thanks, Farah." That is what I love about Farah. She appears to do nothing but think about herself, shop for good clothes, and get entwined in inappropriate dalliances with famous old people. But really she's thinking about you and downloading music of the boy you have a crush on.

"Put it away now," she said, spiking six different vegetables and seeds onto her fork. I put it in a pocket in my binder.

"So," I said, mashing my sandwich down with my hand.

"So, I'm freaking out," she said calmly.

"You really slept with him?"

"Yes, I really did."

"Gosh." I took a bite of the now-flat meat loaf sandwich.

"Wren, when you are a virgin that might seem like a big deal, but for me, it's not."

"How is it not a big deal, Farah?" I looked around at the various girls eating lunch in clusters. Nobody was that close to us, but I whispered to respect her privacy. "You have only slept with Hans."

"Yes, well, I know, but I see him on Fire Island every summer."

"So?"

"So, we have had sex at least"—she tilted her head up and looked at the ceiling, mentally counting—"well, twice last summer."

"Uh-huh." What I wanted to say was *But Cy Dowd is in his thirties and you are fifteen!* I couldn't because Farah doesn't roll like that. She would have shut up like a clam.

"Okay, back the bus up. How did you even start talking to him?" I said.

"After dinner, while your parents, Charlie, and Vati were all mental about finding *you*." She lifted her eyebrows.

"Yeah." I smiled inappropriately.

"Cy," she said his name like he was her husband, "just *found* me. He came right over and started talking to me."

"Were people looking at you?"

"Yes, well I suppose they were looking at him, really. Wren, he's, well, he's a living *genius*. He asked me to come see his studio, so we left together."

"Oh eww, Farah! Did my parents see you?"

"I don't think so." She forked another salad bite into her mouth.

"Why are you so calm about this? Isn't his studio in Brooklyn?"

"Yes! He had a car though." I gave her the you-are-unreal look, and really couldn't think of anything to say.

"I know this is unusual, but then this morning, I started to think it makes all the sense in the world. I've always been mature."

"Okay." I said. I took another bite of my sandwich and chewed slowly. "It was just a one-night thing though. Right?"

"Wrong," she said. "He said he wants to see me again and I want to see him too."

"But, Farah, he's really an adult. It's, well, like Charlie said just yesterday. It's illegal."

"Not if nobody knows."

I looked at my sandwich. "No, not true, Farah. It is totally illegal whether nobody knows or not. And, sorry, but it's weird."

"It's weird to be attracted to one of the most important and famous artists in the country? It's *weird* to respond to the advances of a fascinating, charismatic man?"

"Yeah, I think it's weird." She looked stung and like I was an idiot.

"Just don't tell anyone." She looked at my meat loaf sandwich with disgust. "Got it?"

"Got it. Jeez," I said, widening my eyes at my sandwich.

"I wish I hadn't told you." Now she was staring at me.

"Fine!"

"Fine." She put her fork and knife on the tray to the side of her salad bowl, then she stood up and hoisted her Patagonia backpack over her shoulder. "I have reading to do. I'm going to the library." She stood there for a minute like maybe she thought I might stop her. "If you see Vati, she is really upset, and Reagan isn't even in school today."

"Yeah, I know. I already saw Vati. We're walking home together."

"Fine," she said.

"Fine," I said.

28

Padmavati was already downstairs with her parka, hat, and scarf on, waiting by the front door, when I came down at 3:20.

"Let's go," she said, unchanged from the weepy state I had seen her in hours before.

"Have you signed out?" I asked trying to zip up my backpack and go through the mental list that I am supposed to go through every time I leave the school so I don't space on anything.

> Homework (check)
> Reading book (check)
> Computer (check)
> Notes to parents from teachers (weren't any, check)
> Sign out

"Did it already," she said.

"Okay, let's go," I said, forgetting to sign out.

Vati leaned against the heavy glass door with its shiny brass fixtures, waiting to be buzzed out by Mr. Fisk, the young receptionist guy who sits in a little office in the front of the school and lets people in and out all day. We waved at him and walked through the foyer to the second set of doors to the outside. It was freezing.

"I almost want to take a taxi home. I am so exhausted and starving," Vati whined.

"I have no money," I said, and yanked out my scarf from the middle pocket of my backpack. I tried to tie it in the French way like Farah does, but failed.

"I just have six bucks and my bus pass. Let's take the bus then, six bucks won't get you and me home." Vati said. "It's too cold to walk through the—"

I was already at a dead stop because *right* outside the school, leaning against a car, with a guitar strapped to his back, was Nolan.

"Is that Nolan?" Vati sort of shouted, like she had no impulse control.

"Yes. Hi." He was even better-looking than I remembered, if that was possible. It's because teenagers in suits, even older teenagers, look awkward. There's no way around it. That day he looked like a guy in a J.Crew catalog without the stupid we-have-a-perfect-life thing all their models seem to have.

On the sidewalk, in between his legs, was a beat-up blue backpack, just like mine, which was a hand-me-down from Oliver.

"Hi," he said.

"Hi!" Vati said, and laughed, and snorted.

Let me tell you that it is very, *very* rare to see a boy outside of our school. *Maybe* someone's brother will come to a play, but that's pretty much it. Our school is on a tree-lined side street on the Upper East Side. The boys' schools, of which there are about three, are blocks and blocks away, and St. Tim's, where Charlie and Oliver go, is on the west side. If girls met their boyfriends after school, it was far away in the park or at a remote pizza parlor. It was not customary for a boy, especially a lone boy, to be standing in full view of the faculty and student body as they left the building for the day. It wasn't even a Friday.

I could feel a flush of adrenaline and anxiety rise from my rapidly beating heart and get pumped into my cheeks like a frigging oil spill.

Mary Turnbellow, a senior, walked out of the school, stared at Nolan either out of amazement or because he was so hot, and then gave me a skeptical look.

"Bye, Wren," she said. She had never really spoken to me before.

A gaggle of eighth graders led by Molly Frankel came out of school. All of them stared at Nolan, and I think Sarah Smith's mouth opened in amazement.

I tried to rip my ponytail holder out of my hair so I wasn't wearing a Wilma Flintstone bun on the top of my head. *Please don't let a teacher come out. Please don't let a teacher come out.* No such luck. Miss Bongiorno, one of the gym teachers, emerged from the side door with the track team on their way to a run in the park. I could swear she mouthed to me, *Who is that guy?*

"I don't have your number," he said, and smiled.

"I don't have my phone," I said, and smiled involuntarily at the sound of his voice. Vati pulled my scarf.

"Oh, you remember Padmavati, right?"

"Of course, hey, Padmavati." Long silence as the three of us processed what was going on, or maybe just Vati and I processed. Nolan seemed very comfortable.

"You guys walking home?"

"Actually, we were just talking about taking the bus. *What are you doing here?*" Padmavati asked. Out loud.

"I came to find Wren," he said, as plainly as can be.

"When do you get out?" That sounded weird. "Of school."

"I left a little early today."

"You left school early?" Vati blurted.

"Not too early. I have rehearsal later, so." *Did he cut school? I* thought to myself. *Am I falling for some kind of juvenile delinquent?*

"I have to go home, like right now. My mother was furious with me last night." *Um, Vati? Maybe you could move away by just a few steps and check your phone or something?*

"I know, that's why I'm here, I wanted to make sure you were all right. I got in touch with Oliver and he said you were in deep."

"You spoke to Oliver?" Vati's voice turned to caramel, even though she was supposed to be mad at Oliver. Nolan nodded.

"Forget the bus. Let's walk," I said, and started booking up the street, ahead of Nolan and Vati.

Remember that kissing/body thing I was telling you about? So, at that moment on the street, I had none of those feelings. I felt that kissing/body thing dancing in the club, I felt it on the subway, but I did not feel anything like that walking up Eightieth Street toward Lexington Avenue in the cold. I was all brain. I was on the verge of panic that Nolan was at my school while I was in gallons of trouble at home. What on earth was I supposed to do with him now? Then Padmavati brought up Oliver and Reagan in minute one, and they were off and running.

"I just *can't believe it*," she moaned to him, like he was Charlie or someone close to us. "I have had a thing for him for years, you know? I mean, I can't believe that (A) Reagan, one of my oldest and closest friends, would *butt* in like that—that is *so* against the code, and (B)"—she paused to collect her thoughts—"that *he* would go there, *knowing* how I feel!"

"How do you know he knows you like him?" Nolan asked. I looked back to see how she would answer that one. Padmavati eyed me sheepishly.

"Well, I have sort of made it clear for almost a decade."

"Wren, do you think Oliver knows Padmavati has a thing for him?" I slowed so we were walking in a line, Nolan in the middle.

"Uh, yeah, I think he probably does."

"Has *he ever said* something to you about it?" asked Vati. Nolan looked at me like, *Has he?*

"No, well. I mean, Vati, I think he thinks of it in a sweet way, but I think he thinks of you like he thinks of me, maybe?"

Vati looked crestfallen. "He does?"

"We don't talk about it that much!" Now I felt like I was going to be in trouble with Vati and that would mean I would be in trouble with everyone except for Dinah, and maybe Nolan? But at this point he was not included in the "everyone" category. Not yet.

"But have you talked about me to him, and you never told me?"

"No, we haven't spoken about you, not really, not in words."

"Ooohhhhhhhhhhhhhhhh!" Padmavati moaned. She marched heavily and dramatically up the street. Nolan smiled and winked at me.

She whipped around.

"What do you know about Reagan and Oliver?" She pointed at Nolan. Nolan held up his hands like she had a gun.

"Nothing! I only caught a vibe last night that they hooked up. Don't kill the messenger!" He laughed. "Did you guys even talk to her?"

"She wasn't in school," Vati and I said in unison.

Are you catching this? Nolan had in a matter of two blocks turned into a girl.

"You caught a vibe?" Vati was still walking backward.

Nolan put his hand to his heart and bowed a little, like he was so sorry to have to say "I did."

Padmavati looked sad and turned away from us.

"You guys, I'm going to take a cab, all right? I'm freezing and this stinks and you guys are all—" She waved her hands around. "You probably want to walk alone." By that point we were almost on Madison. Vati ran ahead to the street and hailed a cab like the true New Yorker she is. The taxi zoomed across two lanes and screeched to a halt. She whipped open the door, hopped in, and was gone.

"Wow," I said, watching the taxi barrel down the avenue and eventually nestle into a pile of traffic at the light. "You were brutal with her."

"Brutal?"

"Yeah!" I smacked him with my parka-covered arm. "Yeah!" He looked shocked, and I was thinking, *Are you kidding me?* Vati had been in love with Oliver for years and Oliver had never done anything about it and none of us had ever *said anything* discouraging to her about it, and then in *two blocks* he did?

"Your friend Padmavati is a *sweetheart.* I was just being honest, and anyway, Oliver did text me that he and Reagan hooked up. He said they made out after dinner next to some Egyptian coffins from like 1200 BC."

"What? Oh, that is gross."

"Just sayin'."

We stood there awkwardly.

"Are you mad at me because I got you in trouble?"

I hadn't thought about it that way. "Oh, no. I'm not mad at you. I feel bad because I worried everyone, and now everyone is mad at *me*."

"I want to talk to your parents."

"Oh, I don't think that's a good idea."

"Why? I totally made you come with me last night, which I am grateful for because I'm really into you." I know it's a cliché, but when he said that I really did feel my knees go weak. "But it's my screwup and now you are in trouble and I want to face the music with you."

"I don't think it will be music you are used to."

"How do you know? You're funny." (I so didn't mean to be funny there.)

"I have to go. I have to get home." I said those words because they were true, but really I would have stayed there with him on the corner for the rest of my life.

"Okay, look." He checked his phone, which had been in his hand the entire time. "It's four o'clock and all the cabs will be changing shifts." I looked out into the sea of yellow taxis migrating north up Madison. Not one of them had its light on.

"Let me walk with you across the park." I looked at him like he was nuts. "Listen, if we hustle, we'll be at your house in twenty minutes. That will be exactly one hour after you are dismissed from school, right?"

"Yeah. How do you know when I get out of school?"

"Oliver told me. So forty-five to fifty minutes is not an unusual amount of travel time if you took the bus home, right?"

I thought to myself that it was a little longer than a ride home would usually take, but he was basically right.

"Please? I want to help you with this. I want to take care of it with you so I'm not banished from your life. And I bet you anything that would be a major part of your parents' plan of punishment."

"How do you know?"

"Because that's what I would do if I were your parents."

29

"Isn't it weird, how yesterday we didn't know each other, and now we are each other's person?" Nolan mused as he walked through the gates into Central Park. I walked about ten steps looking down at the slate-gray path, processing this extraordinary statement.

"How am I your person?" I said, stepping directly on a fallen acorn and crunching it under my boot. He smiled at me.

"Well, you're not *mine*, I guess, but here we are"—he reached his arms out wide—"in Central Park, and we're, together." He flopped his arms back down and put his hands on his backpack straps. We walked a few more feet. "And yesterday at this exact same time we were not." I looked at him in astonishment. "I don't know what it is—but here we are, right?" I could feel my face flush and my mouth widen into a way bigger smile than I would have ever planned.

"I guess, yeah."

"Something happened to us last night, and now, we're in it."

I let those words hang over me for a while and held my tongue literally with my teeth so I didn't muck up that unbelievable moment. There were a few park workers in olive-green uniforms and neon-orange vests sawing up branches of trees that had fallen because of the big wind the day before. Blue jays were sweeping past us through the sky, resting on trees in pairs. Were we a pair, like the blue jays?

"Look, there's the echo bridge." He ran ahead. As you leave the east side of the park to make your way into the middle, there is a bridge you have to walk under that looks like an illustration from a Grimms' fairy tale. The acoustics are so good there is usually a musician under it playing saxophone, but not on that day. It was probably too cold and there were hardly any people around. It's the kind of bridge that when you are beneath it, you have to yell, "Echo!"

"I can't believe you call this the echo bridge," I said, out of breath, having run after him. *We* call it the echo bridge.

"Doesn't everyone in New York call it the echo bridge?"

"I don't know, does *everyone* in New York come to this part of the park?" I rocked back and forth on my low boots.

"Touché." He smiled. He had his hands in his jacket pockets.

"So Oliver says you have such a good voice you don't even have to go to college."

"He did, huh?"

I nodded, smiling.

"You were asking about me?"

I nodded again.

"Well, I'm not sure about *not* going to college. I don't think my mom and pop would like that so much . . . I may take a year off though, so my band can tour this album we're working on, see if we can get some buzz. But I want to go to college eventually."

"Yeah, you have to go to college, I guess."

"I don't know if you *have* to go, but I'd love to go."

We stared at each other for a while. We were just *smiling* at each other. It's such a crazy feeling to really like someone and they are there liking you too. It feels like time stops and you are attached to the other person not by touching or talking but by, like, happiness.

"I want to go to an art program next year in France. You get to live and paint where van Gogh painted *The Starry Night*."

"What, like a junior-year-abroad type thing?"

"Yeah, I'll go for a semester. If I get in. It's hard to get in."

"You'd be all the way in France?" He motioned his head in the direction of where I guess he imagined France was.

"Yup. But I have to draw this self-portrait, and I don't know if my grades are good enough."

"Where in France?"

"Saint-Rémy—it's in the south."

"France is *so* far away," he said, like it was sort of a bad thing.

"Well." I looked down, trying to hide whatever goofy expression of joy or shock that he would be disappointed that I might go somewhere as far away as France a year from now, and that seemed strange and wonderful since at that moment France did feel entirely too far away from what was happening under that bridge. I thought he was going to kiss me. I wanted him to. I wanted to stay under that bridge forever in the unfamiliar wonderfulness. I could still hear a distant, tiny voice reminding me I was in a rolling boil of trouble at home, but I ignored it for just a few more moments.

See, that is what this guy did to me. He distracted me with unfamiliar wonderfulness and before I knew it I was as far off the path as Gretel.

30

Nolan came home with me.

"Are you sure you want to come in?" We were on the bottom step of the staircase leading up to my house. The cheerful orange pumpkins and nubby gourds sitting on each step were no indication of the shit storm we would find inside. Nolan's nose and lips were rosy from the cold and his dark brown hair was windblown from running through the park.

"Absolutely."

"My mother can be sort of—" and then the door at the top of the stairs flung open to reveal Dinah, still in her uniform, hand on her hip, head cocked to the side.

"You are going *down*!" she announced, not looking surprised at all that Nolan was standing there. I glared at her.

"Is Mom home?" I whispered loudly as I trotted up.

"Oh yeah, she is, and she's on fire. She had to start knitting because you are so late! It's a total ten."

"I'm *not* late." I pulled off my wool cap and looked back at Nolan. We only had four feet of foyer left before we passed through the second door and entered the lion's den.

"Hey, Dinah, I met you last night, I'm Nolan." Mr. Cool was whispering too. Dinah was the only one speaking at full volume.

"Hi. You have balls of steel showing up here, man."

"Dinah! Shut *up*!"

"What? You are going to get grounded for, like, ever. *Dad* came home from work to be here when you got home."

"What?" The last time Dad had left work early was when Oliver had broken his collarbone at some sort of after-school sports thing. I don't even think Dinah was out of diapers. The second door opened and there was Mom. Her hair had held the blowout from the party the night before, so she looked mad as hell but pretty. She was wearing jeans and a long gray sweater, and in her right hand she was clutching a tangle of knitting needles, chunky yarn, and an unfinished scarfy thing.

"Wren, it is *astonishing* to me that you are late coming home from—what is this?" She stuck out her pile of knitting at to Nolan.

"Mrs. Noorlander, I asked Wren if I could come home with her to talk with you and Mr. Noorlander about last night." I wished I could have taken one of her needles and stuck it in my eye. I looked up and saw Dad standing behind Mom, holding May's collar so she wouldn't jump all over all of us.

"Dinah, go upstairs and start your math, darling. We have to talk with Wren," Dad said totally calmly. Too calmly. The dog was not calm.

"But!"

"Go!" Mom barked at Dinah, who deserved it for being such a smart-ass.

"Aw!" Dinah stamped her moccasin-slippered foot and ran upstairs as Nolan and I started stripping off our outside clothes, me like a guilty dog, and him like he lived there and nothing out of the ordinary was happening. After he hung up his scarf on the hook, Nolan turned around, stuck out his hand to my father and said, "Mr. Noorlander, I don't believe we got a chance to meet last night, sir, but I'm Oliver's friend, Nolan Shop." They shook hands.

"How do you do," said my father solemnly.

"Sir, that was a fine party and show you put on last night. Thank you very much for having me." I gave my mother a quick glance to see the look on her face. Gob-smacked.

"Why don't you two come in. Nolan, this is Wren's mother, Mrs. Noorlander."

"We met yesterday, David." My mother did not have a "how do you do" for Nolan.

"Hi, Mrs. Noorlander," Nolan said cheerfully. Mom looked at him like he had just belched loudly. Dad led us into the kitchen and leaned against the island in the middle. Mom stood next to him. I sat down at the round table and looked at Nolan to sit down next to me, but he didn't. He stood right up in front of my parents. I could see the staircase from where I was sitting, and Dinah's red head was peeking through the balusters at the very top.

"Well, I am at a loss." I detected a slight New Jersey accent from my mother, like she was so upset she had turned into one of the Real Housewives.

"This is such a nice house," Nolan said warmly.

"Thank you, Nolan," my father said politely. "Nolan, we were expecting to speak with Wren alone this afternoon. Wren is our daughter, and I think this is business that belongs in the confines of our family." I looked at Nolan to see how he would return this cannon of a serve.

"I understand, sir." The respectful and steady tone he used is *totally* how to talk to my dad. "I just wanted to speak to you and Mrs. Noorlander before you spoke to Wren. I know she is in trouble, but it is my fault, sir." I saw my father give my mother a very subtle are-you-kidding-me? look.

"You held a gun to her head and took her downtown last night?" my father said.

"No, sir, I didn't, but I don't believe Wren would have ever left the party if I hadn't come up with *many* reasons why it would be a good idea."

"So Wren has no voice of her own? No common sense? No consideration of others? Is that what you are saying?" my father shot back.

When he takes the reins my mother is quiet.

"No, sir."

"Wren? What do you have to say to this? Do you blame this boy for your actions or do you want to take responsibility for making everyone's night far more difficult and unpleasant and worrisome than it had to be?" I looked up at the stairs and Dinah was gone.

"I take responsibility, Dad."

"I should SAY SO, young lady!" My mother couldn't control herself any longer.

"Nan." That is all Dad has to say to get her to pipe down again.

"Sir, if I may just say something? And then I will respect your wishes and butt out, but may I just say one thing?"

We all were looking at each other in a little bit of amazement that this guy was daring to speak. His brown button-down sweater with suede patches on the elbows and worn blue jeans looked like a suit of shining silver armor to me. Dad held out his hand, saying it was okay for Nolan to take the floor.

"I am *not* suggesting that Wren has no mind of her own. In fact"—he reached out his hand like a politician making a salient and moving argument—"last night, when she was describing why she loved that picture you have of that girl on the second floor . . ."

Dad and I looked at each other. I mouthed, "The Vermeer." Dad nodded and turned his focus back to Nolan, who continued. "It was her disarming point of view in particular and her sharp mind that made me want to spend as much time as I could with her, to get to know her better."

"So why not get to know Wren's beautiful mind down in the party where she belonged?" said Dad.

"Well, I get that. In fact, I question myself why I would want to leave that great party, but I can be impulsive. Sometimes I don't think things through, and when my childhood friend, who is by many accounts a flat-out musical genius . . ." My father and mother raised their eyebrows, and I almost said something to stop him going down the musical genius road. Neither of my parents approve of the word "genius" unless you are describing Mozart or Darwin.

"I thought Wren would dig it, and I wanted to bring her." I started to smile. He said "dig it."

"I made a miscalculation by thinking it would be okay to have her back at home in the same time frame that she would be home

161

from the party, and that was a misjudgment and a mistake. I didn't think it through, and I guess neither did you." He looked at me. "Right?" I nodded like Scooby-Doo. "I mean, Wren, you were worried, for sure. But what I wanted to say was that, even though it was a mistake and we definitely messed up—we *both* had a strong instinct to do something"—he paused, looking for the right word—"exciting."

I took in a big breath, besotted.

"We gave into something that, frankly, Mr. and Mrs. Noorlander . . ." He looked at my mother. "I can't really describe. But I want you both to know, the impulse came from someplace good." He put his fist to his heart like he was pledging allegiance to the flag. "Not bad, even though it was ultimately wrong."

"I'm sorry, Dad," I said. Mom put her knitting down and walked around the butcher-block island toward the stove, wrapping her long gray cashmere sweater around her middle.

"Does anyone want tea?" she said flatly.

"Wren, you must think these things through. You must slow down, and think," Dad said. I have heard these two sentences my entire life. Oliver is slow—it takes Oliver ten minutes to put his shoes on. I am fast, too fast. I started to cry, knowing he was correct. In. Front. Of. Nolan.

"I feel *bad* I worried Bennet." I really did feel so terrible about that.

"I bet you do. Maybe you should go see him sometime soon and apologize." He turned to my mother. "I'll have a cup, lovey. Or write him a letter."

"I'll do that, Daddy."

"I will too, Mr. Noorlander."

"I don't think there is a need for that, Nolan. I'm not sure Bennet knows who you are," he said with a dismissive formality as he took from my mother a steaming oversize greenish purple-ish kid-made mug. "It is Wren who put him in a terrible position." He pulled the tea bag string up and down in the boiling liquid. "And it is Wren who has let him down."

"Nolan." My mother turned back to the stove. "I admire what you said."

"Well," Nolan started to reply. Mom turned and silenced Nolan with her hand.

"But I think you should go now. Wren needs to start her homework and we still must discuss what the consequences of her impulsivity will be. Then Mr. Noorlander needs to go back to the office."

"I understand." Nolan looked at me sweetly and then back at my father. "Thank you for hearing me out. I really am sorry."

I stood up and watched as Nolan walked back to the coatrack, wrapped his scarf carefully around his neck, pulled on his army jacket parka, picked up his guitar, and strapped it on his back. While he leaned over to pick up his backpack, May wiggled and lifted her stubby front legs off the ground for a pat, which Nolan obliged. He even let her lick his cheeks.

"Bye," he said, standing up. I put my hand up as still more tears fell out of my eyes.

I was grounded until Thanksgiving, which was a little more than two weeks away. No socializing, certainly not with Nolan, and no phone until then. I was suspended from wearing any of my mother's clothes until she decided otherwise, and I had to once again write a letter to apologize for being unthoughtful and taking advantage of a situation, but this time it wasn't to the seventh grade, it was to Bennet.

31

That night Dad had a work dinner so it was only Dinah, Oliver, Mom, and me who sat at the kitchen table and plowed through leftover Viking stew almost in silence. Viking stew is lentil and sausage stew that my mother makes copiously once the weather turns cold. In order to get Oliver and me to eat it as children (Dinah would try anything in that high chair of hers) she told us it was so good for you and hearty that the Vikings ate it before going into battle. That sold Oliver, and as long as she crumbled the sausage instead of sliced it, and used the little black lentils instead of the big green mushy ones, I would eat it too. Dinah stole the dish for the "Winter Comfort Food" episode in her first season on Bravo.

"Isn't a two-part show on Thanksgiving slightly *bor*-ing?" Dinah said, breaking the silence as she ground more black pepper into her bowl. As far as I know, she is the only person under twenty-five who seasons her food with ground pepper.

"What did Wendy say?" asked my mother as she took the pepper grinder from Dinah and started going at it into her own bowl. Wendy is one of the producers on *Dining with Dinah*.

"She said Thanksgiving has the biggest ratings in all of food television and we have to make hay while the sun shines."

Mom's face contorted at the making-hay comment. She's not so crazy about Dinah talking about making money at age ten (I think she thinks it's crass). But she swallowed it.

"Fair enough." She poured herself a splash more of red wine.

"Turkey, turkey, turkey." Dinah rolled her eyes and looked around the table for a reaction.

"Do like three stuffings, that's the best part anyway." This offering was the first thing to come out of Oliver's mouth since he got home. I gave him a meaningful look—about everything that didn't have to do with stuffing, like Nolan and Reagan.

"What?" Oliver said defensively. "Stuffing is the best part." I didn't respond. Before dinner, Mom had told me that tonight I should just be quiet and think about my actions. I did think two things: one, that Oliver is right about stuffing being the best part of Thanksgiving, but two, that had I given *Nolan* a meaningful look, he would get it and not just think about ripped-up, seasoned bread.

"Wren, are you finished?" Mom asked. "Because I think there is plenty of homework you could be doing upstairs." I hadn't said a word and she was annoyed at me just for existing.

"Yeah, I'll get on it." I took a piece of bread from the basket in the middle of the table and placed it in the bottom of my bowl to soak up the last of my Viking stew.

"Oliver, help me clean up supper, okay? I want to talk to you." My mother was totally going to talk to Oliver about Nolan, and I would have to be three flights away wrestling with math.

"Come talk to me after, will ya?" I said sotto voce to Oliver. He looked at me blankly.

"Wren, I think you should spend tonight staying on target and let Oliver do his own work." The woman has the ears of a wolf.

I gave Oliver another meaningful look, hoping he would tune in and come up anyway, but for all I knew, he was still thinking about stuffing.

Trying to be a very good girl, I cleared my bowl, rinsed it, and put it in the dishwasher. Dinah rooted around in the freezer, probably looking for these tofu ice cream bars called Cuties that she loves.

"Okay," I said, lifting the dishwasher door closed and making the dishes inside rattle too loudly. "I'll be upstairs."

"Don't you want a Cutie?" Dinah asked.

"No thanks, Dinah."

She came up really close to me and said under her voice, *"Nolan* is cute."

I smiled.

"Yeah, right?" She beamed and nodded.

Oliver passed us, opened the freezer, and grabbed two Cuties. "I'll come up later."

"Okay." Thank goodness he's not entirely clueless and stuffing obsessed.

On my way up to my room, I grabbed my backpack that I had leaned against the bottom step when Nolan and I had come in from the park. As I rounded the banister on the last flight of stairs before I got to my floor, a book fell out of the backpack, and then three folders, and a bunch of papers. I had forgotten to zip it. I collapsed on the ground to gather everything that had

tumbled out and saw the Shoppe Boys disk that Farah had downloaded for me at school. I picked it up quickly and got a pang
because I remembered Farah was mad at me and I couldn't text
her to make things right between us. (Being phone-less in the
2000s just doesn't work.) Then I was overcome by the need to get
upstairs to listen to the CD. I looked down again and saw an
unfamiliar folded-up piece of lined paper sitting on the floor with
my name written in blue ballpoint pen. I put the disk in a pocket
of my bag and slowly reached out to touch the paper as if it were
a butterfly and a sudden move would cause it to fly away. When
my fingers touched the stiff edge, I felt a tremble deep in my gut.
I took a steady breath in, pulling the note closer to me as I sat up
on my knees to open it and look inside. On one side, the little
pieces of fringe where the paper had been attached to a spiral
notebook had gently tangled, and I had to tug a bit to open it.
Inside, it said:

Dear Wren (I still can't get over that name),

*Here are the lyrics to a Bruce Springsteen song called
"Rosalita." Actually, just go get on your computer (if your
parents haven't impounded it yet) and Google the song—get
it on YouTube. It's the greatest love song ever written. One
of them anyway. No, I think it's the greatest one. In the
particular circumstance you are in at the moment, this is
the song I would write for you. I toyed with writing you my
own, but we are in such deep shit I thought only Bruce
could get us out.*

*Anyway, I want to liberate you and confiscate you
and I want to be your man.*

I'll find you.

Nolan

*PS: If you can get to a landline, my house number is
212-555-5467*

The breath that I was holding didn't slowly come back out of
my body—it rushed out like someone had just punched me. It
pushed my back against the wall, my feet digging into the hard-
wood floor, my hands pressing the paper onto my chest. I wanted
to shriek, or cry, or hyperventilate. I read the note again and
again. *Do what you have to do to hear "Rosalita."* It's not a slow,
goopy love ballad. It's frenetic, it pounds, it writhes, it yells and
sweats—it's wired and fast. It's hot—it grabs you from wherever
you are and throws you way far away into the ether. In concert
footage, people listening to this song look like they are going
mad. If this were a movie, this song would be playing over images
of me losing my shit on the landing of the staircase, laughing
to myself, feeling my heart pound, and jamming books back into
my bag.

I clutched the note to my chest, ran up the last flight of stairs to
my room, turned on the light next to my bed and the light on my
desk, and got back down on the floor with the note again. Forget
my homework; if I couldn't talk to *anyone*, if I had to be alone with

all the crazy, unbearable feelings, I had to draw. I got up, took the Shoppe Boys disk out of my bag and slid it into the side of my computer on my desk. The opening notes and chords of the first song were hard driving. There must have been three or four guitars, there was an organ and drums and maybe even a horn section. It was big, bigger than I had expected—it was more alive and more exciting and it made me feel all wound up. I hovered over the computer and waited for Nolan's voice. Every note that sounded got me closer and closer to him, and then I heard the words "Wake me in the morning Daddy, when the big old sun shines in the sky. We'll go outside, take a ride, and wait for breakfast to come." And Nolan was in the room with me. His voice, raw and unbridled, almost hurt my feelings. It got to me. I was listening to it the way you drink water in the middle of the night. I felt something boil up inside me, as if someone had jammed a needle of Adrenalin straight into my neck. I pushed the volume button as high up as it could go and twirled around to draw.

I tore off a giant-size piece of drawing paper from a roll that stands in the corner of my room and pulled the huge piece of cardboard that I keep behind my bed to use under the paper so my charcoal doesn't catch on any imperfections on the wooden floor. I laid the paper on top of it, fastening it onto the board with jumbo black paper clips. I lurched over to my desk and pulled open the drawer where I keep supplies. I grabbed a brand-new box of Conté compressed charcoals, ripped the cellophane off, slid the box open, lifted a perfectly square stick out of the box, then folded myself down onto the ground next to *my note* with the music all around me. I spent the next long time lost, feverishly drawing a barn owl rocketing into the night sky, shooting up, wings spread wide, soaring up up up and off the paper with one hundred of her feathers fluttering in the headwinds.

If Oliver came upstairs, I didn't know it. He might have come up and decided not to bother me. I was somewhere far away.

32

Farah was lost too. Really, that night at the museum pushed all of us off our course, but mostly Farah. *She* didn't think she was lost. She thought she was exactly where she should be, wrapped in the arms of Cy Dowd, who was old enough to be her father. Farah, like an anorexic hiding her food compulsion, kept most of us in the dark about this romance as much as she possibly could. But what I learned that semester is there is only so much a person can hide in the dark; a lot of times, you can still see.

"And then what happened?" Reagan said. I was retelling the Nolan-confronting-my-parents story to all the girls at the lunch table in school the next day.

"Then he left and my parents took away my Internet, locked away my phone, and grounded me until Thanksgiving."

"What does getting grounded even mean? That's, like, so 1950," Reagan said, cupping her hand around a cafeteria mug of lentil soup, flicking the carrots to the side with a spoon.

Vati wasn't speaking to Reagan. None of us really were because nobody had gotten to the bottom of what had happened between her and Oliver. I was supposed to get the scoop, but I never got to talk to my brother because I was drawing that owl. So we had to wait for the juice to come directly from Reagan.

"It means I can't do anything but go to school and work on my application for France for like what, two weeks?"

"A little more," Vati said quietly, looking at her bagel and tuna that she lifted up toward her mouth but then put back down again without taking a bite.

"I guess you won't be going to Nolan's gig at Columbia this week then," Reagan said. That was so not what I thought would come out of Reagan's mouth that I audibly gasped.

"How do you know about *that*?" Vati blasted. I was going to say something too, but now the energy had shifted to a Reagan/Padmavati thing and I had to sit back and watch that show.

"Oliver told me," Reagan said, as cool as a cucumber. "He's going."

We all sat in silent shock.

"Reagan, why are you being such a cunt?" said Farah.

"Hey, whoa," I said, feeling panicky—that is quite a word, and I don't think any of us had used it before, let alone directed it at another Turtle.

"You did *not* just call me that," Reagan said, sounding like a Kardashian.

"Yeah, I did." Farah didn't back down for a second. Padmavati's eyes were the size of jelly doughnuts. "You know, Reagan—we all know for a *fact* that Vati has been in love with Oliver for, like, her *whole life* and you are just blindly and *meanly* acting like you had no freaking idea." Vati's bottom lip started to tremble.

"Vati. I. Am. Sorry." Reagan looked around at all of us but Farah. "But what did you want me to do? Oliver totally macked on me."

"Oh yuck," I said, and watched poor Vati go over the edge from about-to-cry to full-on crying.

"See?" said Farah. "What are you even doing? Now she's crying."

173

"I'm *sorry*, but it's not that big a deal, all we did was make out."
Vati made a very sad sound.

"Oh my god, we made out for like two minutes next to dead people. I don't even *like* him."

"Then *why* would you kiss him, Reagan?" Vati wept. *"Why?"* She put her head down dangerously close to her open-faced tuna sandwich.

"You could have said no, Reagan," I said.

Reagan hunched over and looked down, rubbing the side of her tray with her thumb. I felt sorry for her. It wasn't her fault that Oliver chose her. Who wants to be the girl to screw over Padmavati? No one.

"I don't think Reagan was doing something directly mean to you, Vati." I put my hand on her trembling back. "Right, Reagan?"

"No, I just . . . I just kind of didn't think of you, Vati." Well, okay, that came out wrong, but I got what she meant.

"Oh *thanks*," Vati said and wiped her nose with her sleeve, streaking snot along her lilac purple cardigan.

"I'm thinking of you now though, I'm sorry *now*—I just didn't think through what I was doing *then*. Does it really matter if I don't even like him?" Reagan's eyes darted around at all of us.

"Well, you're *stupid*, Reagan." Vati sniffed. "Because, well, you just are." She took a deep breath in and out and stopped crying. "I would do anything to kiss him."

"Maybe you will one day, Padmavati," Farah said.

"Maybe," Vati said dejectedly. Then, right as Vati was getting it together and it seemed like the tension at the table was subsiding, Reagan said, "Farah, what is the deal with you and that artist?"

Farah put her fork down, forgoing the bite of beets she was about to put in her mouth.

"You know, Reagan, I don't think that is your business," she replied. All that tension cranked right back up again.

"Just *asking*. I saw you leave the party with him."

"We did leave together, yes."

"And?"

"And then we went to his studio to see his artwork and then I went home right after that."

What? Farah just lied to Reagan and Vati? I tried not to look surprised, but these were new waters—lying waters.

"Look, he is an extremely interesting person. What was I going to do? *Not* go and get a tour of this famous guy's workspace? We all had spent the entire night looking at his paintings on the walls of the Metropolitan Museum of Art." The expression on her face was like, *Duh?* "Of course I went with him—to see his *process*. And his really tiny pig."

"Ohh, he has one of those teacup pigs? What color?" said Vat, drifting off into a happy piggy place without a shred of distress in her voice. I think in the universe of Vati, miniature pigs and all of their blinding cuteness anesthetize all boy badness. But Reagan was immune to pig cuteness.

"Did he come on to you?"

"No! *God, Reagan*," Farah whispered.

"Okay, sorry." Reagan jutted out her neck, and put her hair behind her ears with both hands. "I just think it's super strange you went home with him, and really, I'm kind of sure everyone here does too."

Farah gave me a look to keep my mouth shut and I totally did. I didn't tell anyone what had happened between Farah and Cy Dowd, at least not for a while.

"Doodle, his pig, *is* unbearably cute." She pulled the dark red beets off her fork with her teeth and started chewing like the cat that ate the canary. "He's adorable."

33

I had to get home. I had so much homework. I had three papers: history, lit, and Latin, all of them mired in briar patches of reading. Primary sources, secondary sources, cross-referencing, translations, biographies, and endnotes, all due before the end of the semester. I had ungodly amounts of math. Math can seem finite because you know there is an end, but that's an illusion, because each problem has at least four additional problems embedded in it like jalapeño peppers in nachos. Hidden, unexpected bummers. A problem looks easy enough with its six numbers all neatly lined in a row, but to solve it you use three sheets of graph paper only to find out the answer is wrong, and if you are me you have no idea where you made the bad turn. I had a science project researching the anatomy of a hummingbird, which sounds fun because hummingbirds fall under the magical creatures category, but like math, this project was more complex than it first seemed. The way hummingbirds fly and their habits are an evolutionary wonder. They are way more technical than their Tinker Bell reputations lead you to believe.

So do the teachers even talk to each other? Does each one have any idea how much work the others are assigning? How do they think we can do it? Do they think we have more hours in the day than they do? And they trick you too. They psych you up for the work way before it starts by giving an inspired introduction to the assignment. They dangle the project in front of your nose like a juicy carrot. You are the dumb horse. When they assign the paper it's their chance to wine and dine you. They suck you in, they wind you up, they make you feel like what they are asking you to do is not only doable, but enthralling. Sure, write a paper on Sense of Place in Faulkner and compare it to your own Sense of Place—what *is it* about *where you come from* that makes you who you *are*. You get so interested in the prospect of figuring out who you are that you lose sight of the fact that you also need to figure out who Faulkner thought he was. And that requires close reading and careful analysis.

Anyone can imagine they will do a good job before the job starts. Anyone can hold the hope that maybe this time they will wail on it and get a big fat A that will raise their grade point average so high they have endless opportunities to *succeed*. But sitting in your room with the task at hand, alone, without the encouragement of your teacher or the determined faces of your classmates providing peer pressure, the bleak and scary reality that you may not be able to accomplish what you want—that shining A, that insightful, fascinating paper—is real and like a cement wall two inches from your face. And you *have to* bust through and just do it, there's no getting out of it, if you don't you fail, you might fail anyway, even if you try. You have to be *brilliant*. You have to be better than you have ever been before.

And if all of that wasn't enough, I *had* to draw myself. I had to, I had to, *I had to*. Within the next month. I had to reproduce who I was on paper and pray it was enough to get me into that school.

If I could get in, if I could go to Saint-Rémy and feel what van Gogh felt, if I could see the colors, smell the air, look into that night sky, I might be able to reach the stars. They felt too far away in New York City. In fact, you can't even see stars in New York City. I felt like if I could just go to France, I would be able to move myself forward and do something important. But here's a secret—you can't find anything worthwhile by simply looking in the mirror. You have to look *beyond* what you see in the mirror. I didn't know that then though; if I had, maybe everything would have been different.

So, I was going straight home and nothing and no one was going to stop me. I had a plan and I was determined. I was going to go directly to my house, be good, put my head down and make my parents happy—make myself happy. Doing the right thing definitely makes everyone very happy. At lunch, Vati and I had decided we would walk home together across the park. A brisk walk would be useful before a long afternoon and night of work and kicking ass. Maybe I would even stop at the deli and get a Diet Coke. There is something about a can of Diet Coke that makes me feel like I can study all night. It's not the caffeine, it's the look of the can. Not a bottle, not a glass with ice, a can. School ended and Vati and I met at sign-out. I definitely signed out that day. I pushed open the heavy brass doors and who-the-freak was standing right outside, leaning on a car, just like the day before—Nolan. But this time *Oliver* was standing right beside him.

Whoosh. That is the sound of all of my determination and every single one of my well-intended-head-in-the-right-place plans blowing away with the mid-November wind.

He found me just like he said he would in the note, the very next day. And not only did he find me, he brought Oliver to Vati.

★ ★ ★

"No, no," protested Nolan. He was wearing his guitar on his back again. In all the time we spent together, I'm not sure I ever saw that guy without his guitar. "It won't take much longer . . . *Don't go, don't go . . .*" he begged, like he knew I wasn't going anywhere. "He's almost done, look." He pointed through the glass windows at Oliver, who was paying for two orders of hot french fries from Le Cafe, a coffee shop on Madison where seniors who are allowed to leave Hatcher for lunch go for chef salads and Diet Cokes. Vati was standing at the cash register looking up at Oliver, talking to him. I couldn't hear what they were saying, but the way Oliver was looking at Vati, it was like he was seeing her for the first time.

"What did you *say* to him?" I asked Nolan.

"I said he had the wrong girl."

"And he changed his mind? He just switched? Like that?" I pulled the sleeves of my sweater down and over my hands, which felt like they were starting to freeze off.

"I don't know—look at them." We watched Vati explode into head-thrown-back laughter at something Oliver said. Sure looked like he dug her.

"Sometimes, guys don't know what's right in front of them. And anyway, your friend told him that night she wasn't into him."

"Really?"

"Yeah, Oliver said he tried to kiss her, and she let him, but she bailed on him pretty soon. I guess she's sort of direct?"

"Yeah, Reagan doesn't mess around. But if she didn't like him, why would she even kiss him at all?"

"Who knows. People are always kissing."

"What? That is insane." I laughed. He turned to me and held the sides of my thin black Patagonia parka that I was wearing over a long almondy-brown sweater—it's probably my nicest sweater and I wonder now in retrospect if I didn't wear it hoping, or knowing, he would show up.

"It's not nuts, I'm right. There are probably hundreds, no, thousands of people kissing in this city right now." I got that sex feeling again. (I'm embarrassed to write about it, but I think the sex feeling you get when you just *kiss* a boy leads to someplace big. It just does.)

"And you think that Vati will just forget that Reagan did that, or Oliver for that matter?"

He shrugged. "I don't know Vati. Or Reagan."

"I have to go home. I can't be late, or bad. I'm not free. My wings are clipped, and it's because of *you*." I pointed at him.

"But—but here's the thing." His big smile made me ask myself, *What is there to lose?* What is more important than this cold, Wednesday afternoon corner in New York City, with Nolan, french fries, Vati, and an afternoon in Central Park? My brother was even there. And couldn't I fly away to somewhere new, with Nolan? Wasn't that what kids are supposed to do? Wouldn't my parents want me to have this brand-new happiness?

"Here. Is. The. Thing," he said right in my face. So close. "How else am I going to see you?" I laughed.

"Yeah, you think it's funny?"

I laughed again.

"I can't stop thinking about you."

"I . . . I . . ." I didn't have any of the words he had, so I copied him. "I can't stop thinking about you either." I held my breath.

"Righteous," he said, to my delight.

"But I'm late," I said almost inaudibly, because I was sick of repeating something that clearly had no meaning for me anymore.

"What *you* are, is beautiful." Nobody, but nobody, has ever called me beautiful the way Nolan did. He said it like it was a fact. Not in some cheesy "Ohhh, you are so beautiful" way. He said it like how you would say a sandwich was good. "Now *that* is a good grilled ham and cheese." He put his arms around me and kissed me like there was nothing else in the world but him and me and the sidewalk under our sneakers, and like that was the way it would always be. It surprised me like you can't believe to be kissed like that, but part of me thought, *Well, my time has come.*

"Hi, guys!" Vati stood in front of us holding bags, ketchup packs, and sodas in paper cups with straws sticking out of them. Oliver came up next to her, tucking his wallet in his back pocket, and took all the french fry stuff from her like a gentleman.

"Let's go to Belvedere Castle and eat those, then you guys can go home. I have rehearsal later downtown," Nolan said, putting his arm around me as he headed in the direction of the park. The light was getting dim, the sky was chalky white. I thought it might snow. I thought I might die.

"Oh, I *love* Belvedere Castle. When I was little my dad used to tell me a princess lived in there, which enraged my mom because she hates the Disney princesses so much, and Dad always let me watch all those movies at his house," Vati said.

"What's up with your mom? She didn't even like Snow White? I don't think she was a princess," Oliver said.

"She was a princess!" Vati skipped in front of Oliver and turned so she was walking backward, facing him. She looked radiant. "But she only wakes up because the prince kisses her. It's one example in many of the *man* coming to save the day and the girl having no part in it. She was asleep," Vati said, sounding flirtatious and not like a feminist.

"Yeah, but she never would have been asleep if that bitch queen hadn't poisoned her. It's not like the prince got paid more for the same job; he just did her a favor and woke her from the dead so she could keep *rocking on*," Nolan said, cracking Oliver up.

"Bitch queen," Oliver repeated, laughing.

"Oh my lord, that queen was such a bitch and she had no hair!" Nolan laughed.

"She was kind of hot though," Oliver said.

"Ol-i-ver—she was hateful and *vain*!" I punched his arm.

"*What? You* spend a ton of time looking in the mirror."

"Shut *up*. I'm drawing myself because I have to." I glared at him.

Vati turned back around, falling in line with the rest of us. "That is another reason my mother couldn't stand all those movies. The mean women who were jealous and ruinous were either gorgeous, with cleavage, or totally bizarre-looking with green skin, or enormously fat. None of them looked real."

"Right, it's totally *not* real. It's Disney," Nolan said.

"Yeah, but real people can be mean. People you know. You don't have to have two-toned hair like Cruella to be a villain," Vati said a little sadly.

Silent walking. I pictured Reagan animated like a Disney character for a minute. She had gigantic purple boobs, thin sexy eyebrows, and a black cape.

"You look like Princess Jasmine," Oliver said to Vati, who actually does look like Princess Jasmine from Aladdin. "And she's strong. I don't think the prince saves her."

"No," Padmavati said as she looked up sweetly. "I think she saves the prince, who wasn't even a prince. He was like a street urchin or a rapscallion."

"Yeah," Oliver said, and I saw him take Vati's hand.

"So, you guys can't come to my gig Thursday, huh?" Nolan asked.

"I can't," I said, and gave Nolan a sad face.

"I can," said Oliver. "Wanna come with me, Vati?"

"Sure, yeah! I mean, I think my mother will let me go."

"How will your mother let you go? It's a school night." I said. Vati is never allowed to go out on a school night.

"I don't know, I think she just will." She looked at Oliver, who was looking down at the ground smiling. It was hard not to be jealous of the plans being made but, (A) I was grounded, (B) I had to be super happy for Vati, and (C) you can't feel that happy and jealous at the same time. Emotions have to take turns.

Once we got to the castle the four of us perched on the huge rocks around the moatlike Turtle Pond that surrounds the fairytale castle.

"There are so many turtles in here, sleeping now of course," Nolan said, ripping into the tinfoil over the french fries. Steam came out as he grabbed a fry and folded it into his mouth. He sucked in cold air to try to cool it before it scorched his tongue.

"It's snowing," said Vati, standing up on her rock and looking into the sky.

"I thought it would snow!" I put my hand up in the air. Crazy little white flakes were zooming though the sky in no particular direction, not even down. It was the first snow of the winter, and I guessed it hadn't gotten the hang of falling right onto the ground to make a blanket.

"I wonder if it's going to be a really snowy year." Oliver put his face up into the whirling flurries. "Last year it only snowed four inches total."

"Yeah, but the year before, we had three snow days. Remember the one we all spent at your house?" Vati said hopefully, looking at Oliver.

"No, I don't remember that." He looked at her. "You were there that day?" He reached out and touched a long loop of hair falling down her back.

"Yeah," Vati said sweetly. "I'm there a lot."

"You want to go up and look at the view?" Oliver pointed up to the tower from which you can see the whole park. "Maybe we can catch a snowflake on our tongues." Vati stood up, gave me an over-the-moon look, and started climbing after Oliver and his dreads.

"Bring the fries!" he called. She scampered back and took a tin-foiled bundle, flashed me the biggest shit-eating grin ever, and ran after him without looking back.

"Hi," Nolan said to me as he set his guitar down on the ground.

"Hi," I said back. "I still don't get how that happened."

"I don't think he knew she liked him," Nolan said, and sat down on the rocks.

"How could that *be*?" I sat down too.

"People don't assume beautiful girls are in love with them." He took a sip of a soda that Oliver and Vati had left with the other order of fries.

"I guess, but she was seriously obvious! He's so smart so I assumed that he was just, well, ignoring her."

"Just because you are smart at math doesn't mean you are smart about girls. Has he ever had a girlfriend?"

"Yeah, he went out with this girl Samara last year."

"Samara Levin?" He handed me the soda.

"Yeah!" I took a sip. (I totally took note of the fact that we were sharing a straw.)

"She's in my class," he said.

"She is?"

"Bronx Science is huge. I don't know her that well, but Oliver once mentioned her in passing so that must be her."

"They went out for a long time, like months. He was quiet about it though. She didn't come over much. I don't even know why they broke up."

"She's quiet. Maybe she was too quiet. Maybe he's more into a girl who skips, like Vati," he said, in a way like he just got people.

"I'm going to get in a lot of trouble. Again." My hands were getting cold on the wet paper cup, so I balanced it on the rock and tucked my fingers into my jacket.

"Then let's get you home. I just wanted to see you. And I wanted to play Cupid." He smiled and pointed up at Vati and Oliver, who were leaning over the edge of the castle looking like a twenty-first-century teenage fairy tale.

"Are you going to Pittsburgh for Thanksgiving?" I asked, a little boldly, as it was still a couple of weeks away.

"Yeah, I'm going to see my pop and stepmom and the kiddo."

"Oh yeah, Bruno?"

"Correct. He is funny. I'm teaching him how to play the ukulele," he said proudly.

"'Cause it's small?" I asked.

"Small and cool," he said, and air-ukuleled.

"I think I'll be released by Thanksgiving, if I don't get grounded until New Year's because of today."

"Today won't be a problem. Oliver and I have a plan."

"You do? What is it?"

"Oliver already texted your mom saying he picked you up from school to help you with your math."

"You guys planned that?" He was killing me.

"Yeah. She already texted back to bring you straight home, but he texted back that if he was going to help you it would have to be at the coffee shop so he could eat."

"Oh my god, she worships him! Because that is sort of a sketchy plan, but whatever, if she bought it. "

"Yeah, but I think you'll be all right. I think she fell for it."

I looked at his guitar.

"Will you sing me a song? Since I won't see you at the concert tomorrow night?"

"Oh, hell yeah." He reached over and pulled his guitar case close to him. Watching him undo the case and cradle the instrument in his lap, you could tell he had made that same motion many times before. Second nature.

His fingers found the strings easily and he started playing the song I had heard the night before in my room, but it was softer, acoustic, and right in front of me.

"Wake me in the morning, Daddy, when the big old sun shines

in the sky. We'll go outside, take a ride, and wait for breakfast to come."

The song is about a boy and his dad on a Saturday. It's as simple and particular as coffee and doughnuts, or baseball. It's a love song, I guess. Not that it's about romantic love, but when you listen to it, you feel love. You can hear it in his voice. Deep, rich, aching love.

"Are you sad your parents are divorced?" I asked, when he strummed the last strum. He looked up at me smiling.

"No, not really." He played a few more notes like he was finishing his thought musically. Then he strummed a flourish of notes, showing off.

"Life is weird, you know? It doesn't always go in a straight line, and then"—he was still playing a little—"you have to figure out how the bent-up line you got works."

"Yeah, I get that. Do you miss him though?"

"Sure, I miss him a lot. A lot of the time I feel like there's a part of me that's waiting for . . . me."

I must have looked confused.

"What I mean is, well, sometimes I think what hurts, or feels complicated, is that I feel him missing me. Like we have to meet each other on the other side of something."

"The other side of what?"

"Just the other side. Maybe of the divorce. I'm not sure when divorces end."

I reached out and cupped my hand around his warm cheek. He tilted his head and let its weight rest on me, closing his eyes for just a minute.

"I'm sorry," I whispered. He opened them back up and lifted his head.

"No, no, it's all good. It's just life. It's what songs and books are written about and movies are made about, it's love, you know? It's just love being love."

"But it sounds hard and sad."

"Sometimes love is hard and sad."

The crazy mixed-up snow started scurrying through the air again. It didn't look like it would snow in earnest, not yet. It was just the beginning of winter.

34

I worked hard for the next two weeks. Dinah shot two episodes of *Dining with Dinah* in one day in preparation for Thanksgiving. Farah didn't come over to see Tom-the-camera-guy, and I had no idea if that was because she had bigger fish to fry or because I was grounded and she wasn't allowed to come over. Something made me think she wasn't into Tom-the-camera-guy anymore.

I didn't get my phone back, my parents didn't lift the punishment, and Nolan didn't show up after school again. It was too risky. We got away with the Belvedere Castle day, but barely. Oliver told me he thought Mom knew something was up. And then she was on me like white on rice every day after that about homework. I did discover a wonderful thing right in our house though: another working *landline* and a solid telephone that connected into the wall with a spiral cord and had a dial. It was my grandmother's and it's been in our living room for as long as I can remember, but I had sort of forgotten about it. It's creamy yellow and heavy. The thing must weigh ten pounds. I never thought it worked because, well, it looked so old I thought it was an antique or something. I knew we had landlines in the kitchen and in my parents' room, not that anyone used them so much. My mother kept the old phone in the living room because, she once told me, she could still detect the smell of her mother's Chanel No. 5 perfume on the receiver.

During my groundation, I was looking for a John Singer Sargent art book for inspiration. He painted a million portraits, really beautiful ones. Not so many self-portraits, but there's one I like a lot. When I look at that painting all I can think is, *That guy looks like he can paint.* He painted really *beautiful* portraits of wealthy people living during the Gilded Age, around the late 1800s, early 1900s. They're not just stiff, jacked-up images of people who could afford to have their portraits painted with their horses and dogs. Sargent must have seen beyond their social standing, or just ignored it for a while to capture these small, human gestures. There is one with a girl slightly lifting her shoulders, her hands clasped together. It looks like the party is about to begin. She could be any girl about to go to any party. Her dress—actually *all* the dresses they wore—are to *die* for. Especially the creamy white diaphanous ones. I can't believe people dressed like that. Sometimes I wish we still dressed like that now. Not fancy so much, just that we could wear long gowns, not these stupid shorts that are entirely too short. Anyway, when I was in the living room, I spotted the old phone on a footstool in the corner, obscured by a pile of books and a big planted palm. Almost as if I thought it might give me an electric shock, I picked up the smooth receiver carefully, and slowly put it up to my ear. It felt cool and weighted in the most satisfying way, as if I was holding a sack of sand. I did smell the faint, powdery perfume, and there was a dial tone. So starting that night, after I was sure everyone was in their rooms, I would tiptoe down the stairs, curl up in my mother's deep armchair, take the note

Nolan gave me with his home number on it, and dial one number at a time, by the light of the street lamp coming in the window. Nolan never failed to pick up and then we would talk, sometimes for hours. I would do my math homework with him. I would read a problem to him and then we worked through each step together until it was solved. He always had the answer way before me, like he could see it without going through the process. But he waited for me, and when I got stuck he was there on the other side of the line to tell me in his adorable voice what to do.

One night after we got off the phone, it must have been around eleven, I was making my way back up the stairs and Dad was standing one flight up, in his long gray bathrobe with dark red piping.

"Just get off the phone?" The hallway lights that recede into the ceiling were dimmed low. His voice is so deep he doesn't really have to whisper to be quiet.

"Yeah," I whispered. I didn't want my mother to hear me.

"Mom and I know you are talking to Nolan. We can hear your feet creeping by the door."

"Oh. Really? Well, I was trying to be quiet." I put my hand on the ball at the end of the banister and sort of yanked it. "I'm getting my work done . . . I haven't seen him or anything." I *so* thought I was about to get reamed.

"We know *everything you do*," he said like Big Brother.

"Well, it's horrible not having a phone," I said, still in a defensive whisper. "I feel so out of the loop. I don't really know what's going on with my friends, I am missing stuff, I feel alienated and left out and it's horrible." I pouted.

"But you only choose to call *him* on the real phone? Not Farah, or Padmavati? Or Charlie? Reagan?"

"No . . ." I only really wanted to talk to Nolan.

"I remember being on the phone with Selina Morton when I was at the University of Chicago."

"Who is that?"

He sat down on one of the steps leading up to my room, so I climbed up a few stairs and sat next to him.

"She was a wonderful girl I went out with in college. She went to Amherst in Massachusetts." He said "Amherst" like it was exceedingly impressive. Dad paused for a second, looking up into the air like he was picturing her. I tried to picture her too, and all I could come up with was Emma Stone. "It was a long-distance love. We must have spent a million dollars on the phone."

"*What?*"

"No, I just mean, we ran up our parents' credit cards with our phone charges. Hours and hours. I talked to her on the pay phone in my dorm hallway."

"It's fun talking on the phone," I said, feeling like maybe this was going to be a good talk. "I always thought that phone in the living room was an antique that didn't work."

"It is practically an antique but it certainly does work. Mom insisted we have it hooked up even though no one ever uses it. It reminds her of her mother."

"I know. She told me she thinks it smells like Granny."

"Yes, Lillian wore Chanel No. 5. It's a rather strong scent, so I'm sure the phone does still smell like her." I smiled. So did he. I think he was remembering my grandmother, who got her PhD in poetry when she was like fifty, and she needlepointed everyone in our family their own Christmas stocking. I remember she made these tiny butter cookies with raspberry jam. I could eat a million of them.

"And it is fun to talk on the phone. You can get lost, no? Lost in conversation," he said.

"Yeah, you really can." I think I sounded a little moony.

"You can't do that on a cell phone—get lost. They weren't set up for real talking." We sat there for a moment. I could hear the faint sound of the television my mother was watching in their bedroom.

"Dad, I know that Nolan kind of screwed up at the start, you know, at the party. But I think you would really like him." I looked at my father to see if he was mad. But he was sort of smiling, like he was really listening to me, so I kept going. "He's different than anyone I've ever met. He reads a ton of books and he plays music and he also kind of reminds me of you, sort of." I looked at him again to see if he was appalled.

"Does he?" He sounded interested, not offended.

"Yeah, you know how you see everything in a big way, like how you don't really care about details?"

"I beg your pardon, my life is a clutter of details."

"No, I know, but Mom's the one who is so specific and who focuses on every little thing. You, well, think about it, you run a museum, you see history and the future every day. That's like the big picture, you know?" He nodded and smiled. I can amuse Dad if I concentrate.

"And that is what Nolan is like? He's a big-picture thinker?"

"Yeah." I smiled. "I think he really is."

"You have a sweet look on your face when you talk about him."

I put my head into my father's shoulder. "I really like him a lot."

"Well." He put his arm around me and pulled me in closer.

"That is good, Wrenny. That is very good." He kissed me on my head. "That is what is supposed to happen to a lovely, big-picture-thinker girl like you."

"Oh, Dad." I pushed in harder, not knowing if I was embarrassed or thrilled.

"Now go to bed, lamby. All this phoning will exhaust you. And we can't have that. Not right before Thanksgiving."

35

Thanksgiving is my absolute favorite holiday, because of food of course, and the general feel-good vibe that pervades everything from school assemblies to the Thanksgiving episode of *Modern Family.*

An extraordinary part of that particular Thanksgiving was that Vati and Oliver were transforming into a couple, *for real.* She had become, in a matter of days, a fixture in the house, so much so that my mother invited Vati and her mother, Dipa, to have Thanksgiving lunch with us. Oliver was not only thrilled, but he was acting like it would be the weirdest thing in the world *not* to have Vati. "Vati and I were thinking of going to a movie after Thanksgiving . . . Vati's mom said she would bring pecan pie so . . ." *We this, us that,* I'm telling you, life did a complete 180 there. But this is what I think: I think that there is a gigantic music studio soundboard in heaven. Angels—I picture them like the music tech guys you see in "the making of" videos—manipulate this huge soundboard controlling where people on Earth move, what decisions they make, what they think about, what they pay attention to. I imagine some angel dude in front of a massive golden mixing console kept Oliver's head in the sands about Vati for years and years so they wouldn't hook up randomly at age thirteen. But then finally the time was right for the angel to fade a dial in, so now they are high school sweethearts, and then maybe they'll be college sweethearts, and then possibly they might, *maybe* (please oh please), get married one day. I can't help it, I jump ahead, I'm impulsive—it's the ADD, or maybe this is just a good idea.

Thanksgiving is also Dinah's day to shine.

"Vati—Vati—*Padmavati!* No! No no no no no. You can't cut the fennel in such large chunks. And look at these, they are *slivers*! No, they must be uniform, like this." Dinah pushed Vati away from her cutting board, took the knife from her, and systematically sliced the white bulb into perfect one-inch fennel wedges.

"Dinah, you are a tyrant, man. Padmavati is only trying to help." Oliver stepped in, coming to his lady's defense. "I *like* it when some parts are burnt."

"We aren't *roasting* this fennel, Oliver, we're braising it in *milk*. You don't want to have some pieces that are mushy nothings and some that are as hard to bite into as a tree root in Central Park, do you?"

"Sorry, Dinah," Vati said, and smiled at Oliver knowingly, like, *Oh, Dinah, you little culinary lunatic.*

"Should I baste, Dine?" I said from my perch on the island.

"Yes! Baste the turkey now, and then set the timer for ten more minutes, so you don't have to *keep asking me*. I have to poach the pears and that will take all my concentration."

The doorbell rang. May erupted in barks and skidded to the door.

197

"Oh my goodness, who could that *be*?" yodeled my mother as she ran down the stairs in her bathrobe and with rollers in her hair. "It's only nine-thirty. God almighty, it smells divine down here. Is it the wine delivery? Oh, hell's bells, I'm running out of time!" She tucked her robe more closely around her and opened the door.

"Nolan, hello." She blanched and looked at all of us like *What the—? Nolan* was supposed to be on a flight to Pittsburgh that very moment, not that my mother knew that, but I did. That morning I had been daydreaming about him at the airport. Would he have breakfast there? Would he be reading a book? Would he be thinking about me? I hadn't seen him in fifteen days, but we had spoken on the telephone for an hour the night before.

"Oh my god," I barely said.

"Oh my god!" Vati pretty much screamed.

"Oh my god," Dinah said, like the fun had just begun.

Nolan was dressed up in a tweed blazer with a checked-blue collared shirt, an orange tie, brown cords, and on top of it all was a thick houndstooth overcoat, hanging open, that looked like it must have been his grandfather's. He was holding a weekend bag. His guitar, as ever, was strapped to his back.

"Nolan." I slid off the island and wished no one were around so I could run into his arms.

"Come in, come in, Nolan. May! Down!" My mother got it together. My punishment had ended that very day. I was waiting for her to give me back my phone and then I would have texted him, but there he was, ten feet away from me. "It's freezing out there," she said, making a wide circle around him to shut the door as if he were a wet, muddy dog. May plopped down at Nolan's feet, panting with her tongue flopping out of her mouth like he was about to give her a piece of bacon.

"Hey, man!" Oliver went and gave him a man hug. "What are you doing here?"

"Hi, everyone. Sorry, Mrs. Noorlander, for just showing up here unannounced." He looked helpless and embarrassed. "I, well, I just found out that my stepmom's mom died."

"Oh, goodness, I'm so sorry, Nolan. Here, Oliver, take his bag. Take your coat off." Mom wrapped her bathrobe around herself again, while at the same time trying to signal to Nolan that he should walk farther into the room.

"She had been sick for a while. I guess they weren't expecting that she would die today, and she did, so now my father and stepmother have to go to where she was in Florida."

"So you're not going to Pittsburgh?" I asked.

"Yeah." He held out his phone in his hand. "My dad just called and said that I shouldn't come. He has to go with Elaine and Bruno. They left the house already. I was on my way to the airport." He looked confused and like a four-year-old teenager.

"And my mother left to go to my aunt's house in Vermont yesterday, so." He looked at me. "I have no place to have Thanksgiving."

And then I walked over fast and hugged him. Right in front of my mother. He smelled like trees.

"Nolan," my mother said eventually. "You must stay here and have lunch with us. Please, you are welcome." She said that very nicely.

I let go of him and looked into his eyes, which were pooling.

"Thanks, Mrs. Noorlander. I am so sorry to barge in like this."

He wiped the tears away before they fell. "I just, I, well, I didn't know where else to go."

"Here, let me get this," Oliver said and took his bag.

The shrill, clamorous ring of the timer went off.

"Wrenny! The *TURKEY*!!!!" Dinah screamed from a footstool where she was hovering over the steaming poaching liquid for the pears. Nothing, not even Nolan showing up unannounced on Thanksgiving Day, would distract that girl from her dessert.

Mom immediately put us to work peeling sweet potatoes. The garbage can was placed in the middle of Vati, Oliver, Nolan, and me. There was a brown paper bag of potatoes next to us on the island. Each of us had a peeler. The amount of cooking shit we have in our house because of the show is unreal.

"You guys were incredible the other night," Vati said, scraping away. She had gone to see the Shoppe Boys with Oliver.

"No kidding, man. It was so fun," Oliver said, and looked at Vati goofily.

"Thanks, guys. I wish you could have been there, Wren," Nolan said. I was still getting used to him standing right there in the middle of my kitchen. Just so you know, I could not have been in a less attractive outfit. I was wearing my worst dark gray sweats that make me feel like an elephant and a dumb, ill-fitting white T-shirt, that I wear to sleep only if everything else is dirty.

"Yeah, me too. But I'll go to another one soon, I hope," I said.

"Oh, you will." He elbowed me with the arm his sweet potato was in and bumped me with his hip.

"Hey, watch it! My peel just went on the floor!" I squealed in my most attractive, flirtatious way.

"Didn't Reagan send you the video?" Vati said.

"Huh? Reagan went?" All the squeal drained out of my voice. They nodded or said yeah. "No, my phone was confiscated. I didn't know she was there." Grrrr.

"What? How did she not tell you at school?" Vati stopped peeling.

"I don't know, I've been in the art studio a lot and I don't know, I go home right after school." Now I was annoyed. Peel, peel. I thought to myself while peeling the living daylights out of the sweet potato, *That is exactly what parents have in mind when they ground you. They separate you from the herd*—peel, peel—*make you have a wicked-bad case of FOMO* [fear of missing out—school shrinks talk to us about it all the time.] *All of them were there, all of them saw Nolan, all of them are now ahead of me and closer to each other. They knew it too—they couldn't even tell me at school. Reagan totally should have told me and she didn't. That is weird and wrong.* Then I thought I was being paranoid. I looked at Nolan.

"Yeah, she was there, so was Farah. Didn't I say that on the phone?" He looked so sincere.

"No," I said softly, and looked to see if Dinah was listening, which she totally was. Mom and Dad were upstairs. "Whatever, Farah has been so weird lately," I said.

"I *know*! She's a total sketch train!" Vati was now madly peeling her sweet potato.

"Did she go to London yet or is she still at that guy Cy's house?" Nolan said, finishing one potato and reaching into the bag for another.

We all stopped peeling.

"Excuse me?" I whispered. Nolan looked like he'd said something he shouldn't have.

"That guy she is seeing? From the museum? The artist?"

"Are you guys done?" Dinah said, with her hands over her head like she was way at the end of her rope. "Can someone *baste the turkey*? Gosh! *Am I the only one focusing on the fact we have like one hundred people coming to lunch in three hours?*"

"Oliver, you deal with the turkey." I signaled with my potato for Vati and Nolan to come over to the stairs out of Dinah's earshot.

"What are you talking about?" Vati and I were looking at Nolan like a team of detectives interrogating the perp on *Law & Order.*

"Okay, hold on." Nolan got really mellow and cool. "We were just talking at the gig."

"Who was talking? You and Farah?" Vati was almost hysterical.

"Yes." He continued speaking to us like you would talk to a crazy person—slowly and calmly. No sudden moves. "She said she had been seeing that guy, Cy Dowd, since the party and they were having a thing." Vati and I looked at each other with that eyes-wide-open-mouth-open-shut-the-front-door face. Like Scooby-Doo and Shaggy when they see the ghost. I hadn't heard a word about Cy since that day at lunch. I had hoped it was a one-night-weird-Farah thing and we would never hear of it again. But then again, I had been in brownstone prison. We looked at Nolan to keep going.

"Did she not tell you guys this?" he asked in his girl/guy way.

"No!" we shout-whispered.

"She told me that she was going to spend the night with him the night before Thanksgiving, last night. Then wake up there today, before she flew to London to go see her dad. You didn't know that?"

"No, no, we didn't. Or I didn't," I said. Vati looked at me like, *Me neither.*

"Oh my *god*, I have to tell Oliver." Vati bolted to the kitchen. I sat down on the bottom step. Nolan sat down next to me.

"How could you not talk to me about that on the phone?"

"I don't know, Wren. I . . . I guess we were talking about other stuff. I wasn't thinking about your friend."

I could sort of see Farah confiding in Nolan, because A) he is the kind of guy that you confide in because he sort of has girl mojo, and B) he's older than us and Farah was doing something out of our sophomore-girl league. I scraped at some gunk in the crevice where the banister met the stair, and we sat in silence for a few minutes.

"And, Wren, *you* never even brought Farah up." That made me scrape the gunk faster.

"I didn't?"

"No, if anything, I thought we were talking about, I don't know, that school in France? Your parents? Not your friends. " He took my hand that was scraping and put it in his.

"You want to come up to my room, just for a second?" I said. I looked at him and then, in a paranoid way, up the stairs, in case my mother heard me through the ceiling. "I want to show you something."

"Yeah. I *totally* want to come up to your room."

36

We stealthily climbed up the stairs, very quickly and smoothly passing my parents' open door. They must have been getting dressed in the bathroom because I didn't see signs of either one of them when I looked in before we beelined past it. I led Nolan up the last flight of stairs to my room and down the hall lined with the artwork from when I was little.

"Hey!" he whispered. I turned around and shushed him with my finger to my lips. "Did you do these?" He pointed at the frames. I nodded and smiled. He mouthed, "Wow!"

The door to my room was open and there, as big as lights, was my unmade bed. What if there was underwear from the night before thrown on the floor, or a box of tampons out in the open? Or a slobbish pile of clothes, an errant apple core . . . ? But before I could worry too much about it, Nolan tumbled into the sheets and duvet and put his arms under his head like he was a sultan on an inflatable pool raft. I closed the door nervously.

"God, I never close the door up here."

"This is an awesome room!" he said, a bit too loudly. "Look at your great windows!" He turned around, pointing at them. "Where are we looking, west? It's like a tree house up here!"

"I always think of it like a greenhouse." I stood between the bed and bathroom, hoping I had remembered to flush the toilet. "I, um." I darted in there for a second to make sure. All clear. "*Totally* lucked out." I came back in. "I used to share Oliver's room with him, then Mom said one of us could have this room and for some weird reason he didn't want it, so."

"He's an idiot not to take this place."

"He wanted to be closer to the kitchen."

"So did you really have something you wanted to show me or was that just an excuse to get me in your bed?" He laughed. I almost threw up.

"No! God!" Suddenly I was blushing and bolting for the door. I had never had a boy in my room before. Charlie had been there, of course, but not a boy like Nolan.

"Sorry, come here." He jumped up and got me. "I am so happy to be up here with you, in your place." He led me back to the bed.

"I didn't bring you up here to—oh, I feel so stupid!"

"Nah." His voice got soft. "That was a dumb thing I said." We sat on the bed.

"What did you want to show me?" he asked. I looked at him and scrunched up my nose. "Come on. Please show me."

"Okay, well." I stood up, slid my hand behind my desk, and got my drawing pad.

"Can I look?" he asked, reaching out. I nodded. "Come down here next to me." He patted the bed then moved over and leaned against the wall, propping himself up with his knee. It was funny seeing him all dressed up for Thanksgiving, in my room, in my bed, in my sheets that I had just gotten out of.

I took a deep breath and nestled myself beside him. He lifted the cover of my drawing pad and started to look at drawing after drawing of my foot.

I burst into giggles, putting my hand over my face. "Oh my god." I tilted over onto him and buried my head in his neck and hair, which smelled like our kitchen.

"Wren," he started, kind of laughing too. "What's making you laugh?" He looked at me. "These are freaking amazing, Wrenny— they are. Shhh. Look at this." I held my breath as he slowly took his thumb and traced along the dusty charcoal line where I had drawn my arch. "Who can do that?" he said in awe. And then he took my hand in his and traced the same line of the arch with my thumb, slowly dragging it down the page. "It's perfect," he whispered. "It looks just like your foot. It even has the personality of your foot." He rubbed his socked foot on mine, pressing with the ball. I pressed back. We pressed our feet together hard until we both pulled back at the same time.

"These are beautiful, Wren," he said, still looking. "You drew all of these when you were held in captivity?"

"Yeah, every afternoon, I would draw until the sun went down. Pathetically, I got obsessed with my foot. I haven't done my self-portrait yet and it's due on December 15!"

"You will. Shit, if you can draw a foot that looks like this, just think what you can do with that face."

He pulled me onto his body and kissed me. My whole self lifted. Not up, but into him. It made me want to bite him, but I didn't.

"Hey, wanna know something?" he asked, kissing me. "Yeah," I said, breathless. I really was breathless.

"You drew those in the afternoon, right?"

"Yeah."

"There's this Van Morrison song [kiss] about [kiss] the afternoon." He stopped kissing me and looked into my eyes. I practically wanted to cry out or bite my own lip. Everything was so quiet and slow, there was only the sound of our breath and the sound of his whispering voice. "It's a really good song." He smiled. I could tell he was hearing it in his head. "I kind of wish it were the afternoon." His other hand moved under me and shifted me down, until I was lying underneath him.

"Me too." I didn't know why, but if he wanted it to be the afternoon, that sounded good to me.

"You got me reelin'," he half sang into my ear and kissed me on my neck and shoulders and slid his hand under my plain old white T-shirt until it touched the very edge of my bra.

We made out for as long as I could take it without freaking that my parents were right downstairs and it was Thanksgiving. I sat up, feeling a sense of impending urgency, like the intercom was about to ring.

"Here's the thing," I said.

"Yeah?" he said, looking scuffed up with painfully adorable boy hair. I took a breath to try to organize my thoughts.

"What is happening?" I let the breath out.

"With us?" he said. That made me punch him on the arm.

"No—with, I don't know, Farah!" I paused and took in his boy hair and cow eyes again.

"Well, Farah, I guess, is in some adventure with that guy." Of course Nolan would see it as an adventure.

"But *why* would she tell you about it—and not me, or Vati or Reagan?"

"Reagan?" he said.

"Yeah. Reagan."

"I didn't think Reagan was so close to you guys."

"Why, because she totally screwed Vati over until Oliver decided to have a come-to-Jesus moment because of, well, because of you?"

"Yeah, and, well, you never talk about her so much. I thought you and Vati were the duo."

"Well, Reagan's tricky," I said, and looked him in the eye.

"Is she nice?"

"Yes. On the outside, she's tough, but inside, she is, well, I think she's lonely a lot of the time. He mother is difficult and not really momlike. I think Reagan spends a lot of time in places with her mother that are too grown up, like they are forever in trendy restaurants."

"That are too grown up?" he asked.

"Well, sort of. I eat with everyone in my family at seven and then have to do my homework. Reagan has tasting menus on school nights. Or she's just alone while her mother is out. So, anyway, I think she's kind of cold on the outside."

"I spend a lot of time alone."

"You do?" He looked like that four-year-old again. "Are you so bummed not to be with your dad?"

"Yeah, I am, but his wife's mother died. What are you going to do?" he said.

"I don't know. I guess come here?"

He smiled kind of sadly at me. "Do you get how lucky you are?"

I must have looked confused.

"Of course you don't get what Farah is doing, or Reagan even, because basically you are *good* and you don't understand screwed-up behavior. You have a charmed life, you know?"

"Charmed? I am so screwed up!"

"How?"

"I can't do anything right. I get the worst grades in my class, I couldn't read until I was nine, and usually I can't get work done unless Mom is standing there holding a club over my head."

"Yeah, but she *does* stand over you. And you *do* get work done. Look at all those beautiful drawings."

"But that's not real work," I said, looking at the drawings of my foot.

"No, man, this"—he pointed to the drawing—"is the most real kind of work." He nodded at me like, *Get it?* "And you have Oliver, and cute little Dinah."

"Dinah is pretty cute."

"She's frigging adorable. I watched her on TV before I knew you."

"Really?"

He nodded. "And your dad," he said. I thought about Dad. He always calls my drawings "work." He believes art can be work just like Nolan does. I guess it's the only thing that feels easy to me, so "work" is not the word I would use—"play" maybe.

"But what about Farah? I am so freaked out by her. I know she feels like she's playing house with this guy, but the guy is a man, an old one."

"Why don't you reach out to her? Text her. She might be freaked too."

"Yeah. I will. I have to get my phone. I bet it's not even charged." I started pacing around my room, pulling on a random sweater that was on the floor. "We have to go downstairs. I have to get dressed. You totally have to go to Oliver's room or something." I started cleaning up the rest of the clothes on the floor but then gave up.

"Come here just for one more second." I wasn't sure I wanted to get back in the bed but I did. He sat up, leaning on his elbow. He tucked a strand of hair behind my ear.

"Are you my girlfriend?"

"Am I?"

"Yes."

37

Downstairs my mother had taken over the kitchen and was standing in the middle of it looking at a yellow pad of paper. Her hair was out of the curlers and looping down, making her look too glamorous for eleven in the morning. She was still in her robe. No one took notice that Nolan and I had been upstairs. Holidays throw everyone off their game.

"Mom, may I please have my phone? It's Thanksgiving."

"If you whip this cream." She signaled to two pint-size boxes and a large whisk on the island. "I will get your phone, Wren. But let this be a lesson to you both." She turned and pointed two fingers at us. "Don't mess with me."

"We won't, Mrs. Noorlander, and again, I'm sorry," said Nolan.

"No, no." She held her hand up, blocking the apology. "It's water under the bridge, no need to apologize again."

"Okay, cool. Can I help?"

"You can help Wren when her arm gets sore. *Wren*, you aren't showered? What is that ratty sweater?" she said as she made her way to wherever she'd hidden my phone. "People will be here at noon. You know Marian. She waits on a park bench until 11:58," she called from the other room.

"Who is Marian?" Nolan asked.

"My father's secretary." I poured the quart of heavy cream into the bowl.

"Want me to do that?" Nolan put his hand out with confidence.

"Oh, I can beat the daylights out of this cream, you just sit back and watch, my friend." (I LOVED having a boyfriend!)

"Stiff peaks, Wren, don't make butter," Dinah called over from the dining room table where she was drawing turkeys on place cards.

"What, you just whip this until it turns into Cool Whip, right?" Nolan asked.

"Yup," I said, taking the whisk in my hand and the big copper bowl in my arm. "Then you add a little vanilla and sugar."

"We only ever had it from the can."

"Yeah, that is contraband here. But I like it. I wish we had stuff like that. I always wanted Lunchables."

"I never had a Lunchables either, but they did look good on TV. I was a PB&J guy."

"I never brought my lunch to school, and all nuts and seeds have been banned from the entire cafeteria since I was in kindergarten because so many girls had allergies. I don't think I've had a PB&J since Pre-K." I was starting to get out of breath, but there was no way I was going to give him a turn.

"That is so tremendously weird."

"I know. But have you ever had sun nut butter?" He just laughed at me.

Mom returned, holding my beloved sparkly pink phone.

"*Thank yoooooou!* Oh my gosh." I had no free hands to take it. "Hello, phone. I have missed you." Mom rolled her eyes.

"I'm putting it down here and you can reunite when you are

finished with your task!" She put my precious phone on the butcher-block counter.

"Where did Oliver go?" Nolan asked.

"I sent him and Vati out with Mr. Noorlander to get tonic and more olive oil. How we ran out of olive oil I have no idea . . ." She drifted off to the dining room with her seating list.

Nolan picked up my phone, pressed the power button, and looked at the screen, which was a little weird, but maybe that is what boyfriends and girlfriends do. No secrets, everything shared and out in the open.

"You have, like, a thousand texts."

"I do? Here take this and keep beating on the side of the bowl until it starts to thicken up. *Don't* overdo it, or we'll have five pounds of butter."

"I remember that from fourth grade. I think we made butter in school as part of our Colonial study."

My phone was fully charged. "She charged it, that was nice," I said.

"This isn't easy." He started whipping the cream then shifted the bowl in his arm and went at it with more resolve.

"Oh jeez, Nolan. There are so many texts from Farah." I scrolled down. "From days and days ago. Listen."

> W—God why don't u have your phone??? He is calling me. Like every hour. He is sending a car to pick me up. R u getting these???

"When was that?"

"Um—it was, I think, like, two days after the party. Maybe it was that weekend. I don't know, she didn't say any of this in school. Listen to this one."

W—At his loft. Have been here all afternoon.

"When was *that*?" He was still whipping.

"I think the same day, no! It was the next day. Sunday." I read on.

W—He gave me a necklace he made. It's amazing. He is amazing.

"Oh my god." I looked at Nolan. "This is so weird, Nolan. He is in his forties!"

"He's in his thirties, I think."

"*Whatever!* She is fifteen!" I stared at the phone and saw a bunch of cute texts from Charlie.

Hang in there Wrenny. We miss you!!!

"I'm calling her. At least she was texting me," I said to myself.

"I think this is done." He held up the whisk and there indeed was a beautiful white peak of transformed heavy cream.

I pulled up Farah's contact. Her picture is her jumping in the air in front of a car. One time her mom told us about an old Toyota car ad where people jumped up in the air when they bought their car. They sang, "Oh oh oh what a feeling to driiiive . . . TOYOTA!" We thought it was so hysterical we spent the next few days taking pictures of each other jumping in front of random cars on the street and then laughing until we almost peed in our pants.

"Go show Dinah." I pointed to the dining room with the phone. He looked terrified, which made me laugh. *I loved having a boyfriend!*

My call went right to voice mail.

Hi this is Farah. I'm out of the country. Thanks.

"She must be on the plane!" I called to no one.

"Who?" Dinah shouted.

"Never mind!" I yelled. I looked into the dining room and saw Dinah inspecting Nolan's work. She nodded her head approvingly. He held up the whisk for my mom, who also smiled. She once said to me having a husband who can cook is easier than having a husband who can't cook. Maybe the same was true for boyfriends. And my boyfriend could whip cream.

38

The first twenty minutes of people arriving for Thanksgiving at our house is mayhem. Sometimes Thanksgiving with my family will be twenty-five people who might never have met, or haven't seen each other in a year since the last Thanksgiving. Both my parents are only children, so we don't have any cousins. Mom's parents both died and the Noorlander grandparents are in Holland. Our Thanksgiving guests are mostly people my parents know socially or from the museum or my mom's pottery studio who don't have anywhere else to go. New York City is full of people with no cousins, and nowhere to go.

Charlie and his parents walked in the door at ten after twelve. I didn't even realize how much I had missed him until I saw his sticking-up hair, apple cheeks, and his new purple bow tie.

"Oh, Charlie!" I flung my arms around him. Sometimes my father will say I am "a sight for sore eyes" and that's how I felt about seeing Charlie.

"Hi!" he said, like he was totally happy to see me too.

"Hi!" And then I leaned into him again and whispered, "Nolan is here! He's somewhere in this house!"

We pulled away. Charlie didn't look as happy as he had a second before.

"I hate when you don't have a phone, Wren. I feel like you disappeared." We moved over to the side of the hallway so our parents could say hello to each other and my father could take the serving dishes full of food that Winston had brought for the feast.

"I know, I did kind of disappear. I got in so much trouble for leaving that night."

"Well, that was," he whispered, "*really messed up*, Wren."

"I know. I totally know. I got grounded and my parents made me do my Internet homework in the kitchen."

"I was worried about you." He sounded kind of pissed.

"I'm sorry!" I squeezed his hand.

"You don't even know that I got into the Bard Ornithology program."

"You did?"

"Yes, and I get to go to *Bard College* this summer and do intensive bird-watching. It's pre-college."

"That is so great, Charlie. Vati told me you were worried about getting in."

"Well, it's very competitive, especially for a sophomore." I nodded and gave him a fist bump. He looked more like himself again and not so disgruntled at me for being the spaz who left the party without telling him. "What about France? Have you sent in the application?"

"It's not due until December 15."

"Well that's soon. Are you done?"

"No. But I'm getting there. When I was grounded I drew the bike and my sneaker. I've done everything but the essay and self-portrait. Did you hear me that Nolan is *here*?"

"Yeah. Why?" *Why?* Was he *jealous* of Nolan? How could that be? None of us had ever felt that Charlie "liked" us. He had never had a crush on a girl as far as I knew—well, Kate Middleton, but I thought that was because she was a princess.

"Well," I said. Now I was getting a big vibe that I just should have shut up about Nolan altogether, but maybe if Charlie felt sorry for him . . . "Because he was supposed to go to his dad's who he only sees once a month," I paused for dramatic effect. "But, his step-grandmother died." I looked at Charlie for a reaction. Nothing. "And I guess his mom is in Vermont, so. He came here this morning."

"Why *here*? Because of Oliver? I didn't think they really even knew each other."

"Well, first of all, Oliver and Nolan do know each other, but really, I suppose it's because . . ." I felt like I had to be brave to say this. "I'm here. We are sort of a"—his face was so blank it looked mean—"couple."

"I'm going to take off my coat, get a drink or something." He looked around me, like he didn't care at all that I had basically just told him I had a boyfriend.

"Oh, okay, yeah."

"Happy Thanksgiving!" Vati came rushing down the stairs from the living room where most of the guests were around the fire. "Charlie! Come upstairs! Are your parents here? Did you guys bring that shrimp?" She gave Charlie a hug. "Come on, Wren! Nolan was asking where you were."

Charlie took his coat off and hung it on the coatrack.

"I'm just going to help my parents for a second." He made his way to the kitchen where his parents were instructing Dinah and my mother on what to do with the shrimp hors d'oeuvres that really are the best thing you will ever put in your mouth.

"What's up with him?" said Vati, whose face was flushed from either the fire or from being near Oliver.

"I don't know. I think he's still mad at me that I left my phone with him that night at the museum."

"How can you blame him? Remember, you were MIA, for real," she said.

"I know, I guess," I said, unsure.

"What do you mean, he's *not* mad about the phone?" she said.

"Do you think he's mad about Nolan? He was annoyed that Nolan was here." Vati's eyes widened.

"Is Charlie in love with *you*?" She took a big breath in like suddenly it all made sense.

"No!" I whispered, and looked up the stairs to see if Nolan was coming, and then I quickly peeked into the kitchen at Charlie who was carefully arranging the shrimp on a tray with Dinah. "No, Charlie is like my brother."

"But he could have been secretly in love with you all these years." She clutched her hands to her chest. I love Vati, but any whiff of potential romance for anyone, even movie stars she doesn't know, sends her into a tizzy. Her pupils turn into hearts.

"No! Vati, stop." I pulled her closer to the front door so we would be farther away from all the action in the kitchen. "I don't know who Charlie loves, but it's not me."

"He never talks about girls, all he does is hang out with us here, and *you* live here!"

"Just because *you* hung out here, totally in love with Oliver

219

month after month after month, does not mean that we all are in love! Charlie is our friend. He's my friend." I could feel my heart get heavy, and at the same time I could feel the neurons in my brain leaping around trying desperately to make all the connections they had to make to deal with this day. "I think Charlie just doesn't like Nolan. He got a terrible look on his face when I said he was here, like he had had a sip of bad milk." Vati's face fell.

"Well, he will like him when he spends time with him today. It's Thanksgiving." She linked her arm in mine and that felt as good as someone putting a blanket on me in the middle of the night. "Come on, let's get some of those shrimp and go upstairs."

It was a Thanksgiving like I had never had. Nolan held my hand under the table while my father said grace. On our walk to the park to play touch football, Mom wrapped her arm around me and told me it was "good" that Nolan was there with us, and not in some airport waiting to fly to Vermont. Vati and Oliver were openly being lovey-dovey all day, like they were not aware of anyone else in the room, and it was charming, even if it was unfamiliar. Charlie turned it around with Nolan over washing dishes when they discovered Nolan knew Charlie's guitar teacher. But the part that made that Thanksgiving feel the most remarkable was, before everyone left, Nolan took out his guitar and played "Edelweiss," that beautiful song Christopher Plummer sings in *The Sound of Music*. It was a perfect song for that day because it's sweet and old-fashioned, and Nolan singing it made me swoon in my own living room. But it's a sad song too, in the way lullabies can make you wistful. Lullabies can make you long for something. I think maybe, even if you are a kid, they make you long for your childhood.

39

First period, the Monday morning after Thanksgiving, I was in Studio Art, in one of the deepest seven-mile stares I had ever had. It was like I would never have to blink again, and it felt so totally good. I was *feel-thinking* about Nolan. Feel-thinking is more than just thinking. You *think* about lunch. You *think* about what's going to happen on the next episode of some TV show, you *think* about what to wear—you *feel-think* about boys. Right then I was feel-thinking about Nolan. Nolan at the table talking smack with my father about the touch football game. Nolan plotting with Dinah about what cookies to make for the Christmas episode. (Nolan is nuts about Linzer tarts, but Dinah argued quite rightly that they are way too difficult for a half-hour TV show. She would make them with him another time.) Nolan's forearms, his fist bumping with Oliver's. His eyes . . . I was feeling him, in a thinking way. And the steady, romantic snowfall out the paned glass window wasn't helping matters.

"Wren, *Wr-E-Nnnn*, where on *earth* a-rrrr-e yoooou?" Mrs. Rousseau sang, waving her hand in front of my face.

"Sorry! Ugh, sorry, Mrs. Rousseau. I . . ." I took my chalk that had almost melted in my hand and randomly started shading on my still life.

"I thought you were going to bring a self-portrait for me to look at. It's the beginning of December, and I don't think I have to tell you that December 15 is right around the corner."

"Oh, I know. I will, I mean, I totally will. I just, well . . ."

"You haven't done it?"

"No."

"Woe is me, my dear. What is keeping you?" She clutched her hands together in the middle of her bosoms and looked at me over her reading glasses.

"I don't know. I'm having a hard time."

"*Stop.*"

Huh?

"I won't have it, Wren. I will not have you whining at me about not being able to *do it*." She imitated me whining. "Do you think you get more than one shot, Wren?" I didn't know what to say. "Do you think that this talent of yours will keep moving forward, will keep progressing by itself? Do you think you are above putting in the work you need to *get this done?*"

I shook my head back and forth.

"No! I *know* you know better than that. I won't have it. I have taught you that. You have been doing *so well*." She grabbed my cheeks with her hand. I could feel the edges of her fingernails digging into my jaw. "What has happened to you?" She shook my face back and forth just the tiniest bit. "What has come over you? You are out to lunch!"

"I'm so sorry," I said, while she had my face in a death grip. "I thought I was doing okay, I'm almost finished with this, see?" I lifted my chalk up to indicate my crazy medieval town still life.

"This?" She let go. "Wren, this is like playing hopscotch for you. And it's *not* the assignment for Saint-Rémy." She lost her fire and suddenly didn't sound angry anymore, just disappointed. "I don't understand. I thought we had a plan."

"We do, Mrs. Rousseau, I swear. I will do it."

"Good."

And then just when it could have been over, I felt an overpowering need to confess. "Something is happening, sort of," I ventured, not really sure it was the right thing to do. "I met a boy and he's changing things." I should have stopped there, but it was too late. "He's . . . altering the way I feel."

"About art?"

"Well, no." I thought about it and changed my mind. "Yes. About art and other things. I feel differently about everything." She squinted at me and took in a breath for a good thirty seconds.

"All of that may very well be true, dear heart, but you are running out of time. Don't let your life become too dramatic."

40

Life *was* getting sort of dramatic. After class I saw Farah and Reagan in the hall on our way to Life Science elective, the one class we were in together. The one where we were studying the hummingbirds.

"Hey!" we all said, and awkwardly hugged each other, not really wanting to.

"How was London?" I said to Farah in an overly formal tone.

"Fine, lovely. It was good to see Daddy. Ronica was all about the triplets and I didn't really deal with her. I think it was part of the plan that Daddy take me to so much theater and to museums and meals out, it would somehow escape me that they have fully started a new family."

"Oh, did you get to have turkey? I mean, I know they don't have Thanksgiving over there, but . . ."

"No, it was on the menu at Claridge's of course, for Americans, but I didn't order it."

"I didn't have turkey either," said Reagan, and then the two of them looked at each other in some sort of unpatriotic solidarity.

"Oh." If it's lame that I felt insecure about having turkey on the day most of the country has turkey, I get it, but I did. I felt lame about having a real Thanksgiving.

"Where were you, Reag? With your mom?" asked Farah.

"Yeah, we bailed on the whole big meal thing and spun."

"Like at a spinning class?" said Farah.

"Yeah, the place my mom goes does three-hour classes on Thanksgiving—turkey burns."

"Genius," Farah said, sounding fake. "So, tell me about Nolan!" she said, sounding normal. "Vati texted me the whole story, but it was so long and rambling I stopped reading it. I totally want to hear, so spill it, *s'il vous plaît.*"

"Ohhh, it's kind of wild. He's, he's, wonderful." We exploded in giggles, which was the biggest relief. I had my friends back. Turtles. Farah even raised her eyebrows really high and did a little excited dance.

"Yeah, it's really, really wonderful. I thought that time I was being punished was going to be horrendous, but it wasn't. We talked on the phone, the real phone, for hours. And he picked me up from school . . . did I tell you that?"

"I actually heard that from, like, six people," Farah said.

"You did?"

She nodded. "Um, yes, you were the only ninny who didn't have her phone."

"Oh yeah, I got all of your texts on Thanksgiving—and he actually came to Thanksgiving!" I said.

"Wow," Reagan said in sort of a weird way. Did she know that Padmavati was there too? Did she know that Oliver and Padmavati were a couple? Did she care? Reagan is so hard to read. She's socially awkward; people never think she likes them.

"It's out of nowhere, right? Sort of?" I said, and Farah shrugged.

"But I feel close to him. He's, well, he's my boyfriend," I said, like I was still trying out the term.

"He said he was really into you," Reagan said.

"Yeah, he did—I think you *totally* have a boyfriend," said Farah.

"When did he say that to you guys?" I asked, bracing myself with excitement.

"At his gig, where he was *unreal*. That band is amazing," Farah said. And then the first bell rang.

"He really said he was into me? That is so sweet, right? Oh my god."

They both nodded and Reagan went into the classroom.

"Farah, Nolan told me something . . . did you see Cy Dowd last week?"

Second bell.

"Totally." She sounded so normal about it.

"Girls!" Mr. Trevor bellowed from the science lab. Farah gave a thousand-watt smile and sauntered into science.

41

I only went over to Nolan's apartment once during the entire
time we were together, which seems really strange to me now. But
it was far uptown and, not that he ever said it, but Nolan seemed
to want to be at our house. So I only went that one time. My parents knew I was going. It was on a Saturday afternoon.

Nolan and his mom lived on Saint Nicholas Avenue on the top
two floors of a brownstone. The day I went to see him, Nolan met
me at the subway stop. A lot of times when I was going to see Nolan,
right before I saw him, the minutes before, I felt alone—isolated. I
think it was the almost unbearable anticipation; it separated me
from anyone else who was around, or the entire human *race*. I saw
a movie once called *Billy Elliot*. It was about a boy ballet dancer.
During most of the movie he is a young boy, maybe eleven. At the
end of the movie you skip ahead in his life and he is a grown man.
There is a very specific moment that stuck with me: The grownup
Billy is standing offstage, in the wings of a theater, waiting to make
an entrance. I'm not even sure you see him, but by the way the
camera moves and the sound, you can feel what he is going through.
The lights onstage are brighter than anything else in the frame.
You hear the music, but it's muted like you are hearing it through
his skull. You can also hear his controlled but heavy breathing, and

you might even be able to hear his heart beat, like a thoroughbred before a race. You can't see the expression on his face at all, but you know he is waiting for it all to happen. There is a real anxiety in the scene, it's almost agonizing, and it feels lonely, but then he leaps onto the stage, like a strong stag leaping over a fallen tree in the forest. Once he goes, you know it all turned out okay. You know he is exactly where he wants to be, where he needs to be. That is what it felt like before I saw Nolan, like I was about to go onstage. The light was a little too bright, the sound was muted, and I was alone. But then I would see his face, like I did that Saturday when I was walking up the unfamiliar subway steps; I saw his face looking over the gate at me, and in an instant all the fear and isolation were gone. I was in mid-leap, and exactly where I wanted and needed to be.

"You must be Wren. Come in, come in. I'm Jessica Nolan."

"Hi," I said. Nolan, my Nolan, kissed me on the mouth right in front of his mother like we were thirty years old.

The bottom floor of their apartment was small and filled with light. The kitchen, living room, and dining room were all one room. There was a round table with four chairs and a small vase right in the middle, filled with what looked like silk flowers, close to a big light gray L-shaped sofa, with lots of mismatched pillows piled in the corner of the L. There was a flat-screen TV on one wall, and on the other walls were framed posters of famous paintings like Matisse's painting of pink onions and Picasso's hand holding flowers. The flowers in the vase looked like the flowers on the poster. It smelled like bark in there, and then I remembered that Nolan sometimes smells like trees.

"Well, I am so glad to meet you, Wren. Nolan just doesn't stop talking about you." She reached up and gently grabbed Nolan's ear and gave it a tug.

"True enough." He came over and took my coat and bag.

"Oh." Was I in some kind of indie movie? I went over to the Matisse. "I've always loved this painting."

"Nolan tells me you are a wonderful artist."

"Well, he's only seen drawings of my feet," I said, looking at Nolan like he was a weirdo.

"He says there is a lot about you that is artistic, not only your work. He says you have the *soul* of an artist." She gave me a how-about-that look. If Nolan was the prince of confidence, his mother was the queen. Her hair was darker than Nolan's but it had the same thickness and shiny texture. It was all wrapped up in a bun with one of those leather bun holders that has a stick that you put through it to hold it in place. I think those hair things were made for professors and shrinks—she was both.

"You two should have something to eat. There's plenty in there, there's stew from last night."

"Are you hungry?" Nolan looked at me, tilting his head.

"Not really."

"Me neither."

"We're just going up to my room, Mom."

"Okay, I'll be down here. I have finals to grade. So great to meet you, Wren. I hope I see lots of you!"

Nolan led me up a winding spiral staircase to the second floor, where there was a door open to one room, clearly his mother's. Her bed had a pretty white, green, and red patchwork quilt spread over it. Each square had two cherries sewn onto its center. It looked like something you would find in the country, and I wondered if maybe she got it when Nolan was a little boy and they lived with his dad. Down the hall was the bathroom, and at the other end there was another door. It had a DANGER NO CROSSING sign that I thought might be left over from when Nolan was in seventh grade. He stepped in front of me and opened the door to a large room that looked like a recording studio. On the side closest to the door there was a window that looked out on the back windows and rooftops of other buildings. It was a lot like the view out my window. On the other side was a bunk bed. The top bed was made, but was piled high with books, and the bottom bed looked like someone had thrown a bunch of sheets and blankets at it. The entire other side of the room was full of guitars, banjos, a keyboard, and an arrangement of hand drums. There was one desk covered with books, papers, binders, and empty water bottles and one bookshelf packed so tightly with books I don't think you could fit another one in it. Actually there were books everywhere in piles. There were no Tonka trucks or Dungeons & Dragons boards left over from when he was little, like there are in Oliver's room. Oliver even has a few long-loved stuffed animals that stay very purposefully in the corner of his bed where his mattress meets the wall. Nolan's room was more like what I think a boy's room in college would be like. I felt like I was stepping into the future when I walked into that room.

We climbed into the bottom bunk, that smelled musty and like sleep. He lay on his side and I fitted myself into him, flat on my back with my knees up.

"How about my mom?" he said, raising his eyebrows.

"I liked her."

"My friends are kind of scared of her."

"I can see that."

"'Cause she's no bullshit, right?"

"Yeah, she vibes 'shrink' a lot. It feels like she knows something about you, or I wonder if we think that because we know she is a shrink?" I thought for a second. "I think it's her hair."

"I get what you mean. She has warrior hair."

"Yeah," I said, loving that he understood hair mojo. "Reagan has warrior hair too. All her power is in her hair," I said, thinking of her ponytail that's like two inches thick at its base.

"Reagan's hair protects her, I think," he said.

"Yeah . . . from what?" I said, sort of getting what he meant.

"Reagan's scared," he said.

"Maybe you'll be a shrink too one day?" I said.

"Maybe. " He looked like he was losing his train of thought because he did the thing he does when he takes a piece of my hair and wraps it around my ear. Then he snapped out of it. "No! That's her deal. I'm a musician." He put his hands out toward all the music stuff in his room like, *See?* I laughed.

"What was your mom like when you were little?" I asked.

"The same. Mom."

I smiled because that is the thing I most wanted to do when I was around him.

"Do you remember your mom when you were little?" he asked me.

"I remember that she hated that I got knots in my hair." He smiled. "I used to get really bad ones."

"Oh yeah?"

"Yeah. I think she thought I was going to be a good-for-nothing because of those knots." That really made him laugh.

"A good-for-nothing! What kind of thing is that to say? That's like what they called people in eighteenth-century England."

I flopped over, embarrassed. He poked my back, so I lifted my head.

"Do you remember anything else she thought of you? Or did you always think she thought you were a good-for-nothing?"

"Now you really do sound like a shrink."

"Well, maybe the apple doesn't fall far from the tree."

I smiled again and thought about it for a while. "No. She's always loved the way I draw."

"I'll bet."

"Even if I was doodling on one of those paper tablecloths in restaurants where they give the kids crayons, she would say, 'Oh, look at Wren's elephant,' or whatever I had doodled. 'Who can draw like that?' And she would look around the table like she was really asking them. Like she really thought I was something special."

We lay there for a while looking at the slats of the upper bunk.

"Nolan." I turned to him and sat up a little. " Can I tell you something?"

"Yeah, tell me everything."

"Okay, well, I just feel so . . . so full of emotion and *happy*, but more than that. Something feels really big, like I can't get enough air in my lungs. I'm always overwhelmed, but in a way that feels all right, you know? And, Nolan, it's a lot about you. In fact, it's all kind of about you. I just feel so . . ."

"I'm in love with you too," he said very simply.

I shot up to my knees. *Love?*

"That's what this is, Wren, it's love. We're in love."

The afternoon light was filtering in sideways through the window. In the rays you could see those tiny, floating specks of dust in the air, just like I had seen when I was little in my dad's arms. It was also like the light in the Vermeer painting we looked at that night in the museum. Have you ever seen a Vermeer painting? That is what this light was doing. One side of Nolan's face was illuminated so I could see the curve of his lip and the straight edge of his nose. The side that was resting on his hand was in warm shadow.

"I'm in love with you." He smiled like he knew he was blowing my mind.

"This is *love*?" I said quietly.

"This is love."

Love. Streaming light. Nolan. Love.

"I love you too. *I am in love with you too.*" I felt like I was trying the words on, like I was being crowned and was repeating a two-thousand-year-old oath that I had never said before but that I implicitly believed in. The words shocked a universe of untapped energy into my body, catapulting me off his bed and to the closed, mirrored door of his closet. Nolan followed me and came up right beside me, as if to catch me from running away. Putting his head next to mine, he wrapped his arm around me, securing me, both of us looking at our reflection, which we did silently for a few moments.

"We're the same," he guaranteed.

"Really? Do you feel the exact same way as I do? Because,

Nolan, I am feeling this very strongly." There was nothing I could do about the tears that had welled up in my eyes and were making their way down my cheeks. "It's scaring me."

"Wren, you can't feel this way unless the other person feels it too. If you are scared, so am I; if you are happy, so am I; if you want to go somewhere, so do I. It's the same. We are the same."

That was the day I lost my virginity. And here's the thing about that. It may be true *now* that Nolan turned out not to be the love of my life, but on that afternoon, it sure felt like he was.

42

If you think I had lost sight of the fact that Farah was in a Lolita affair with a famous artist, I had not. However, it was hard to tell how serious it was at first. It was like when there is a big storm coming. On the television, news reporters are listing what supplies to stock in your house, the mayor is calling for evacuations, stores are running out of batteries. You know a storm is on its way but you have no idea if it will really hit and cause destruction, or if it will blow out to sea. And sometimes, even when the first winds start rushing and the skies darken, you can still find yourself saying, "I don't think it's gonna be that bad."

The loss of my virginity called for a group Turtle meeting, sans Charlie. I texted everyone to meet at my house that Sunday afternoon for a "study session." Oliver had an away basketball game, my parents were going to Philly (something for Dad's work), and Dinah was spending the afternoon with one of the only friends that poor little working girl has, Zoe Powers, who lives on the East Side. So I asked Farah, Reagan, and Vati to come over for lunch.

"You guys," I said, pulling a loaf of bread out of the fridge. "I have something to tell you." I flopped the bag of bread on the island that we were all standing around.

"I knew you hadn't really called a study session," Farah said.

"Yeah, no." And then I got super nervous to say it out loud.

"Yes?" Padmavati looked like she knew what I was going to say. Her voice sang.

"So yesterday," I began. Reagan had her eyes fixed on me and shifted her weight from one hip to the other. "I went over to Nolan's apartment and—"

"Oh my god!" Vati is clairvoyant.

"It's just that we . . . we had sex." Squeals from all of them, but not in the same tone. Farah's was more of a laugh, Vati's was very high pitched, and Reagan sort of said, "Oh yeah!"

"I know!" And then we hugged.

"What was it like?" Vati said once we had calmed down.

"You did it during the day? That is *sexy*." Farah asked like she had sex every day, which she might have been for all we knew at that point.

"His mother was there."

"*What?* That is insane," said Reagan.

"Yeah, I know, but she was downstairs and besides, she's a shrink."

"That's sort of nice, right? That she was there. Makes it less scary," Vati said.

"You must have had to be quiet!" Farah teased.

"Eww, Farah! But you know, it was quiet, and it wasn't scary." Everyone piped down and listened.

"We were in his room, and there was this beautiful light coming through the window. We were all snuggled into his bunk bed."

"He sleeps in a *bunk bed*?" Reagan gasped.

"Yeah, on the bottom, but it's one of those ones where the bottom is bigger than the top. It felt like a nest—a grownup nest."

"Was he nice about it?" Padmavati asked tentatively.

"Yeah, he really was. He had protection and everything."

"Like he planned it? That's weird," said Reagan, the nonromantic.

"I'm sure he didn't plan it, Reagan," Vati shot back. There was still some friend-yuck there.

"I'm just saying. Why else would he have condoms?"

I had not thought of that, but I thought it was good that we didn't have unprotected sex, the very thing I had been forbidden from doing since I was nine and my mother told Oliver and me in the greatest detail about how babies were made, puberty, homosexuality, sexting, and anything else she wanted to be the first one to tell us. ("I would *much* rather have *my* morals, ideals, and values get in your brains first before some dingbat kid in your school tells you masturbating will make you go blind.")

"Doesn't every senior guy have condoms?" I said.

"Oh *yeah*," Farah-the-sex-expert chimed in. She also broke out the sun nut butter, took a spoon, scooped it, and then sucked it off with no bread or anything.

"Anyway, he was really sweet and he . . ." This was harder to say out loud than the sex part. I could have easily said it if it had just been Vati. ". . . said he loved me."

"He did?" all of them said in unison. I just nodded. "I said I loved him too!"

"Oh, Wren, that is so great," Reagan said, sort of surprisingly.

"It *is*! Oh my gosh, Wren, it's all happening," Vati said.

"Well, whatever, I just wanted to tell you guys." I felt bashful, maybe because I was talking about sex, not in the abstract, but for real.

"Did it hurt?" Vati asked.

"No, it didn't, which I guess is weird?"

"No, it's a myth that it hurts and that you bleed all over the place," said Farah.

"I bled," said Reagan.

"When did you lose your virginity?" I said, and looked at the other girls to see if they knew.

"Oh god, I don't know, not so long ago. It was with someone I met over the summer, when my mom and I went to visit her friends in Maine."

"How could you not tell us?" Vati said.

"I just didn't. It wasn't a big deal. I never even saw the guy again."

"That's sort of sad, Reagan," I said.

"It didn't feel sad," she said, and opened a can of seltzer.

"I think Oliver and I will wait," Vati said. "I just want to be sure that it's all real."

"It's real, Vats," I said. "He's nuts about you."

"Isn't that weird? It's like Reagan brought you two together," Farah said to a flabbergasted audience. "Oh come on. If Reagan hadn't kissed Oliver at the museum, Vati would still be having a huge crush on him from afar, like way afar."

"Vati." Reagan stepped up. "I am sorry about that. It was just a thing. It was kind of an accident."

"I know. It's okay, I don't think you could have really known how much I actually liked him. After all these years, it may have seemed unreal."

"No, I knew how you felt about him. I—I just wasn't thinking it through. Thoughtless is the wrong word, it was more like stupidity."

"Oliver told me he was flirting with you pretty hard," Vati said. "We're talking about what happened so we can get past it." I knew Vati *loved* that she was having "relationship talk" with Oliver.

"Well, we were both being stupid," Reagan said.

And then Vats and Reagan gave each other a girl hug where you kind of laugh and get weepy at the same time.

"Whew," I said. "That was like, a really weird month, with you two on the outs. It was weird, right?" I started making a sun nut butter and raspberry jam sandwich.

"Farah, what is up with you?" Reagan said, pulling away from Vats.

"Well . . . I'm in love too."

"With *Cy Dowd*?" I flipped up the knife and jam flew onto the kitchen floor.

"Yes of course. Who else?"

"Well, I don't know, Farah, you just met him." I went to the sink, ripped off a piece of paper towel (even though we are supposed to clean up spills with a sponge so as not to waste paper), and bent over to wipe up the blop of jam.

"You just met Nolan," she shot back.

"Yeah, I know, but we're teenagers. He's a senior, not a senior citizen."

Vati laughed. I hadn't even meant to make a joke.

"Oh my god, that is so judgmental," Farah said.

"Sorry. I just thought you . . . that it was a mistake, like Reagan and Oliver," I said.

"You can't help who you love, Wren," Farah said.

"I can't believe you are saying you *love* him. Does he love you?" I asked.

"Well, I don't know, but I would say yes. We don't talk about it. We just hang out."

"What does that mean, you just hang out? Where? How come everyone is suddenly talking about love?" Reagan walked to the yellow sofa and fell onto it, making her big boobs bounce up and down.

"Oh my god, Reagan, you guys, forget it, I shouldn't have said anything." Farah tossed her spoon in the porcelain farm sink, making a loud clatter. She winced at the sound of it.

"No, you should, you should tell us," I said.

"Well, don't tell anyone—like *your parents*, Wren." She looked at me, and I have to say it *was* my first instinct, to tell my parents. I wanted to blab the entire story the second they got home. Once my father told Oliver and me that if we ever found ourselves over our heads, say if there were drugs at a party or if someone was vomiting from drinking too much, we had to call them. Those circumstances would get us a free pass from getting in trouble. He said that he and Mom could be relied on to be a "safe haven" and we could count on them to get us out of a bad situation that was beyond us. Free. Of. Trouble. This felt like that. This felt like a bad situation, and my parents felt like a safe haven from it. Where was Farah's mother anyway?

"Just *don't*, okay?" she said, looking at me doubtfully. "Cy said it would be a shit show if people found out."

"How do you even see him?" Vati said.

"He texts me and then sends a car, and I go to his loft. I tell my mom I'm with you guys or at the movies or whatever."

"Just be careful, Farah," I said.

"You too, Wrenny," she shot back.

Vati took a bite of my sandwich that I hadn't eaten.

"I don't think I have to be careful, Farah," I said quietly.

Later that afternoon when everyone was gone, the doorbell rang. I was still in the kitchen attempting to read my Lit homework, a good book called *The Outsiders*, but even with its pretty engrossing plot, I was drifting. I popped up, went to the door, and asked who it was. Nothing. I went to the window and tried to see if anyone was standing on the steps. No one. I opened the first door to the vestibule and felt the cold through my sweater.

"Who is it?" I said again. Nothing. I opened the front door carefully because we are not supposed to open the door if we don't know who it is, and there on the top step was a small pot of paperwhites. Paperwhites are tiny white flowers with long bright green stems that only come at Christmastime. They were wrapped in brown kraft paper and tied with a red satin ribbon. The note said,

> *I really can't stop thinking about you. It hurts.*
> *Love, Nolan*

I took the little plant up to my room and put it on my windowsill. The white flowers looked like stars. *Was he giving me the stars?* I took out my drawing pad and started sketching the flowers, which stood up proudly in front of the Upper West Side rooftops extending behind them. I became extremely focused—my brain was a microscope. I could feel myself zoom in, scrutinizing the tiny, winding pale gray veins embedded in the silken petals. My pencil recorded photographic replicas of each flower as if I were an architect drafting the plans for a building. It was as if I needed my brain to have an imprint of them so I would be able to go back to them for years and years. And then, maybe from exhaustion or just because of the way my brain works with its ADD, I let go of the intense focus and I drew from another place, a fuzzier place, a place where I am closer to my soul. I let the flowers turn into the stars I wanted them to be. I drew the story of Nolan and me spinning and rolling through the night sky together—dancing in the Milky Way, soaring on a moonbeam.

43

It was astounding to get paperwhites on my front steps—even my mother said, "Now *that* is nice." And it does feel great to believe that a boy really loves you. But I didn't see Nolan that much, so I questioned whether the afternoon in his room, or the flowers, or even my feelings, were real. There was a declaration of love and then no path to follow. What does one do after saying "I love you"?

Nolan did come pick me up from school again. It was getting closer to Christmas; the city was starting to put on its sparkle. The fir trees on the oblong islands that run down the middle of Park Avenue were all lit up. The story goes that years ago, in 1945, a few wealthy families that lived on Park Avenue got money together to wrap the trees that stand on the islands in white lights to honor those who died in World War II. The trees are still lit up every winter. Since my school is on the East Side and I have to cross Park Avenue on most afternoons, those pretty illuminated trees mean the start of the holiday season. You can't imagine how fairy-tale-like it is to stand on a corner and look downtown for blocks and blocks of twinkling trees. Anyway, one afternoon that week when Nolan picked me up after school and we went to get milk shakes at the coffee shop on Madison Avenue where we got french fries that one time, the trees were twinkling.

"I think I am going to take a year off before college," Nolan said, holding my hands across a little table-for-two next to the window.

"Oh yeah?" His hair was in a loose ponytail and he hadn't taken his scarf off. Sometimes he looked like this actor Olivier Martinez, who was in this old movie called *Unfaithful* that my mother inappropriately let me see when I was still a little kid. The movie was scary. It's about a woman who has an affair with this hot guy, played by Martinez, and then her nice husband finds out and gets so jealous and enraged that he sort of accidentally kills the lover with a snow globe! Once Mom realized what I was watching she almost made me turn it off, but it was too late and I begged her and she spent the rest of the movie anxiously explaining everything she thought was too mature for me. Anyway, Nolan looked like that hot, straight-nosed French actor and I was proud to be sitting with him.

"Yeah, if it all comes through, we are going to tour with this band Triumph—they are out of Atlanta and sort of sound like the Black Crowes." We had ordered fries too. He let go of my hand to take a fry and swiped it in ketchup.

"I think I know who they are. Do they sing that song that goes . . ." and then I had to sing, which was mortifying. " 'Dooonnn't stay . . . something, something, back me up, back me up,' something like that?"

"Yes! Oh my lord, you are so cute! Yes! That is their song! How did you hear that?"

"Oliver plays it constantly."

"Oh yeah, I gave him the CD. They are coming to New York

soon, and we are going to open for them at the Palladium, and if it goes how we think it will, it's going to happen, and we'll travel all over America with them starting next year when their album is released."

"That is amazing!" I really thought it was amazing.

"So." He took a sip of his milk shake and looked at me kind of skeptically. "Are you still all gung ho about going to France? To that program?"

"Yeah, I mean, I am so up a creek because I haven't finished my application yet, but yeah." I dipped a fry in the milk shake and ate it.

"It sounds fantastic and you should finish—you will get in. You totally should." I didn't at all think he was going where he ended up going. I nodded, and swallowed.

"But." He took another a sip of milk shake. "What if you didn't go?" I looked at him like he was speaking Icelandic. "I know, but just listen. I was going to go to college, right? But now I'm not going to go, until the next year. I was freaked out about that because, well, it's a good thing to go to college and I totally want to go to college, but the thing is, I don't have to go right away, you know? Like, we don't have to do everything in the exact way we think we are supposed to."

"Uh-huh." He kept going. I was following, but I sort of do try to do everything in the way that you are supposed to, so I felt muddled.

"I'm going to be in New York all summer until November. If you go away, you will go for the fall, right?"

"Yeah, it'd be from September through December."

"*Right.* We will miss each other. I'll be gone when you get back."

"So what are you saying?" Suddenly I felt really stupid in what seemed to be a pretty important conversation, with a huge, foaming chocolate milk shake in front of me.

"I'm saying, isn't there some amazing art program in New York that you could do?"

"And not apply to Saint-Rémy?"

"I guess, yeah, don't apply. I want you to stay here." He was asking me to be with him all the way until the following year. This was not just a flimsy tenth-grade romance, this was *real*. My heart rate went up dramatically.

"I don't know . . . I have wanted to go to Saint-Rémy for so long. It's been a dream of mine for—ever, and, well, I have a plan with Mrs. Rousseau and my parents and everyone."

"I know. This is stupid. I am being totally selfish and crazy, actually. If this is meant to be, you and me, which I think it is . . ." He smiled in his easygoing, confident, friendly way. "It doesn't matter where we are. I'm just saying that sometimes life can change our paths, and that's okay. I think that is part of the deal."

I was speechless.

"Hey, you know what?" he said cheerfully.

"What?"

"I was Googling that Cy Dowd. He seems like a creep."

"Yeah?" I felt my body relax at the change of subject, and I took a long drink of my milk shake like you see people take long drinks of a scotch in a movie. "I think you're right. But what do you mean specifically?"

"I mean, he's definitely a genius and everything, but he's blatantly with a different model every night all over *Page Six* and the blogs. Is Farah still messing around with him?"

"Yeah, I think so, and you know, I'm kind of freaked out by it. *Really* freaked out."

"You should be. It's sick that he is taking advantage of her." *Right!* I thought. He was taking *advantage* of her in his creepy, genius art loft with his tiny pig running around, and she was clueless about it. Nolan's assessment made me crazy in love with him. His protective instinct reminded me of my father.

"I want to tell my *dad*." I pointed at him with another french fry.

"Oh, I don't think you should do that."

"No?"

"No, no. Just wait. If you involve parents, it could get out of hand. What he is doing is illegal."

"But Dad will help her, and if it's illegal—which I know it is, by the way—then it should be stopped." I pictured telling Dad at the kitchen island. I pictured his face turning red and him rushing to the closet to get his Barbour coat to go find Cy Dowd. "Or he will challenge him to a duel and kill him."

"That's hilarious. Your dad would totally wield a sword instead of beating the daylights out of the guy. He's so civilized."

"Maybe he would call the police!" I was getting excited.

"Maybe." He thought for a moment. "But perhaps, instead of totally ruining the life of a mack-daddy artist, we should talk to Farah and get her to stop. No harm, no foul," Nolan said earnestly.

"I don't think she would listen to me," I said, and sucked more sweet comforting milk shake into my mouth.

"She would listen to all of us."

All of us. I loved that Nolan felt like he was included in "all of us." Like he was a Turtle, or the boyfriend of a Turtle.

"I wonder if there *are* any good after-school art programs in

New York?" he said, looking at me with a half smile. "I mean, I don't know, but I wonder." He put his hand up between us in the air, with his elbow still on the table. I put my hand up on his, like we were seeing whose fingers were longer. I thought to myself that if I didn't have to apply to Saint-Rémy, if I didn't have to draw that self-portrait, I would feel the weight of a thousand stones tumble off my shoulders.

"You have big hands for a girl." I clenched my hand into a tight fist of embarrassment. Like one of those sea creatures that are all open and flowing, but then something scares them and they retract into a little ball.

"No, stop!" He pried open my fingers and pressed them back onto each of his fingers.

"That is terrible, I don't want to have big hands!" I was laughing, but dying the curse-of-the-tall-girl death inside.

"No, nooo, it's badass. It's strong." I could feel the heat in my face as I eased up on my hand, letting our fingers touch lightly and then collapse and intertwine and be together.

44

"Oh my god. You look so pretty right now," Reagan said, looking up from her math homework on my bed. It was the Wednesday before the December 15 deadline and I was attempting to draw myself. Reagan said she would keep me company and finish a bunch of corrected math assignments she had piled up. (In Math C, which Reagan and I both take, our teachers make us take the problems we get wrong home to "rework." It's such a pain in the butt to do homework not once, but twice. *However,* "We learn from our mistakes," Mrs. Hotchkiss loves to remind us.)

"Eww, no I don't—I'm totally Wilma Flintstone. I have charcoal everywhere."

"No, you have that I-don't-know-I-look-pretty-but-I-do thing going on. You look pretty when you draw."

"That's whack," I said, and went back to fixing the curve of my ear on the smudgy paper.

"You do," she said. "I remember thinking it in sixth grade when we had art together. You concentrate when you draw in a way that makes you look like you're thirty."

"What's pretty about being thirty?" I looked up at Reagan. From where I was sitting on the floor, and how she was sitting on the bed, I could only see half of her face, and her crossed legs.

"Because when we're thirty, we'll be in the groove of our lives and it'll be badass. When you draw, you can tell that it's what *you* are supposed to do," she said, and sat up. "Like, you can see your badass-who-you-are-going-to-be self on your face. It's more than pretty . . . see, you have that look on right now. I'm going to take a picture of you and post it on Quickypic." She swiped on her phone, typed in the password, and then put it in front of her face to take the picture. "And then Nolan will see it and he will so fall even more in love with you."

Click.

"Nolan follows you on Quickypic?"

"Yeah." I felt a little jealous ripple in the back of my throat. "He follows me too. But I only post my drawings," I said.

"I'll hashtag it #wrendraws," she said while typing with both thumbs.

"Can I see it?" She handed her phone over. My hair was piled on top of my head, and there was even a smudge of charcoal on my forehead, but I have to say I liked the picture. I wasn't smiling or anything, but it looked like a me that I would want Nolan to see.

"That is so Cyrano of you," I said, handing her back the phone.

"Who's Cyrano?" Reagan said and took a nonsmiling selfie. Click.

"Cyrano was a smart poet guy who loved this woman, Roxanne, but he had a big nose so he didn't think she would love him. And this other guy, I forget his name, loved Roxanne too, but he was a dumbass, good-looking, but not a poet. So, for some reason, Cyrano said he would write really beautiful, smart love letters for the dumb guy, so Roxanne would fall in love with him. And she did. I don't think she ever found out that Cyrano was the one writing the letters. But I do think she died."

"But I don't love Nolan," Reagan said.

"Right, but you are helping me by sending him a picture of me drawing and looking pretty, so you are kind of doing a selfless thing in the name of someone else's love," I said.

"Well, I don't have a big nose," she said and took another selfie, this time giving the camera a wink.

"No, you do not." She showed me her selfie. Reagan had *Mad Men* looks. Her thick black Welsh, mojo hair naturally tumbled around her shoulders and fell on her soft black angora sweater. All the black made her skin white as half and half cream. She could really bring it in a picture.

"Want to take one together?" I asked.

And we did.

45

I guess it's global warming, but that December, instead of snow, the city was enveloped in fog. The weather warmed, you didn't need your parka, and Manhattan had a bank of mist rolling across it all month. It was supremely cozy. You kind of felt like you lived in Scotland, and each morning when you woke up you could hardly make out the branches on the trees. This fog fed Nolan's and my knights-of-the-round-table plans to kidnap the fair Farah away from the dubious, older, mysterious Cy Dowd.

As much as we wanted to meet and scheme in a tree house or somewhere (we, meaning Nolan, Oliver, Padmavati, Charlie, Reagan, and myself), we lived in the city and couldn't see each other all that much. We didn't live in the suburbs with basements and garages, where I imagine kids in the suburbs gather. In any case, this plan took shape on our phones in text messages. Facebook ended up playing a key role too, but I was a little out of it there because my parents had ironclad restrictions on my computer for all social media. Reagan and Nolan, however, had free rein in their houses, so they could spy on Farah, who, like a dingbat, posted every move she made or was going to make, even parties and gallery openings that were obviously all about Cy. And as it turned out, even though Cy Dowd was ancient, he was as deft at social media as us teenagers and his Facebook page was a road map.

GROUP MESSAGE

Charlie: Farah is in trouble. I read on Gawker Cy Dowd was married.

Me: I think he was married. Dad said divorced.

Reagan: U told ur dad?

Me: No way. I asked in a totally nonobvious way.

Nolan: Mr. Noorlander would never suspect someone his daughter's age would be with that guy.

Vati: Farah said she thinks she has crabs.

Me: What????

Charlie: That is disgusting.

Nolan: Doesn't surprise me. The guy gets around.

Oliver: Don't talk about that shit. Farah is like my sister.

Me: She's like *my* sister.

Oliver: I'm going to throw up.

Reagan: She didn't come to a sleepover at my house but told her mother she was here.

Me: Why isn't she talking to me?

Vati: She thinks you are judging her. :(

Me: Aren't we all worried?

Vati: Worried is different than judgmental.

Nolan: She might be freaked because Cy is in the same circles as Wren's parents.

Reagan: He is having a "Not So Silent Night" party right before Xmas. Saw on FB.

Me: U r his "friend"?

Reagan: He is everyone's friend. Has like 60k friends.

Nolan: Anyone know if she is going?

Charlie: Of course she'll go. She's a super freak about him.

Nolan: Just found the party on his FB page. I think we are all going to this. It's on the 19th. Friday night.

Me: Last day of finals. My parents will let me go out that nite I'm almost sure.

Oliver: I'll say I'm taking you and Vats to a party. I'm golden now that I got in to MIT early.

Vati: ☺☺☺☺

Reagan: Cambridge is f-ing cold.

Nolan: I have a gig that night but it's early. I will meet up with you guys.

Reagan: I'm in.

Charlie: I'm in.

Me: We'll go get her.

Nolan: Intervention style. Peace out. W—call you later.

Vati: Awwww

46

The last episode of the season that Dinah shoots is the New Year's episode. This year she decided to ask the network if she could do something different and have five of her school friends in the episode. In some version of *The View* format, the girls would sit around the kitchen table, eat hoppin' John, a black-eyed pea dish that Dinah wanted to make for the show, and tell their resolutions. (Apparently it's like a three-hundred-year-old tradition to eat black-eyed peas in the South on New Year's Day—it brings you good luck.) Dinah said it would connect her with her audience if they saw she actually had friends, and I think she saw a similar year-end episode on *Barefoot Contessa*, where Ina Garten had a bunch of her friends over. Dinah is so ambitious, I am telling you.

So anyway, Mom wanted me around to help with the girls. In real life, none of the ten-year-olds were allowed to wear anything but ChapStick yet so the TV hair/makeup part was insanity. The girls went crazy trying on fifty different colors of lip gloss and having their hair blown out with a hair dryer the size of their arms. It was like *Alvin and the Chipmunks* meets *Little Women*.

Once they were lit and sitting around the table eating and talking, Mom and I sat on the stairs in the shadows and watched.

"My New Year's resolution is to remember to feed and change the water of my lovebird, Pinky. I always forget and my mom yells at me," Susan Meyers said. All of these girls were in Dinah's class at Hatcher. I recognized some of them from school assemblies. Dinah doesn't have a lot of playdates because of her show. It's kind of sad, but I guess it's a trade-off for fame and fortune.

"Cut! Camera reload!" yelled the director. Dinah and the rest of the girls used the break to say what a good job Susan had done.

"What is *your* New Year's resolution this year, Wrenny?" Mom was still in her pottery clothes. She wears bandannas on her head so her hair doesn't fall into her students' work when she bends over to help them make pots on the wheel. That day she was wearing a light blue bandanna with little yellow rosebuds on it. She smelled like clay.

"I don't know, what's yours?"

"What do you mean you don't know? I don't like that answer." I'm sure I sighed. *I don't know* is never a good answer for my mother.

"Um, well, I always can be better at putting my stuff in my backpack before bed."

"Yeah, that would be good . . . nothing else? I don't know, something more meaningful? Oh wait, they are starting. Shh."

"*Aannnnnd* action," said Jeff, the director, from "the village," which is where the video monitor stands so the director and the key people can watch and see that everything looks okay while they shoot. This time it was Max Burns's time to share. (Max is a girl.)

"I resolve"—they were told that they couldn't all say "My New

Year's resolution will be . . .": they each had to come up with something more interesting—"to write to my pen pal in Honduras. It's fascinating to learn about a different culture, but if I don't write, I'll never learn."

"Cut. Let's try that one again. Dinah, maybe you could be passing the hoppin' John during this take," Jeff said.

"Okay, Jeff. Got it," Dinah said, like a seasoned pro. The other girls sat up a little straighter and nodded like they were in the loop too. I thought it was good if they were impressed with her.

"Thanks, Dinah. Give us one second and we'll start from the top with Max."

"You know," my mother continued (I was hoping she might have forgotten her train of thought). "Is there anything you are aspiring to this year?" she whispered while keeping her eyes on what was going on in the shot.

"Well . . ." I felt a surge of blood rush to my face and knew I was about to say something I hadn't fully thought through. "I was thinking instead of going to France next year . . ." She turned her head to me and looked like the word "instead" was vinegar in her mouth, but I continued. "I was thinking I would stay in New York and maybe take classes at the Art Students League?" Then she looked at me like I had slapped her.

"What?" She spasmed. Her neck jutted out at me like she was a lizard about to attack. "What are you talking about?" she hissed.

"I, just, I mean, France is far . . . and maybe I don't want to go so far away?"

"When," she said too loudly, quickly calmed herself, and went

back to a whisper as there were fifteen people in our kitchen. "When did you start to think about *that*? You have been dreaming and wanting Saint-Rémy for *so long*, Wren."

"I know, I know, but maybe, I'm changing my mind."

"Oh, Wren, you're breaking my heart."

"What?"

"Yes, yes you are. I don't understand why you would out of nowhere change your mind. Is it because you think you will fail math?"

"No, no that's not it."

"Jesus, this is going to kill your father," she said quietly, while pinching the rim of her nose with her pointer finger and thumb.

"I didn't say it was for sure, I just . . ."

"Have you not finished your portrait?" She looked straight at me again.

"*Annnnddd* action," the director called.

"I resolve to write my book buddy," Max Burns said.

"*Cut!* Book buddy?" Jeff almost yelled.

"Sorry, sorry, I'm so sorry. I meant pen pal, sorry!" Poor Max.

"*Reset!*" Jeff was going bonkers. It's like Dinah was the only kid he had ever met. And Dinah really isn't a kid.

"Mom, I've tried so hard, but I haven't finished my self-portrait," I admitted.

"Oh god." She put her bandanna-covered head in her hands.

"But that isn't why I don't want to go, or why I am changing my mind." She looked up at me like, *Well, what is then?*

"I don't want to leave New York."

She put her head back down. "Come up to my room."

★ ★ ★

My parents' neutrally toned, quiet, mohair and plumped-pillowed room usually felt like a sanctuary, but at that moment it made me think of a padded cell.

"Now, what in the hell are you talking about, Wren?" My mother went to her dressing table, sat on the stool, crossed her legs, and whipped her kerchief off like it was a stupid hat she suddenly was embarrassed to be wearing.

"Mom, calm down."

"DON'T tell me to calm down. God *almighty*, I hate it when children tell me to calm down."

"It's not that big a deal," I lied.

"Goddamn it!" she slapped her knee. "It *is* a big deal. God, how I hate it when kids say it's no big deal."

"It's not like I'm failing out of school, or I'm freaking doing drugs!"

"No, no, it isn't, Wren—and there is absolutely no reason to attempt to distract me from the matter at hand by reminding me you don't do drugs—that's a cheap tactic. Here is why it's a big deal." She spread her legs open and put one hand on each knee.

"It's a big deal because *France* is your dream, Wren. You have been focused on going to *France* since Mrs. Rousseau suggested it was something for you to aim for two years ago."

"I know," I said.

She pulled her phone out of her back pocket and zoomed her way to the calendar. "It's—my god, Wren—it's due on the *fifteenth*. It's the tenth!" She clicked off her phone. "It's the tenth," she repeated sadly.

"Nolan said . . ." Mom sat straight up and let the hand with her phone in it drop.

"Nolan? *Nolan* has something to do with this?" She stood up with her hands gripping into the sides of her hair and started walking back and forth across the plush woolen wall-to-wall carpeting.

"No, totally not. It's my idea," I lied.

"That makes no sense. Why did you say Nolan?"

"Because he is supportive of me."

"And he *supports* this terrible idea of yours that you STOP TRYING?"

"*I AM TRYING!*" That was louder than I meant it to be but she started it.

"Do you know what I think?" she said, zeroing in on me.

"No." I took one step back.

"I think that this *is* Nolan's idea," she said, while pointing at me.

"It isn't."

She looked at me the same way she used to look at me when I said I had brushed my teeth and hadn't, but this time she couldn't smell my breath.

"*It isn't,*" I insisted. "I just don't want to go anymore."

"Well, that makes me want to cry." She did look like she was going to cry.

"Well, I'm sorry." I felt panicky, like the walls were going to collapse on us. She stood in the middle of the room and looked at her bedside table. On it is a picture of Oliver, Dinah, and me taken from behind so you just see our backs. We are walking on one of the paths in Central Park. I couldn't help but think she was wishing it was that day in the park, when we had a picnic of deli sandwiches on the Great Lawn, and that it wasn't five years later, dealing with me, her failure daughter.

"I'm going downstairs to see Dinah. I can't think of what to say to you." She steadily walked by me with a steely look on her face. "But I'm sure your father will come up with something."

47

I did not go back down to the New Year's Eve taping. For the rest of that day I resolved to lie low. I was dying to commiserate with Oliver, but he wasn't home, so I texted with Nolan.

> **Me:** Hi :-)
> **Nolan:** Just found out Dad will be in Florida for Xmas dealing with Elaine's dead mom's house.
> **Me:** Aren't you going to Pittsburgh for Xmas???
> **Nolan:** Thought so.
> **Me:** I don't get it.
> **Nolan:** If I want to see Dad I Have to go to Fla. Not happening.
> **Me:** Bummed?
> **Nolan:** Yes.

Then my phone rang.

"Yeah, I'm totally freaking bummed. I can't believe he has to deal so much with *Elaine's shit*. Can't she go by herself?" He sounded mad.

"You would think. Did you tell him you were upset?"

"If he can't figure out I would be upset, then they should freaking take back his PhD."

"I'm sorry, Nolan."

"It's okay, it's just, I don't know. Why would I want to go to Florida and stay in some old, deceased woman's house?"

"Wasn't she your step-grandmother?"

"Yes. I'm an asshole, I know, I just really wanted to go to my home in Pittsburgh and see Emme and just hang out."

"I get it."

"You do, how?" He sounded cold.

"Maybe I don't get it," I said quietly.

"I'm sorry, I'm just upset and I don't know what to do."

"Where are you?"

"Rehearsal, where are you?"

"Home, in my room. I'm studying. I just told my mother that I might not apply to Saint-Rémy."

"Whoa—wait—you are thinking about that?" His voice melted.

"Yeah."

"Wow, Wren, that is, god, that is amazing."

"Well, my mother was rip-shit and I don't think it's going to go over well at all with my father."

"No, of course not. They want you to go, and there is a huge case for you to go, but . . ." He was quiet.

"Nolan?"

"I hope there is a case for you to stay. I mean, I really don't want you to go . . ."

I got up from my desk and went to my window seat. I looked into the sky to see if there were any stars—it gets dark so early in

December. I saw an airplane that looked like a moving star, took a shaky breath in, and closed my eyes as if I was going to wish on it.

"I don't want to go either."

Later that evening, my father said quite clearly that I would be making a detrimental, gigantic mistake if I didn't apply. But he said he couldn't make me do it, that ultimately it was my decision. I didn't finish my self-portrait, and I didn't make the deadline for Saint-Rémy. I had completed all the other required drawings, I had my portfolio in a JPEG, I had my recommendation from Mrs. Rousseau, and by a miracle (and I think because of that time I was grounded) I ended up getting a B average that semester, which is what you need to apply. The December 15 deadline eased on by like the mist outside my windows. Nolan had changed my mind about doing something I'd wanted to do with all my heart. That is the thing about love—for better or worse, it changes you. I *know* that is something no parent wants to hear. There is not a parent out there who can tolerate hearing their kid say, "Even though I got into the University of Success and Happiness, I'm going to defer and not go because of Mark/Madeline/David/Debbie/Troy/Una/Frank. I'm in love." I think more people than you can imagine have changed the course of their lives because they were grabbed by love and thrown in another direction. And as not-strong as this sounds, I don't think you have much control over it.

There is one part of the conversation-I-had-with-my-father-whom I-chose-to-defy that has stuck with me to this day. We were in the living room. He was sitting by the fireplace with no fire lit. There was no need for it because of the warmer weather and all that fog.

He was sitting in his chair in his work clothes—a dark suit and a silk tie from the Met Museum gift shop. Usually he takes his work clothes off and gets into his "at homes," but not that night. He had a dictionary-size report of some kind on his lap—work. It looked hard and boring. In fact, he told me it was hard and boring, which was weird because he never complains. I was standing in the room, but close enough to the door that I had a clear path out of there. Mom had prepped Dad, and instead of looking mad, he looked exhausted and irritated. The part that got me was he didn't even mention Nolan. It was like Nolan was beside the point. I couldn't understand why the central thing on my mind was the furthest thing from his.

"Wren, I would never in a million years expect this from you."

"I'm not making some *gargantuan* change, Dad. I just don't want to leave New York right in the middle of *everything*." I could tell he was wondering what exactly "everything" meant.

"I'm sure it doesn't seem like you are changing anything in the big picture, my darling. I bet you think that you are honoring something as creative and important as the dreams you have for yourself, but you are simply too young to know that kind of thing with certainty and I am here to tell you that you are wrong." He was carefully choosing the right words. "To compromise *who you are* and where you are going because of *emotion* is bullshit."

"Dad! No, you don't get it. I *am* feeling emotion and having feelings, big feelings, and it's not bullshit. It's real. I'm not so young." He stared me down, and that made me feel pretty young, especially since he was wearing his suit.

"No, you are right, you are not so young. You are old enough that I can't *make* you send in that application. But I wish I could. I would do anything to draw that self-portrait for you and get it in on time. But I can't."

"I know." My head was down.

"You would get accepted, Wren. You are that talented."

"My talent isn't going to go away."

And then he lifted his eyebrows and said, as if he were speaking to a fool, "Let's hope not."

48

I can hear my mother yelling to no one in particular, while decorating the Christmas tree or getting a notification in one of our backpacks about yet another holiday concert at Hatcher or at St. Tim's, "December is the most *insane* month!" I never got what she was talking about because for a long time, December, for me, was angel-shaped sugar cookies and cocoa by the fire, and personally, I always loved the Hatcher holiday assembly. But that year December lost some of its charm.

The very next night after my heart-to-heart with Dad, my parents' book club met at our house—the book group where it all started. Needless to say I was persona non grata around the house. I think the sight of me was making my mother's blood boil, because even on a school night (when I thought I would be relegated to my room to eat gravel and toothpaste for supper) she asked Oliver to take me to Big Tony's, the best pizza place in New York, so we wouldn't bother them. (Dinah was asked to make finger food for the book club, so she was in the kitchen mashing avocados for guacamole.) Being in a house with not only my own but a multitude of Turtle parents magnified the feeling that I was a rogue-bandit bad girl, even if none of the Turtle parents knew yet that I had blown my future. We left at six-thirty, missing Farah, Vati, Reagan, and Charlie's parents by a solid half hour. We chose Broadway for the walk downtown.

"I guess I'm just surprised," Oliver said. He was wearing a maroon Hatcher skullcap Vati had given him as an early Christmas present. His blond dreads were sticking out the bottom.

"Well, what I don't get is *what* is the real difference between going to the Art Students League here—where many, many people from around the world come to study—and going to France? I mean, really?" I asked defensively.

"That's BS and you know it," Oliver said as we trudged past a Korean deli selling fir trees and wreaths. "I like Nolan a lot. He's not like guys at St. Tim's . . . I think he's smarter than most people I know." I smiled at him and pushed my hair out of my face, wishing I had a hat on. "Do you know he's read *The Brothers Karamazov* like three times? He always has a paperback copy of it with him in his guitar case."

"That's a difficult book, right? Dostoevsky?" I said now, beaming at him. Knowing Nolan read and re-read any book, much less important Russian literature, made my deep insides tingle and reinforced my conviction that I had made the right decision, to stay in New York.

"*Yeah*, it's a difficult book." He paused while we waited for the light. "It's political and complex, all about social injustice and is-there-a-god, and good and evil. It's the real deal, man." He walked ahead and I followed him like a peppy miniature poodle.

"Have you read it?" I asked.

"No. But I know it's intense and I am going to read it."

"Yeah, see! Nolan is amazing," I oozed.

"My point is, Wren, that is *his* thing. *He's* smart and a great musician and he's on a serious path to something and I'm sure he will be really successful. But he's on his own path."

I wanted to interrupt him and say I was on Nolan's path too. That was why he asked me to stay. We were on a path together.

"But—" I said. I was now sashaying beside Oliver instead of walking.

"No, let me finish," Oliver interrupted. I stopped leaping and calmed down because he almost sounded annoyed.

"*Your* thing is art, Wren. That is what you are really good at. You love drawing. Do you know you draw without even knowing you're drawing?"

"What do you mean?"

"You are always picking up some pencil and drawing on something. All of our school directories in the kitchen have your sketches all over them. You draw in the sand on a beach. When you were little you drew in the bubbles in your bath. It's like you can't help it." I walked quietly now, listening.

"Did Nolan really ask you not to go? Mom thinks he did. And I can't believe that, because of all people, I would think Nolan, if he liked you or loved you or whatever, would want you to follow your dreams just like he does. Not keep you here. Not make you miss something special."

"Do you think Vati is special?" I said, walking with my hands way down in my parka pockets.

"Yes," he said, looking ahead at where his feet were going.

"Would you want her to go away?"

"No, but she's not. And I think even if she did, she would come back and we could do what we do then. And anyway, I'm going to MIT next year, so, what will be will be."

"Nobody is understanding me," I said. We were at Big Tony's. There are tables outside even in the dead of winter with green awnings over them. All over the storefront there are a bunch of signs saying BEST BURGER IN TOWN! SUMO PIZZA! ITALIAN HEROES! I pulled the door open and led Oliver inside where it smelled of hot cheese, sauce, and baking bread.

"Are *you* understanding you?" he asked, pulling off the skullcap and shaking out his dreads.

49

Even with talks from Mom, Dad, and Oliver, I bizarrely didn't get punished for not submitting my application. In fact, the subject was ignored. It almost felt like *I* was being ignored altogether even though I had exams and it was Christmastime, and my parents never ignore me. Life went on, except I had a dark-purplish swirling black hole of anxiety in my stomach. I couldn't tell if it was because I hadn't turned in the application or if it was just a loving-Nolan feeling. Love can make you feel sick just as easily as it can make you feel blissed out. I wasn't even seeing Nolan that much, but that didn't seem to matter. It's like how some girls are in love with guys from boy bands they never have laid real eyes on. I once saw Padmavati cry because of how much she loved some dude from One Direction. Not seeing Nolan in no way kept me from daydreaming obsessively about his teeth, or replaying how he held my hand in the coffee shop, or thinking about how he called me when he was upset about not seeing his dad for Christmas. Sometimes it felt like I loved him by myself. But if he didn't love me back, why would *I* be the one that he called when he was sad? Why would he have sex with me that one time? He must have loved me. I really think he did love me—that's what he said, that's what it felt like. Sometimes.

The day before we were all going to do an intervention on Farah, Charlie came over out of the blue. It was a late Thursday afternoon, December 18. I was leaving my house to walk May and he was walking up the street.

"Hey! What are you doing here?" I asked, and held up the arm not holding May for a hug. He was wearing his rather bright green parka with a furry trim on the hood.

"Hey." He hugged me back. "Nosh is catering a holiday party on Eighty-Fourth." He hiked his thumb backward indicating farther west down the block. "And I was done with my homework, so I thought I'd see if you were home."

"Cool! Want to walk May with me? I haven't seen you much."

"Yup."

"Why are you doing your homework at a Nosh party?"

"My mom is at some other holiday thing and I didn't want to be home alone so my dad said I could come and sit in these people's kitchen."

"Was the food good?"

"Of course. Latkes."

"Oh yeah, it's Hanukkah."

"Yup."

We walked up to Columbus. "Wanna keep going up to Central Park West?" I said.

"Yeah, why not."

"You seem bummed. Oh, good girl, Mayzer." May stopped to do her thing, so we waited and I got the bag ready.

"I *am* bummed!" He sort of exploded there.

"Whoa, why?"

"Well, what is going on? You and Vati don't even call me any-more. It's like you've been captured by aliens."

"Well, Vati has been captured by an alien—Oli."

"It all sucks. Farah is acting like Miley Cyrus."

"I know, she looks exhausted at school."

"She goes to school from his loft!"

"How do you know that?"

"I think she is scared to tell you, or any of the girls, so she tells me."

"When has Farah ever been scared to tell me anything?"

"Since she started *having relations* with your dad's friend."

"Oh, yuck." I wasn't talking about dog poop.

"Tell me about it. She made me buy rubbers."

Charlie held May while I ran back to the corner, threw the crap in the garbage can, and ran back.

"She made *you* do it?"

"Yeah, I guess Mr. Dowd doesn't have the decency."

"That's awful. Having a rubber is rule number one."

"Please, I know." I didn't think Charlie had come close to having sex, but I let that go, because he was all upset.

"I didn't send in my application to Saint-Rémy," I said, and braced myself.

"They give extensions?"

"No, I just didn't send it in because . . ." He looked up at me like a horrified Eskimo in his green parka.

"Why?"

"I didn't send it in because of Nolan," I blurted out.

Charlie thrust his hands in his pockets and walked with his head down.

273

"Why does this bum *you* out, Charlie? Now we can all hang out next year and, well, aren't you happy?"

"Not really, Wren. I think you're being stupid."

"*Stupid?* You know I hate that, Charlie! I hate being called stupid. I am *not* stupid!" Even May looked shocked he'd called me stupid. "That is a *terrible* thing to say to someone, especially someone like me who thinks she's stupid."

"Sorry." He looked a little panicked.

"You know who doesn't think I'm stupid, Charlie? Nolan. Nolan thinks I have a cool mind. Nolan thinks I say funny things and he looks at me like I invented something awesome like, like, crunchy French toast or something."

"What? That makes no sense." He didn't look like he felt so bad anymore.

"Whatever. He looks at me like I'm the only girl in New York."

"But you're not."

"What? I know that, Charlie," I snapped. "But he makes me *feel* like I am the only girl in New York." He pushed his hood back and started spiking up his hair in an anxious way like a parrot.

"I'm sorry I yelled at you," I said, hoping we could start that bad conversation over again.

"How do you know he doesn't make other girls feel like that?"

I paused, as it had never occurred to me one way or the other. I had just thrown that "only girl in New York" thing out there.

"Have you ever—no you haven't, you haven't been to one of his shows, which is so strange, but I have, and let me tell you, all the girls in the room feel like they are the only girl in New York when he plays. That's just how he is with everyone. I feel like *I'm* the only girl in New York when he talks to me."

274

"No, you don't. And that's a thing, that's like a rock thing." I gave May a scratch behind the ears because she was being such a good girl waiting for us while we stood arguing. "I *will* go to a show . . . I haven't been able to because I was grounded and sometimes they are too late and my parents would never let me go, but I will. I will go to a show."

"Reagan goes to his shows," he said.

I started walking. "What? What do you mean? She went to one."

"No, she goes to all of them." He walked quickly to catch up with me.

"How do you know?"

"My guitar teacher goes to all his shows and he sees her there. I introduced them once."

We were walking pretty fast now and I was yanking poor May when she wanted to sniff the tree guardrails.

"Well, so?" I was starting to feel a cold sweat come on.

"So, nothing. But did you know that?"

"No."

He lifted his eyebrows in a that's-weird way, and then he said, "Did you really not apply or are you just thinking about not applying?"

"I really didn't apply. I didn't send it in."

"That's screwed up."

"You're screwed up, Charlie!"

"No, I'm not, Wrenny. When you get freaked out or hurt, you blame other people. Remember when you fell down the stairs at your house and I went to help you out and you threw Dinah's boot at me?" I did remember that.

"You probably made a mistake—a big mistake—and now you

are saying that I'm screwed up. But I'm *not*! My *acceptance* letter from the Bard bird program is in my special box under my desk, Wren, so I'm not screwed up at *all*."

"Well, I have a boyfriend who wants me to stay."

"Okay. There is nothing I can do about that."

"Okay." We stopped walking and stood there for a minute or two in silence.

"Charlie?" I said, wanting to be in a better place.

"Yeah."

I waited for a second to see if I could use any of my tools to not be impulsive and to not ask a risky question, but I couldn't stop myself, because as intrusive as it might have been it also felt right to ask.

"Why do you go to so many Nosh events? Are they really so interesting to you?"

"Um, why are you asking me this now?" he said, like I'd started to talk about global warming or something.

"Because I'm thinking a lot about love, and sometimes I wonder why you don't ever have crushes on anyone."

"I do have crushes on people," he said simply.

"Are they all those cute Nosh waiters?"

Charlie looked at the lit-up windows of the buildings on Central Park West and squinted as if he were trying to see the people inside. "Yeah," he said, still looking up. I took his hand with my hand not holding May's leash.

"Does that mean, well . . ." I don't know why, but it felt natural to ask him. Like we had had the conversation before. "Do you think you're gay?"

"Maybe," he said calmly. "I think so." He was still looking at the windows of the building across the street. His hair was sticking up, but he looked handsome. He looked grownup.

"Why wouldn't you tell me?" I said.

"I don't know, I guess I thought, of all people, you would know." He looked at me and kind of shrugged his shoulders.

"Well, I did," I said.

He squeezed my hand and I squeezed his back. We turned around and looked straight ahead into the park. The trees were black against the dark gray sky. The night sky in New York never gets truly black because of all the lights in the city. But that night, even the New York sky looked as close as it comes to total darkness, so we kept holding hands.

50

"Ridiculous! What are you speaking to me about?" Mrs. Rousseau had been out with acute bronchitis the entire week before my deadline, so I didn't have to face her wrath until my application deadline had passed.

Mrs. Rousseau has a desk in the corner of the art studio behind some palm trees and easels. It looks like you might imagine—lots of different-colored folders, Buddhas, piles of *The New York Times*, a fancy ebony pen with a gold-plated clip, Sharpies, rubber bands, a box of Kleenex, and a computer.

"I think I am going to look for another art program in New York for next year," I said, and held my breath.

She put her hand to her chest like she was having a heart attack.

"You didn't complete or hand in your application." She blinked hard four or five times. "I think I might faint, Wren."

I didn't think she was kidding.

"I'm sorry, I thought about this a lot." *Had I?* I wondered. Was I impulsive? Had I been thoughtless?

"When you say 'a lot,' how does that amount of time compare with the amount of time we have been thinking and preparing for you to apply to Saint-Rémy?"

"Well, it doesn't. But I did think about it."

She looked crestfallen. "And you think there might be something in New York?"

"Maybe?"

"There is not."

"How do you know?" I did *not* mean to sound like I was giving her lip there, but I think she thought I was.

"Because I know with full certainty that there isn't." She looked down at a paper on her desk like she was done with me, and then she changed her mind and wasn't done with me.

"I am so *disappointed*, Wren." And then she literally howled. I knew not to speak, but I did peer through the leaves of the palm to see if the girls who were in the studio finishing up their projects noticed that Mrs. Rousseau was freaking out. They did, but they looked down as soon as our eyes met. "I am so *distraught*." She threw her hands in the air and set them down on her desk as if she might get up. "And confused." She waited to collect herself. "Do you know I went to study at that *very* program, oh, forty-some years ago?"

"No—you never told me that," I said, and picked up her nice pen to fiddle the anxiety out of my body.

"I did. I did and I loved it. I learned everything I know about light in that school, and not because someone *told* me about it, no. Because I could see it and feel it and study it, *because I was there*! The light *moves* differently there. It is unexpected, it tricks you, there is an ethereal quality to it, and it mesmerizes you. It's challenging. It will teach you and you won't find it in your bedroom at home or in the *goddamned* studio at the Art Students League!" Her voice had lowered to a shame-inducing whisper.

"I'm sorry." I *was* sorry.

"Don't say you're sorry unless you are, Wren. You have *everything* at your fingertips and you chose to turn your back on it, for what? Fear? Laziness? I don't comprehend it."

"I am *not turning my back on art! Gosh.*" Tears came to my eyes.

"What happened, Wren?"

"I just want to stay here. I want to make art here. I want to make art in New York." She looked at me funny, like she knew I wasn't telling her the truth, and I wasn't. I wanted to stay because Nolan had asked me to. It had nothing to do with art at all.

51

That afternoon when I got home from school, I felt like I was getting a rash from shame about Saint-Rémy. I was also getting texts from Nolan saying he couldn't wait to see me at Cy's party. My confusion felt tangible, like a Rubik's Cube I couldn't solve. I bet Romeo and Juliet felt like they were doing the wrong thing too when they ran away into the woods to get married by the friar, but they did it. Okay, they died in the end, and it's a fictional story, but the point is, they still left the safety of what they knew and charged into the woods—for love.

The other thing that was bugging me like crazy was Reagan. Was Charlie right? Was she going to Nolan's shows and not telling me? But maybe that's not such a big deal? I was looking at my phone every two seconds, and just as I was planning on texting Vati to see what she thought about it, my phone rang. The picture of me and Reagan we had taken in my room that day when she said I looked pretty filled up the screen and suddenly she was on the phone.

"Hi!" she said, her voice friendly, friendly, friendly.

"Hi," I said warily. I went and sat on the top of the stairs on my floor. It was getting dark out already even though it was only four o'clock.

"Oh my god, I have been wanting to talk to you desperately," she said. "Nolan told me the *whole plan* for tonight."

"Wait—what do you mean?" I said, reaching up and peeling off some blue tape that was holding one of my owl drawings onto the wall.

"I mean the other night when I saw him at his gig, we talked about ambushing Farah."

"Do you go to all his gigs?" I said, trying to restick the blue tape on the wall because the drawing was starting to fall down.

"Yeah," she said point-blank.

"Oh," I said. The drawing fell.

"What? That's weird?"

"Well, I'm never allowed to go out that late, so I don't even think to ask my parents. And you didn't even tell me you were going, so that is a little weird, right?" Even though I think I'm nonconfrontational, impulsivity sometimes feels confrontational. Having ADD can feel like having a truth serum constantly coursing through your veins.

"Oh, you know, my mom doesn't care what I do," she said in a nondefensive tone. "And I am *so* into the bass player of Shoppe Boys—this guy Aaron. Did Vati tell you?"

"No," I said, now looking at the owl I must have drawn two years before and thinking it needed improvements.

"Didn't Nolan tell you?" she asked.

"No, nobody told me that you are into the bass player. *Charlie* said you are always there at the gigs, and honestly it made me feel weird because, well, it's weird that you see Nolan more than I do." I stood up holding the drawing, went into my room, and got a purple colored pencil. I sat on the floor and started working on the shape of the owl's eyes.

"What is weird is Charlie telling you anything, because he's never there."

"His guitar teacher sees you," I said and stopped coloring.

"Well, I don't even see Nolan, not really, he's playing and singing and doing his whole band thing." *Gosh,* I thought, *I don't really know what that is.*

"I don't even talk to *Aaron*, I just *watch* him!" I had seen pictures of Aaron on the Shoppe Boys website. He looked like Jaden Smith.

"Well, I'm going to go to a gig during break," I said, putting the phone on speaker and setting it next to the drawing.

"Yeah totally, we'll go together! My mom's not taking me anywhere this Christmas." Her voice echoed out of the tiny phone speaker.

"Okay," I said, feeling a little better about Reagan, and about the owl.

"Word," she said, and sounded like she was going to get off, but she didn't.

"So, have you and Nolan slept together again?"

I looked down at the phone. The selfie of us was still lit up. "Oh, no—we haven't," I said, taking the phone off speaker and putting to my ear.

"Really?"

I had an overwhelming urge to throw my phone out the window. "No," I said. "But I don't know, isn't that something you do like once a month?"

"Once a month? Did you just say once a month?" I swear I heard her laugh. Then she said, "I don't think you put a number on it—usually it just happens naturally—but more than once a month, I'm pretty sure."

I had been treasuring the one and only time Nolan and I had had sex and wondering when it would happen again, but I wasn't worried about it. In fact if it took more than a month for us to do it again that would have been all right with me. I would be happy with just kissing.

"It's all right," she said.

"Reag—I didn't send in my application to that program in France because Nolan asked me not to."

"So?" she said.

"So? I don't know, everyone is pretty shocked by it and I'm a little freaked. I mean, I feel so happy about Nolan, but it was kind of a big deal of him to ask me, don't you think?"

"Yeah—sure it is. But, Wrenny, do you think one program in France is going to change your life if you do it or not?"

"My parents are hardly speaking to me, Oliver thinks I'm whack, and Mrs. Rousseau thinks I'm an idiot," I said, and pushed the drawing away from me.

"Mrs. Rousseau is an old bat. I know you love her, but please. She's like a hundred years old."

"I think she's in her sixties."

"Whatever. Follow your heart, Wren."

Yeah—*yeah*, I thought. Follow your heart. That is a *tried and true* solid theory about how to go along in life. Grownups are always telling you to follow your heart. My mother must have said it to me a million times. Follow your heart; it will lead you to the right place.

52

"So when we get there, just stay with me. Okay, Charlie? Vats? Reagan? You?" Nolan squeezed my hips with his hands and tugged me more up on his lap. We were all shoved into the number 2 subway train careening downtown to Brooklyn. (Sitting on Nolan's lap was giving me a feeling that maybe I wanted to have sex more than once a month, but we were on a mission, so I ignored it as much as I could.) "Oliver and I will deal with whoever is at the door. Just look like you know where you are going and like you are supposed to be there." He held my hand. "Obviously there will be underage people around, he doesn't seem to have a problem with that."

"Wrenny, I think you and Vati and Reagan should find Farah right away, and I don't know, just see what you vibe," Nolan said. We pulled into the Fourteenth Street station. This is a stop near New York University and it's in the middle of the West Village. Seeing people way cooler than me in their granny boots and ironic eyewear ease onto the train as it headed even deeper into the land of coolness forced a rush of adrenaline up my spine. I did regret that I hadn't piled on more bracelets, like the girl who stood in front of me had, and I thought that maybe it was time to purchase a fedora, but I did have on a very wrappy gray scarf that put me in the game. Nolan was wearing a similar scarf in a dark army green. Truth be told, I had copied him. If I could have worn all his clothes, I would have. Rattling along on that train, I had a small fantasy that maybe the next fall, since I was going to be in New York, we would wear the same clothes—all the time. He would leave a sweater at my house and I would wear it to school—maybe he would wear the very scarf I was wearing! Maybe he would wear it to gigs. Sadly, I think we could even wear the same jeans. Anyway, soon we would look like those couples, like Jennifer Aniston and Justin Theroux, or Gwen Stefani and Gavin What's-his-name, couples who dress out of the same closet, or look like they do. We would grow more and more alike and people would say, "Wren and Nolan are two peas in a pod, it's so cute." Maybe one day my art would be used on his album covers and websites. We could work on movies together; he could direct and I could do the art direction. We could move to California!

"What if we are blowing this up and it's nothing and she's just hanging out with him? Are we going a little Homeland Security on her?" said Reagan.

"Reagan, what? No, no. Farah usually knows what she is doing, but I absolutely think this time she is in the weeds." That is a restaurant term for being in trouble. Charlie tosses in things that waiters and line cooks say now and again because he grew up in a catering kitchen.

"I just want to get her, get the hell out of that place, get back on this train and go to a coffee shop on the Upper West Side where we all belong," Charlie said, almost pouting.

"I am not a fighting man, but I feel like I want to sock that guy," Oliver said, with one arm draped around his girl Vati and the other making its way into a fist. Vati snuggled closer into him and pushed his dreads out of the way so they wouldn't poke her in the eye.

"Bring it, babe!" Vati said. *Babe?* Who calls anyone "babe"? Just so you know, those two are still together. I have a feeling they always will be.

53

Oh my goodness, you should have seen this place. First of all it was way the heck out in Brooklyn. We had to walk for fifteen minutes from the Junius Street station until we got to the deserted strip where Cy Dowd had his den. This was not *The Cosby Show*. This was not BAM or the Brooklyn Museum of Art or the hip streets with organic ice cream shops and knitting stores. No, this place felt as if we had walked to the end of the earth, or at least to the end of Brooklyn.

It wasn't hard to get into the party. You would think from what we were seeing on the Internet that it would be like getting into Buckingham Palace, but there wasn't even a bouncer. We all just walked right through the banged-up door and climbed the narrow staircase. The steps were wooden, like we were in a factory from the 1800s, but in contrast to that ancient feeling there was also a black light that made anything white that we were wearing glow. The thumping of the music from the party closely mimicked my pounding heart.

Inside, the party felt like what I had imagined Andy Warhol's factory was like. The electronic music penetrated everything. It was overwhelmingly loud and unfamiliar, but you could tell it was coming out of expensive speakers. Well, Nolan told me that.

"This place is sick. Those are Grand Utopia EM speakers. They're like $200,000. Who the freak is this guy?" Nolan took my hand protectively as we made our way into the gigantic room.

"This is wild, I mean, we should get her, but it's kind of cool." Charlie was moving to the music and looked like he would stay if we were not on a mission.

"I think this is scary. I can't believe she's even in here." It did *not* feel like the night when Nolan took me to see Mikey. That felt like a dancing bunch of kids where I belonged, even if I was in that huge red dress. (The dress, thankfully, was successfully cleaned, but I don't think I will be wearing it again anytime soon. When it came back from the cleaners, Mom held it up for me to see, lifted her eyebrows and the cleaning bill, and said, *"Eighty-seven dollars!"* and pointedly took the dress upstairs, away from me and my wrong-doing.) *This* gathering of, let's face it, adults, felt like we had entered another stage of life that we weren't supposed to see yet. It was a vibe more than anything. Like, have you ever been to a party where you think you will know everyone, but then there are some kids from another school there, and maybe they are in a higher grade? Just those five or six older kids can make you question what you are wearing, your place in the universe, and possibly relegate you into a huddle in the corner with the people you do know, because the unfamiliarity feels chancy and awkward. Cy's party was that feeling times one thousand. Plus it was dark, plus people were drinking cocktails, plus people were smoking, plus some men had goatees. It was just wrong, as Dinah would say.

"I'm going to go to the back, it looks like there are some more rooms that way. Do you see Cy?" asked Nolan. I was standing next to cool-as-a-cucumber Reagan, and even she was flipping her hair repeatedly, revealing insecurity.

"No. But I think I just saw the guy that does the website for the Met," I whispered to everyone. *"Oh my god, if my parents find out we are here, we are going to fry."*

"I'm getting a beer," Oliver said. "Come with me, Vats. You guys, these are all just poseurs. They're like loser hipsters, hangers-on."

"Has anyone seen the little pig?" said Vati.

"You guys go back and try to find Farah. We'll hang out in this room," said Oliver.

"And keep your eye out for Doodle, his little pig. I need to see that thing," Vati said. I'm telling you the girl is driven mad by tiny cute creatures.

"Oliver, do you think Dad will find out we're here?" I said.

"Don't freak out, Wren, just go get Farah. They think we're at a St. Tim's Christmas party at Benjer's house," Oliver said, and gave me a little push.

"I'll stay here with them," Reagan said, gesturing to Oliver and Vati.

Charlie was already making his way through the moving, dancing crowd. It felt like we were in a sea filled with fish that moved and turned together. The light was even blue. I held on tightly to Nolan's hand. "I bet she's back there," I said, looking deeper into the cavernous loft space.

"I bet he is back there too. By this point, she's in his inner circle," Nolan said. He did not seem freaked out, but I sure was. I didn't like the term "inner circle." It sounded sinister.

Sure enough, Farah *was* there. Unlike the dark front room, the back was a brightly lit kitchen. This was not your average home kitchen; this looked like the kitchen on *Top Chef Masters*. It was all souped up, with stainless-steel ten-thousand-dollar Sub-Zero fridges. (I know how much refrigerators cost because of *Dining with Dinah*. The network paid to replace our old one to accommodate the food for the show.) There was a long, thin table running down the length of the room with chairs that, thanks to my art history classes, I was sure were designed by Mies van der Rohe, the hugely famous German-American architect. On the table were perfectly spaced alabaster eggs that must have been designed with flat bottoms to sit there because they were not rolling around. A few women stood across from the table leaning against sleek black cabinets, drinking from wineglasses with no stems. When we walked in the room, they looked at us like we were the Bad News Bears. Even Nolan looked like a scruffy kid compared to these women, who for sure worked at *Vogue*. I felt like a less-mature Dinah. I actually felt like May.

Sitting at the table in a long sheath of a silvery-gray dress was Farah, drinking deeply colored red wine out of one of those stemless glasses too. She looked like she lived there, and a little bit like an alien because she was wearing plum lipstick that was so dark it looked black. Sitting right next to her was Cy Dowd. No sign of the little pig.

"Farah!" I ran over, squatted down, and hugged her.

"Wren," she said very slowly, calmly and controlled. "Oh my god, *what are you doing here?*" She had a smile plastered to her face, but she was mad.

"What do you mean? You don't think I can see things on Face-book? Nolan is my boyfriend. Just because my parents don't let me have social media doesn't mean the rest of the free world isn't on it. We all know about this party."

Farah froze and gave a guilty look at Cy, like maybe she had screwed up by posting everything on her Facebook page. It didn't look like he gave a shit, but then out of the side of my eye I saw Cy Dowd take a thin rectangular piece of slate or something off the table.

"Hello, Wrenny," he said, in what I perceived as a mocking tone. And I immediately thought it was freakish that he knew my name at all, much less called me Wrenny, which is what my father and my close friends call me.

"Oh, by the way, everyone is here," I said. Now Farah didn't look so calm, and she sounded edgy.

"Oliver, Padmavati, and Reagan are here too, but they are in there." I pointed to the room we had just come from. "We've come to take you home." I did not look up at Cy Dowd. Nolan was standing behind me.

"Cy, wait here, okay? These are my friends and I have to deal for a minute." He nodded and didn't seem to care at all where she went.

Farah got up and led Nolan, Charlie, and me even farther back into some kind of grownup video game room. She whipped around.

"Nolan, don't you have a gig or something?"

"Farah, what the—? Why wouldn't we all come to a party where we know you are going to be?" Charlie said. "And you look super-strange in that lipstick, you haven't found your color yet."

Farah looked like a trapped silver fox standing next to an ancient Pac-Man video game machine.

"We think you are in trouble with this guy, Farah," I said, putting my arms on her shoulders, attempting to calm the beast.

"I am certainly not in any trouble, Wren. I'm totally fine here. I'm here all the time, for your information. This is just a party."

"What was Cy taking off the table, Farah?" Nolan asked.

"What *was* Cy taking off the table?" I asked too, because I actually didn't know.

"What? What the hell, Nolan, who even are you?" Farah's eyes darted in the direction of the kitchen room with the *Vogue* girls in it.

"What was he taking off the table? Drugs?" Nolan asked steadily.

"DRUGS?" both Charlie and I said. Somehow, like an idiot, I'd thought this intervention was all about sex. Drugs had never crossed my mind.

"He totally slipped lines or something off the table when we came in. I saw him," Nolan assured us.

"I'm not doing coke," Farah quickly said, looking at the video game.

"God, Farah! Are you doing *coke*?" I whispered.

"*No!* God." She was so lying—or was she? I wasn't sure.

"Farah, look in my eyes," Charlie demanded.

"Oh, this is insane," she said, peering into Charlie's eyes.

"Huh." He sounded confused.

"What?" I said, watching him stare into Farah's widened eyes.

"If she was doing coke, her pupils would be as big as Frisbees," Charlie said. "They don't look that big, but how can you tell in this crazy light?"

"I *know* I saw him hide something," Nolan said, almost to himself.

Farah was standing there in what was clearly her mother's dress. I thought she was about to tae kwon do and kick her way out of there (like she said she would do in seventh grade if anyone took advantage of her).

"Farah." Charlie took her hands. "I think I get why you are here." She let him talk—we all did. "You are getting swept away by something so riveting and so powerful you can't help but go with it. But I don't think you should. Cy Dowd is a genius and one day you will be surrounded by men like that, but now is not the right time. We're too young. You are too young for him." Farah looked at all of us and chewed her lipsticked bottom lip.

"You all came down here," Farah said, buckling. Her shoulders crumpled and she started to cry into Charlie's arms.

"I can't believe you guys are here," she said, muffled in Charlie's shoulder. Then she pulled away from Charlie for a second. "And it *was* coke." She looked at Nolan. "He always has it. Everyone here is doing it," she blurted out as she cried. "I don't do it." She used both hands to put her hair behind her ears and looked down. "Well, I did it once. That first night." Then she really started crying. "It was awful. I couldn't sleep and I felt like there were these black lacquer devils in my brain, but I haven't done it since. I hate it, and I just want to get out of here now."

Nolan looked at me and mouthed, "See?"

Charlie took her in his arms and gave her a big Charlie hug. He was still in his green coat.

"Let's get out of here," Nolan said and put his hand on Farah's back.

"I have things here—in his bedroom," she said, looking wet-eyed and exhausted.

"Can you just leave them?" I said, putting my hand on her back too. She rested her head like a little kid on Charlie's shoulder.

"Yeah, I mean, I'd have to leave my favorite desert boots but . . ."

"I say bag the boots and let's go," Nolan said.

"Do you want to say goodbye to Cy?" I asked, even after what she had told us. She shook her head no.

"Do you have a coat?" Nolan asked.

"It's in the bedroom."

"Here, take mine." Nolan took off his grandpa's overcoat and draped it around Farah.

Cy Dowd was gone from the kitchen when we came back. There was no fight for Farah. The most romantic part of myself thought maybe he would have tried to convince us that he really loved her, but who was I kidding? One word from me to my father about that tryst and his massive career would be in ashes.

Farah, who I thought would give a fight to stay, led us through the party, down the flights of nasty industrial stairs, and out onto the street. Maybe she was waiting to be saved all along. We stood in a circle looking at each other.

"Is your Christmas tree up, Wrenny?" Farah asked.

"Yeah, it is! And Dinah made eggnog today. Oh, let's go home!"

"Yeah, let's go home. It's only ten," Oliver said, looking at his phone.

"Maybe we can get *It's a Wonderful Life* on Netflix?" Vati said and took Farah's hand.

"That is an awesome idea," Oliver said, looking at Vati like she was a Christmas angel. Neither one of them knew what Farah had told us yet.

"Oh my god, I can't stand that movie, it was made a hundred years ago!" Reagan whined. She also didn't know what Farah had been doing with Cy Dowd. If she had maybe she wouldn't have put up a fight about *It's a Wonderful Life*.

"Oh come on, you Grinch," said Nolan, as he threw one arm

around Reagan and the other around me. Charlie linked arms with Farah, who linked arms with Oliver, who was Velcroed to Padmavati. We made our way back through the fog that was also rolling through Brooklyn and onto the subway, uptown to our house. When we got there, we saw that the tree lights were on, and even though Dinah was asleep, her creamy, nutmegy eggnog was in the fridge. I made popcorn, and if you can believe it, we did go upstairs and watch *It's a Wonderful Life*—with my parents. "Hi, *guys!*" my mother said when she saw us come up the stairs. It was the first time since I'd told her I wasn't going to France that she seemed happy to see me.

Nobody talked about Cy Dowd or my missed application to Saint-Rémy. Sometimes at Christmas, when you have just escaped a famous-artist-pedophile-cocaine-guy or missed an opportunity of a lifetime, you have to pretend everything's okay and just get cozy, even if it's only for one night. I think parents even do that. I think even though they were worried about me (and maybe Farah, who looked like a tramp), they had to put it to the side, because we were there. Everyone, for just one night, wanted to forget what was worrisome, pile on the sofa, get blankets, turn down the lights to watch an old black-and-white movie about the meaning of Christmas, with eggnog, May-the-corgi curled at our feet, and a ten-year-old asleep upstairs.

During the opening credits, Nolan did one small thing that, if I'm being honest, felt weird to me. He stood up from where he was sitting next to me on the sofa, took a throw blanket that was folded on the same sofa behind where Oliver was sitting with Vati, and tossed it to Reagan, who was snuggled on an armchair on the other side of the coffee table. "Here, you look cold," he said. She looked up at him and smiled, unfolded the blanket and wrapped it around her feet. He came back to me, got under our blanket, grabbed a handful of popcorn from the mixing bowl resting on my stomach, and settled in for the movie.

In retrospect, getting that blanket for Reagan was meaningful, and maybe I knew it at the time, but I chose to put that troubling feeling somewhere else, just for that one night.

54

My father has a saying about what one is supposed to do on vacations. "Eat, sleep, a little fresh air." And happily that is all my family did that weekend. I slept like I was under a spell until I woke up Monday morning with a bad pit in my stomach. I picked up my phone and texted Charlie.

> **Me:** Are you up?
> **Charlie:** No
> **Me:** Call me.

Two seconds later my phone rang. I had set my ringer to the Shoppe Boys song that Nolan sings about his dad. The one he sang to me in the park.

"Hi," I said, pushing a pillow behind my back.

"Hi," Charlie said, sounding very awake.

"Listen—remember when you said Reagan went to all of the Shoppe Boys shows?"

"Yes I do."

"Your guitar teacher told you, right?"

"Right."

"I want you to text him and ask him if he ever sees Reagan with Nolan at the shows."

Silence.

"Charlie, hello?"

Silence.

I looked at my phone to see if the call was still connected. It was.

"Did you hear me? Do you think he ever has seen Nolan with Reagan? Charlie?" My heart was beating fast fast fast, like the heart of a frightened rabbit.

More silence.

"*Charlie*—you are totally freaking me."

"I don't want to say anything." Then my rabbit heart plummeted deep into my gut.

"What is it, Charlie? Please tell me. You can tell me."

"I think something is going on between them, Wren." I felt my feet break out in a sweat. I moved them around in a cool part of the bottom of my bed.

"I don't get it." I slid down under the blanket and looked at the ceiling.

"I don't get it either. Paul, my guitar teacher, thought Reagan was Nolan's girlfriend because of the way they act at the concerts. I guess it looks like Nolan thinks *Reagan* is the only girl in New York."

I felt my throat constrict.

"I have to go," I barely said.

"Maybe I'm wrong, Wrenny. Maybe Paul doesn't know what he is talking about. But . . ."

"What?" I felt two thin lines of hot tears race from the corners of my eyes and into my ears.

"There is a picture of them on Facebook that I don't think you would like." I turned away from the phone and squashed my face into my pillow. *Oh no, no, no, no, no, nooooooo.* "Oh my god, I don't have Facebook!" I whipped around and looked at my stupid, parentally restricted computer.

"I know. Everyone knows you aren't on Facebook because it's so weird."

"I have to go, I have to call him," I said frantically.

"Okay, Wrenny. I'm going to go see the *Messiah* with this friend that I met in my bird-watching class in Central Park this fall. It turns out that he's also going to Bard this summer and, well, we both like the *Messiah*, and there is a great choir singing it today at St. John the Divine's, so I invited him to go."

"Okay, thanks, Charlie," I said, feeling impatient that he was banging on about birds and a concert, but then, through my panic about Nolan, I tuned in to what he was saying.

"Charlie, are you going on, like, a date with this guy?"

"His name is Arthur."

I could hear the smile in his voice as he said Arthur's name.

"Arthur!" I felt a surge of happiness for Charlie.

"Yeah, Arthur. He's really cute. And really into birds." Charlie laughed.

"So are you!" I laughed.

"I know." There was a nice silence. "Wait, Wrenny, how did you know? About Nolan and Reagan? How did you find out?"

"I didn't—I think I was just following my heart."

"Okay. I'm sorry, Wren. I hope it's not true."

"Yeah, it may not be true, right?"

"Right, maybe." He sounded like he thought it was true.

"Okay, bye. Have fun today. Bye."

"Okay, I will. Good luck. Bye." He hung up.

I tried to catch my breath. I had to pee. I was thirsty. It was dark in my room because the curtains were closed, and all of a sudden I couldn't stand the darkness, so I got out of bed and ripped them open. It was bright bright bright outside. The fog was gone. The sun was blaring and the sky was a terrible shade of the most shocking blue—too blue. I texted Nolan.

Me: Can you meet me on the Met steps?

Nolan: Yeah, when? Good morning btw.

Me: Eleven. I have to get my dad a tie.

Nolan: See you there. xxxx

I threw my phone on my bed with all my might. It bounced and flipped down into the space between the bed and the wall. I scrambled over the sheets and pillows. My hair was in my face. I reached behind the mattress and jammed my arm down along the wall. My phone had gone to a place on the floor where I couldn't reach so I'd have to pull the bed away from the wall to get it. I jumped up and yanked back the cast-iron headboard. My huge drawings portfolio that I keep between the bed and the wall opened—I must have forgotten to tie the ribbon on the top the last time I drew. The two sides separated like a huge cardboard mouth and a piece of newsprint that had been trapped wavered and buckled in the empty space. It was the picture I drew of the owl flying into the air. The picture I drew right after Nolan gave me that beautiful note. The picture that made me feel like the two of us could fly away together. I took it to the open space in the middle of the room and let it float out of my hands onto the floor. The feathers in the drawing fluttered and shimmered in the light. I didn't remember drawing so many. The owl's face was turned up, her fierce, delighted eyes looking at the edge of the paper where she would soon blast off so she could fly way, way up. It was a breathtaking, big, bold drawing made when I felt that crazy flush of infatuation and excitement and promise and happiness. And love.

I got down on my knees and ripped it into a thousand pieces.

55

I hoped I would be able to escape out the door without anyone asking where I was going, as I was on vacation, but no, Mom was in the kitchen wrapping presents. She was still in her bathrobe. The radio was on. Two women were talking about a bestselling novel in hushed, oily tones.

"What's up, buttercup? Hey, give me your finger, will you?" She held up both ends of a two-inch-thick blood-red ribbon and nodded her head down, indicating that I had to put my finger in the middle so she could tie a bow. I did it. My mother wraps everything in newspaper and burlap sacks but uses really fancy ribbon. "Thank you!" she said, and tugged the loops into a bow that would make Martha Stewart weep.

"I gotta go, Mom."

"Hey—you look worried." She stood up and pulled my hair back into a ponytail (something she does to see if I'm sick or not). "Are you sick?"

"Well, I feel like I'm going to throw up, so yes. Sort of."

"Tell me. I know something is wrong. Where is Oliver?" she said, with her most concerned look on her face.

"How am I supposed to know?"

"I don't know—what's the matter?" She sat on a chair and pulled out the one next to her and gave it a pat.

"Sit. Or do you want to eat something? You're not taking your pill today, right?" I shook my head back and forth—there was no school.

"No, no, Mom. I feel awful."

"*Why*, darling? God, will you turn off NPR? I can't concentrate."

I stood up, walked around the island, got the clicker for the Bose, and muted the radio. The silence made a space for me to burst into tears.

"Oh, my baby." I heard the hornlike noise of her chair pushing back on the floor. "No no no no, what is happening?" My mother was reaching out to hug me.

"Nothing, stop, Mom." But she got to me before I could push her away. Her hands on my face, her smell, maybe just because she was my mother, made me cry harder but now in her arms.

"Oh, my lovey. Tell me." I just cried and cried.

"I have made such a mess of everything." I finally managed to get that out, but it only made me cry harder.

"Shhhh." I felt her hands in my hair.

"I am *such* an idiot. *I am stupid.*"

"No, no . . . shhh." I was doing that thing of sucking in breath and letting it out in fits, like I was three years old.

"Is it Nolan?"

I lifted my head and nodded.

"Okay." She took chunks of my hair and put them behind my ears. "Okay," she said again. Her voice was soothing.

"I have to go meet him at *eleven*." She and I both looked up at the kitchen clock. It was ten-thirty.

"You have time, where are you meeting?"

"The Met steps." I was still trying to stop crying.

"Dad's there, you know. It's a workday for him."

"I have to get Dad a tie. For Christmas."

"He'll like that," she said.

I nodded.

"Listen, Wren, you don't have to tell me what's the matter, but listen to me, okay?"

I nodded.

"You are my wonderful girl."

I started crying again. Nothing is worse for crying than someone being nice to you.

"You are," she said.

"I'm not so sure."

"I am."

I sniffed a big sniff and wiped snot on my sleeve by mistake.

"Here's the other thing," she said.

I rubbed the snot into my shirt hoping it would go away.

"It's all going to be okay."

56

It was too cold to walk through the park so Mom gave me money for a cab. I was doing everything I could so I wouldn't cry during the ride through the transverse. Deep breathing, tugging at my sleeve, biting my lip, it worked enough so I wasn't crying, but I felt tight in my chest and like I was holding back a sneeze that was going to come out of me eventually whether I liked it or not. I didn't know what it was going to feel like to have my heart broken, but the fracture felt pretty bad already. Nolan was standing on the Met steps when the cab pulled up to the curb. There were about a million tourists and museumgoers out there with him. People on the steps have been doing the same things for as long as I can remember. They drink coffee, eat Sabrett hot dogs from the nearby carts, take pictures, talk to each other, look at their phones, think, sketch, chat, smoke. And there were swarms of them doing all that stuff, but I saw Nolan right away. He was waiting for me, so good-looking in his grandfather's overcoat, the same dark army-green scarf wrapped around his neck, jeans, and his purple high-tops. He had a big smile for me. It was so normal and friendly that for one gloriously relaxing moment I let myself think: *Charlie is wrong.*

I paid the driver with the ten-dollar bill that had been folded in my hand since my mother gave it to me on our stoop and got out of the taxi. It really was freezing outside. A big wind must have come in the middle of the night and pushed the warm, soupy weather away. It felt like Christmas, but I was cold for the first time since the day of the party when I met Nolan.

"Hi," I said.

"Hi," he said, and kissed me on the cheek. Every molecule in my body wanted to be wrapped up in his arms, like I had been on the subway on the night we escaped my father's party, and in the park and at his house. There wasn't an inch of me that wanted him at a distance, but that is where he stayed—at a distance.

"You want to go in?" he said cheerfully. I shook my head. "No?" I shook it again. Did he really think we were going tie shopping?

"Nolan?" I looked up at him, but my eyes squinted shut because of the sun, or because I had been crying. They felt raw, and suddenly I felt weak, so I sat down on the stone step. He sat next to me. I decided not to look at him. I could hear the rush of traffic stop when the light turned red.

"So." I didn't know how to get the words out.

"Wren." His voice startled me, his beautiful voice.

"Yeah." I felt like I was going to cry again.

"I think I know what you are going to say, and I feel sick," he said.

"What?" I looked into his face.

"I haven't been honest with you." He said that *so slowly* and almost nobody on Earth would mistake what it meant, but I kept looking in his face hoping he wasn't going to say what I knew he was going to say.

"I—I'm afraid that I . . ." he began. I kept looking right at him, holding back tears with all my might.

"Reagan and me are, we are together. Something happened when she came to one of our gigs and we talked, and that led to . . ." His voice faded into the traffic noise and the frigid air and the roar in my head.

Have you ever been in a place, not an emotional place—like a room or on a bus or a train—where you know you shouldn't be? Like every instinct in your body tells you that you need to get out of there? Once I got on a subway going uptown when I was sup-posed to be going downtown. All I wanted to do was get on the right train. If I could have jumped off that train going in the wrong direction I would have. Of course I couldn't, I would have gotten killed. But now I could.

I looked at him for what I was pretty sure would be the last time.

"I changed my life for you. Do you get that?" He didn't say any-thing. I was talking about Saint-Rémy, and the words were coming out of me like I was possessed—maybe by my mother, or Mrs. Rousseau, or just a better version of myself. "I didn't apply and now it's over." I looked up at the huge museum where my father was probably sitting at his desk and got even more resolve. "I missed the deadline on purpose—*for you!*" I pointed at him. "Because you said I shouldn't do it and that we should be together! I believed you and it was totally stupid, because, because, well, now it's over." He looked so stunned, like I had slapped him.

"But, Wren—"

"No!" I held out my hand. "Maybe . . . ultimately it was my fault, because, well, because it was mine to give away, not yours, but I can't get it back. Everything, *everything* is changed!"

And then I ran.

I ran down Fifth Avenue. For about half a block I could hear him running behind me calling my name, but I ran faster and soon his voice was gone. I ran across Seventy-Ninth Street with so many cars turning out of the park transverse I felt like I was going to get hit. I ran past the Frick Museum on Seventieth Street. I ran past people and strollers and bus stops. I ran past the Central Park Zoo on Sixty-Fifth Street, I ran past the people selling books on Fifty-Ninth Street, I ran past the Plaza and past the horses and carriages lined up to take people for a holiday ride in the park. My mind was blank. I ran past the Bergdorf windows, and at St. Thomas Church on Fifty-Third, I turned right and ran straight up to the doors of the Museum of Modern Art.

57

I handed over my family membership card to the guy sitting behind the admission desk, and while he looked at his computer, I checked my phone, trying to catch my breath.

> **Nolan:** Come back! Please I am so sorry.
> **Nolan:** I am still at the steps. Please
> Missed call—Nolan
> Missed call—Nolan
> Missed call (VM)—Reagan
> Missed call—Nolan
> **Nolan:** Wren. I am sorry. Come back. Need to explain.
> **CLEAR ALL.**

I didn't need an explanation. Not then. I took my pass back, put it in my wallet, and listened to the low, hollow rumble of foreign languages and footsteps while I rode the smooth escalators to the fifth floor. The hum of the museum carried me until I turned the corner into the gallery and could see *The Starry Night*. I hadn't seen it in person since I met Nolan. *How did I never take him here?* There were people looking at it when I arrived and people lined up behind me for their turn to see it. Being in front of *The Starry Night* felt like seeing my oldest friend, or our kitchen table, or a family photo album that every once in a while you find yourself thumbing through even though you have seen it a zillion times. I was reminded by the French or Italian or German conversations around me that some of these people lived far away and this could easily be their very first time to see the swirling, bright stars, the mystery of the deep blue sky, the steeple in the village, and the looming cypress trees in the foreground. I wondered if they loved it.

You can't really sit on the floor in the museum. I don't think it's allowed, and at that time of year it's downright stupid because there are so many people milling around, but I did. I meant to only put my bag between my legs while I stood, but either from the running or the slow realization that everything was not as it seemed, I just sank down until I was on the floor. I saw a guard look at me funny. How I wished *The Starry Night* was at the Met, with Dad and Bennet and the other guards I knew close by, and carpet beneath me that I had sat on since I was a little girl. But the Met didn't have that painting, and that was the painting I needed.

I looked up at van Gogh's masterpiece and counted the bursting yellow stars. One, two, three—all the way until I got to eleven. I let my eyes drift to the biggest one, the one I wish on.

Please let him love me. I shut my eyes tight but I could still see the star in the darkness of my mind. *Please, please let him still love me.* Tears squeezed out of the sides of my eyes, and I could feel my mouth turn down. "Please let him still love me," I said in a trembling whisper. I felt a bump of a leg.

"Pardon me," said an older, elegant woman, frowning and probably annoyed that I was on the floor.

I scrambled up. "I'm sorry," I said.

"Oh—you are just a young girl!" the woman said in a French accent. She was wearing a camel-colored woolen coat that was cinched at her waist by a belt of the same color. Around her neck was an Hermès scarf with a pattern of gold buckles and brown horses. She had a short haircut that looked done, as if she had been to the salon that day. She looked like once upon a time she might have been a movie actress.

"What were you doing down zere? Wishing for love *out loud*?"

I was stunned she had heard me, and I stood frozen and speechless.

"Please, come look." She gently took my shoulders and moved me in front of her so we were both facing forward. "*Zis* is one of ze great paintings in all of time, in all of ze world. It's *Ze Starry Night* by Vincent van Gogh, a genius."

I looked at the sleeping town of Saint-Rémy.

"He knew his destiny, and he painted it here," she said, pointing and smiling at the stars in the swirling heavens. "What are you crying about, dear girl? Your destiny?"

"A boy that I love doesn't love me," I said.

"Well zen, zis boy, he is not your destiny. He is just a boy."

58

What was my destiny? Well, I will tell you, it wasn't to sit under those stars and paint in France. No, when I missed that chance, I really missed it. Some things you can't get back. For a while my destiny was to live through the drama that is heartbreak. I found out that for a bunch of friends, breakups are far more exciting than hookups. I will tell you why I think that is: there are a million stories about falling in love, from Tristan and Iseult to *Twilight*, but when it happens to you, it is a brand-new feeling. And as much as you want to describe it to someone who hasn't experienced it, you can't. When the universe decides to give you love, it's like you have gotten an A on a test when everyone else got a C—you keep it to yourself.

But unlike love, everyone gets breakups—even if they have never gone through a breakup. Breakups are mechanical. They have parts, twists, and layers, and as I found out, your friends will talk endlessly about *what happened*. I'm not sure if you ever get to the bottom of it. Even Dinah tried.

"So that's it?" Dinah said, taking down a silvery glass ball from the Christmas tree and putting it into one of those ornament boxes from the Container Store. "Nolan is just outty?"

I twirled a candy cane around my finger. "Seems to be." I kept twirling and not doing my job of taking down the decorations from the tree.

"And he's with *Reagan*?" she said, looking at me wide eyed.

"Yup."

"That is messed up. Are you *so* mad at her? Isn't that *so* against the code?" She held her hands out to the side like Dad does if he gets cut off in traffic by another car.

"I guess people have different codes," I said, and bit the cellophane wrapper off the tip of the candy cane and started sucking it like a pacifier, then took it out again. "And some people, like Reagan, have no codes or morals." I put the candy back in my mouth and sucked harder.

"Are you going to yell at her and so not be her best friend?"

"I want to yell at her, but I weirdly also want to be her friend, I think." I lay down on the sofa with my candy cane, exhausted. "Maybe not her best friend."

Dinah scurried over holding a fox ornament with a Santa hat on, and tucked herself in a corner of the sofa. She tugged at my big toe. "Did she like steal him from you? Like a sly fox!" She laughed her head off that she actually had a fox in her hand. I kicked her to shut up. "Okay, okay." She calmed herself. "But are your friends going to give her the Heisman? Like, talk-to-the-hand?" She held her hand out in the talk-to-the-hand motion. "*And* is Nolan such a *dick*?"

"Dinah!" If Mom were there Dinah would get a point for using that word (three points and you get no media all weekend. It's been a rule since Oliver was eleven and started swearing around the house).

"Well, I thought he loved *you*!"

"Well, so did I."

"That's confusing," she said, and tilted her little red head to the side. "But," she held up her pointer finger, "I guess you aren't grown-ups."

"What is that supposed to mean?"

"It means that you are still learning—you're not *parents* yet!"

"*Still learning?* That's something they said in Montessori nursery school."

"So? Everything you learn in nursery school is like the most important stuff you ever learn." She lifted her skinny arms up straight over her head and clasped her fingers together.

"Well, I don't remember learning what to do when the boy that you love falls in love with your friend, so." I looked up at the half-naked tree and had a flash of Nolan putting the blanket on Reagan. My heart felt separate from my body. Like it had its own set of arms and legs and muscles and wanted to pull away from me and go wherever Nolan was. Was he playing music? Reading? In the park? Was he with her?

"You should *yell* at Reagan. Like yell your head off at her." She arched over the arm of the sofa until she was doing a back bend and I could only see her legs and tummy.

"I am giving her the silent treatment." I sighed.

"Thaaaattttssss nottt satttisssfyyying." Her voice was straining and all weird because she was upside down. I had sucked a really pointy tip on my candy cane. I stuck it between my eyes, hoping the tip would be like an acupuncture needle and would hit some chakra in my face and all of my sorrow and confusion could pour out of that tiny, important hole.

59

To say that fifth-period lunch on the first day back from the holiday break was awkward is a huge understatement. Maybe if I had been in my thirties and got my heart broken, I could have gone away on a trip abroad to recover, like the characters do in E. M. Forster novels, but being fifteen, there was no escape from seeing Reagan at school. I avoided her for the morning, but the minute I walked in the lunchroom, there she was at our table, eating a grilled cheese bagel and reading a book.

"Okay. Let's just calmly get our lunches and discuss what we will do about this situation," said Vati, pulling a pumpkin-colored plastic lunch tray off the pile.

"I feel like if I ate even a *grape* I would throw it up," I said, taking the next tray.

"Just have milk maybe. And maybe crackers," she said, as she headed down the lunch line.

"Oh wait, they have chicken soup. I think I can eat that." I looked ahead at Emma Fox waiting for Mrs. Posner, the lunch lady, to ladle her a soup.

"Good idea, protein. Do you want to sit with Reagan and just have it out? I don't know where else we can sit without it being a major statement, and I think the stronger choice would be just to confront her and get it over with. You guys can't not talk to each other for the rest of your lives."

"Chicken soup please, Mrs. Posner," I said when it was my turn to be served. "Okay, but maybe you should say something first. I think if I try to talk to her I'll cry and that would be stupid."

"Totally, I can do that, but crying isn't stupid. This is a big-time situation," Vati said, and took a grilled cheese bagel from the rack.

Vati looked at me with her big brown Indian Katy Perry eyes, and blinked very seriously and very purposefully. It meant solidarity.

As we neared the table Reagan looked up, dog-eared the page she was on, and *smiled* at me. At the same time, from the corner of my eye I saw Farah heading straight for the table, almost running, as if she wanted to get there before the action started. Reagan's smile was not what I was expecting and it triggered my impulses before the plan could go into action. I slammed my tray down on the table, spilling my soup.

"Wipe that smile off your face!" I said, so loudly that the girls at other tables looked over. "*What* is your problem, Reagan?" I said in my most vicious tone.

She didn't say anything, but I saw tears come into her eyes.

"Talk!" I commanded. Vati and Farah didn't say a word.

"I'm sorry, Wren," Reagan said, tears falling.

"Sorry?" Now I felt like I was in a movie. "*Sorry?*"

"Yes," Reagan said.

I was out of breath and still clutching the sides of the tray. There was even some soup on my hand.

"Sorry doesn't mean anything, Reagan!" My mother says that

to me sometimes when I mess up and say sorry defensively. "Unless you mean it!" I was panting.

"Well, I *do* mean it," Reagan said steadily. I looked to Farah for some guidance or a snappy comeback. She had nothing but wide eyes for me.

"Are you together with Nolan?" I felt my ears get hot, and when that happens it means my chest is blotchy. I can never hide that I am upset, which is so uncool.

"Yes," said Reagan. She kept looking at me. Vati put her tray down on the table and then put her hand on my back. All the burn came to my eyes and I started to cry.

"Well, I *know* that already and I have to say, that it Really. Hurts. My. *Feelings!*" I tell you, it did kind of feel like nursery school where you are encouraged to tell a friend you're having an altercation with how they are making you feel. I was using my words.

"I'm *sorry*," she said again. It was her mantra. I didn't know what else to say so I sat down. Farah marched over to the condiment table, took about fifty napkins, came back, and cleaned up my soup. Vati sat down next to me and took a big bite of her cheesy bagel. You would think that Reagan might have gotten up, in shame or fear or something. But she didn't. After Farah helped me wipe up the chicken soup, she threw away the napkins and constructed a big colorful salad. And then the four of us ate lunch in silence. I didn't leave.

I wanted to storm out, turn my back, smack her, whatever, but I didn't do any of that stuff. I knew because of the Saint-Rémy fiasco what it was to be held accountable for something you did wrong and I guess I wanted answers from her.

"Um, so what did happen?" I asked Reagan.

Vati looked at me with the widest eyes I have ever seen her make, like she wasn't sure *at all* I should be asking such a risky question, and I sort of agreed, but it was too late. We both looked at Reagan, who responded by lifting her shoulders up to her ears with her head down.

"You are lucky that Wren isn't ripping all that black hair out of your scalp right now, Reagan," Farah said. "I would look up and answer her if I were you."

"What the hell, Farah?" Reagan looked around the table with her mouth formed in the shape of *Wha?*

"Am I wrong?" Farah asked like a seasoned prosecuting attorney. "You are being exceedingly disloyal and Wren has been just taking it. Now she is asking you what happened, so I suggest you answer her."

"*Okay*, it wasn't such a big deal," Reagan said, and rolled her eyes.

"Yes, it is a big deal!" I burst out. "You always say things aren't a big deal, and lots of things are big deals. This is a big deal." I pointed at her.

"Okay, *sorry*, but honestly it started by just talking." When a girl throws down the "talking" card, it's code for, this is *serious*. If you "talked for hours" or "just talked and talked" to a cute boy, it's like declaring you will be married one day. Fooling around with a boy is a joke compared to talking. I felt like I would vomit. Reagan sat up straighter. I could see girls at other tables starting to clear their trays and carry them over to the dish slot. After ten years of eating lunch in forty-minute blocks you have a good sense of beginning, middle, and end, and this period was coming to its end. We needed to start talking faster to finish the conversation before we had to go to the next class.

"Okay. One night, after one of his shows, Nolan asked me if my parents were divorced, or something like that."

I *couldn't believe* she said his name. It sounded so easy coming off her tongue. His name was *mine* to say, *I* had a boyfriend with a cool name and a guitar and a big smile and purple high-tops and a high IQ that I talked to all night. *I* did, not her. I felt breath fill my lungs and get trapped.

Reagan continued. "I said my parents had been divorced for a long time, and then Nolan said that *you* had said I was alone a lot."

A sharp feeling of betrayal shot into my gut like an arrow. *How could he tell her what we had spoken about?* All the breath pushed out of my lungs and I held on to the sides of my tray to steady myself. The orange plastic felt greasy from the cleaned-up chicken soup. I thought I might have a panic attack.

Reagan resumed. "Then he, Nolan—"

"*I know who he is!*" I said sharply.

"Okay." She took a big breath and kept going. "He said his parents were divorced too. Then he asked why I was the last one of us"—Reagan looked at Vati and Farah, so they must have been there that night too—"at the gig, and I said my mother was out and I didn't have to be home. And then, I don't know, we started talking about all that stuff. I guess he didn't have to be home either."

"And what, you had so much in common because of your no-curfew-Facebook-cooler-than-me lives, you just forgot that you were my friend and I was his *girlfriend*?"

"It's not like we did anything that night. We just talked."

"Oh god, forget it. You're together, right?" I asked again, standing up.

The bell rang.

"Yes," Reagan said very simply. It was hard to hear her with the increasingly loud sounds of chairs being pushed away from tables, trays clattering loudly down, the lunchroom staff replacing food on the metal racks for the next class, teachers moving girls along, laughing, books closing, sneakers thwacking on linoleum, but through all of that noise, it was clear. She definitely said, "Yes."

60

So Nolan and Reagan fell in love and it was stronger, or better than the love that he and I had. Even his mother said that to me. I did the thing you are not supposed to do: I called the boy who dumped me. I couldn't help it. I called him on his mother's home number instead of his cell phone. I did that because even though it was almost February, I was reading the note he gave me (the one with the Bruce Springsteen lyrics) over and over again in lovesick pain. His home number was written on it. Remembering our late-night conversations on my grandmother's old Chanel No. 5 phone, I decided to use it one last time hoping it might have some 1970s magical powers that would change his mind. Jessica Nolan answered.

"Hi. It's Wren," I said.

"Oh, Wren." She sounded sorry for me. "Hello."

"I was just calling to see if Nolan was there."

"He's not, dear. He's at school. There's a basketball game."

"Uh-huh. Okay, well." I started to cry.

"Oh, Wren," she said again, but that time her voice dropped an octave when she said "Wren."

"I'm sorry, this is so stupid. I should go."

"No, no. Please talk to me for a little. I would really like that."

Maybe because she is a shrink, I stayed on the phone. Or maybe it was because it was his mother and that was the next best thing to talking to him.

"I'm just so *sad*." I wept. If you think I was crazy for telling his mother I was sad, you are sort of wrong. It was comforting to speak to her.

"I know. It must feel awful."

"I just don't get it."

"Well . . ." She sounded like she was really considering my statement. "I'm not sure there is anything to get. It's just the way the world works sometimes."

"But it's unfair."

"Yes, it is unfair. And I am not proud of how Nolan handled it, but he and Reagan"—those three words stung worse than a real bee sting—"truly have feelings for each other."

"But he told me he had feelings for me."

"*He did!* He did have feelings for you. He had big feelings, Wren." That made me cry even harder. "I know he did. I could tell."

"But those feelings can go away, and it can just stop?" I blubbered.

"I don't know that it stops, but especially at his age, and your age—you are both so young—really at any age—sometimes, even if you have very strong feelings and commitments to one person, another person can come along and challenge them. And sometimes, for whatever reason, things change." Her voice sounded soft and gentle, and it occurred to me Nolan's dad had chosen Elaine over Nolan's mom. Even though his parents had been married, even though they had Nolan and his Kermit the Frog–green bedroom and a promising life together in Pittsburgh.

"Okay." I guess sometimes things stink but you have to live with them.

"I know it doesn't make anything better, and I know it hurts."

"I feel like I did something wrong."

"You didn't, Wren. It must feel that way, but you didn't. Nolan feels like he did something wrong, you know. He did do something wrong."

"Oh." That *did* make me feel better, but sad too. It seems like none of us knew what we were doing, not really.

"Please don't tell him I called, okay?"

"If you don't want me to, I won't."

"Or tell him." I laughed at my confusion. "I don't know."

"Okay." She laughed a little too. "Goodbye, Wren."

I hung the heavy cream-colored phone receiver in between the plastic holders. Its weight sank down on two little clear knobs and disconnected the call. That was probably my favorite part of using that old thing. Hanging up was so satisfying.

It was that night that I drew my self-portrait. I walked up the stairs to my room, got out my drawing pad and charcoal pencils, and sat in front of the mirror on the back of my bathroom door. I could hear the voices and music of my family on the floors below me like a layer cake. I took in a big, deep breath.

There must have been something about me that he had loved. Where was it? How could I find it? I looked and looked into my eyes, right into their centers. It felt like they were pools that I could jump into. And I did. Suddenly I was inside myself. I was at the museum as a little girl running through the halls. I was in fourth grade, struggling and frustrated with punctuation. I was lying on the floor with Vati daydreaming about our weddings and laughing with Farah in the hallways of Hatcher. I was a Turtle in fold-over white socks and a bob haircut. I was in my father's arms reaching for the light and I was at my mother's dressing table getting the knots brushed out of my almost waist-length hair. I could smell Dinah's first chicken potpie and hear Oliver's thumping music from behind his closed door. I could see Mrs. Rousseau's silver rings on her fingers as she adjusted a line I had drawn almost correctly, and I could hear Charlie's sweet voice bucking me up whenever I lost my footing. I even saw Reagan and that hair of hers. I felt sorry for her that she had done something seemingly so mean and hurt my feelings. Maybe she couldn't help it; maybe she is just trying to figure out everything too. She still felt like my friend. Maybe she was. Or maybe she would be again, someday. I felt my body lift up to press against Nolan's. I felt how much I loved standing next to him and feeling his hand take mine. I saw his smile. At least I got to know what that kind of love felt like. I could feel my whole life, and when the time was right, I looked down and there I was on the page. Imperfect and hopeful.

Epilogue

I didn't go to France during my junior year, but that self-portrait got me into an art program in Savannah, Georgia, for the summer. It's a *great* art school—one of the best in the country. They say if you do the summer program you have a better chance of getting into the college, and I hope that is true.

I'm in Savannah now. It's warm here, hot. I have a funny roommate named Marni who comes from New Jersey and wears a real diamond engagement ring on her wedding finger. Her mother gave it to her so she wouldn't get married too early just for a piece of jewelry. I think it's a sparkly reminder that her life is her own.

At night the students hang out on a quad in the middle of campus. There are ancient trees with sage-colored moss hanging from the branches like shredded old blankets. Apparently they have been there since the Civil War. We all sit around and talk about the teachers and what we did in studio that day. We drink endless Dr Peppers that we get in the machine in the dorm and we always have our sketchpads, like bird-watchers have binoculars. There is even a kid I think might have a crush on me. His name is Vernon Veve if you can believe it. He's from Virginia Beach. We have gone on walks a couple times. I don't know for sure if he likes me, but I think he does. He's quiet and sweet. He's a really good artist.

On clear nights, like tonight, I'll take my pad and walk up the hill where there is a sturdy bench. You can even lie down on it it's so big. From there you can see the back of the campus, and beyond, a road that leads to town. If you lean back and let your head rest on the wood, there are the infinite stars peering at you through the darkness, shining and steady. I think about van Gogh painting the same stars so long ago. I think about all the artists and lovers and just regular people who have looked up at them, wished on them, found direction from them. And then I think wouldn't it be fun if the stars are watching us too, watching what we do and waiting for what will happen next.

Acknowledgments

My wonderful mother worked at the Metropolitan Museum of Art when I was very young. I would like to thank her from the bottom of my heart for taking me to that place, and many other places, and pointing out big and very small extraordinary things throughout my life. She is the one who taught me how to marvel at this beautiful world. And I would like to thank my boundlessly enthusiastic, supportive, and loving father, who believed that a dyslexic kid could, and indeed should, reach for the stars. And while we are on the subject of parents, love and thanks to my terrific in-laws, Ellen and Stanley Lattman.

I want to give huge shout-outs to my beloved brothers, and the brothers of my friends growing up, who taught me a lot about what good guys were like. Thank you, dear friends, all of you—the ones I met when I was five and the ones I met in my forties—for being Sams. ("Sam" is a word my father uses when describing someone who is by your side and helps you along the way.)

I would love it if every single teacher and tutor in my life read this page so I could say thank you to them—especially the drama and art teachers, but really all of them. And I want to thank all the schools I ever went to, and everyone inside them.

I would like to thank every boyfriend I ever had. Nothing is better than a boyfriend.

I am calling loudly up to heaven to thank the great Nora Ephron. I didn't know her very well, but she was my north star, especially with this book.

Bill Clegg, to whom this book is dedicated: I will spend the rest of my life grateful that he made me feel like a writer—for real. I heartily also thank his assistants Shaun Dolan and Chris Clemans for being so *on it* and helpful, always.

FSG!!! A tornado of thanks must sweep through the FSG offices, hitting everyone in its path, but the first office it must tear through is that of my editor, Joy Peskin. Thank you, Joy, for finding me and pulling *Starry Night* out of me so calmly, with huge encouragement and careful, smart guidance. I adore and appreciate working with you. This tornado must also hit the copy editors Karen Ninnis (whose red markings and comments I fell in love with) and Karla Reganold, for overseeing everything. It is no small task copyediting a dyslexic. Thank you to the fun and sharp publicity whiz, Molly Brouillette! And Kathryn Little for her great work on marketing. Angie Chen for all of her help; Beth Clark, who designed this beautiful cover; and a huge, crashing thank-you to Simon Boughton, whose support I am so grateful for.

Thank you, Mikey, Cat, Grace, Max, and Deirdre for taking care of the kids while I was writing this book and getting it out into the world. I could not ask for smarter, more creative, loving wing-people.

THANK YOU to our kids' other parents, DeSales, Laura, and Gillian. I am extremely fond of our little ecosystem and endlessly grateful for it.

I must thank Maude, our dog, who is now my writing partner.

It makes me cry when I think about how to thank you, husband Peter Lattman, because if there is such a thing as the brightest star in a starry night, you are it. How do you thank the person who is relentlessly by your side? Who continuously gives you joy and happiness and who never stops moving forward with you? It's like trying to thank your breath, or your heartbeat. I guess I'll just say: Thanks, babe. XOXOXOXOXOXOX

Hugh, Sage, and Thomas, thank the Lord for you, darling hearts, for being wonderfully YOU, and for helping me understand more and more about everything—even spelling. This book is being published just as you three are on the cusp of becoming teenagers. Is it weird for me to tell you that I can't wait? I can't wait to see you all fall in love and navigate school and beyond! Ups, downs, whatever, I am by your side cheering for you even when it seems like I'm not and that I don't get it at all. And if I may use a sports metaphor: remember always, I don't care if you make the winning goal, I just *love* watching you play.

—I.G.